THE MOLTEN CITY

Also by Chris Nickson from Severn House

The Inspector Tom Harper mysteries

GODS OF GOLD
TWO BRONZE PENNIES
SKIN LIKE SILVER
THE IRON WATER
ON COPPER STREET
THE TIN GOD
THE LEADEN HEART

The Richard Nottingham mysteries

COLD CRUEL WINTER
THE CONSTANT LOVERS
COME THE FEAR
AT THE DYING OF THE YEAR
FAIR AND TENDER LADIES
FREE FROM ALL DANGER

The Simon Westow mysteries

THE HANGING PSALM
THE HOCUS GIRL

C29 0000 0846 259

THE MOLTEN CITY

Chris Nickson

This first world edition published 2020
in Great Britain and the USA by
SEVERN HOUSE PUBLISHERS LTD of
Eardley House, 4 Uxbridge Street, London W8 7SY.
Trade paperback edition first published
in Great Britain and the USA 2020 by
SEVERN HOUSE PUBLISHERS LTD.

British Library Cataloguing in Publication Data
A CIP catalogue record for this title is available from the British Library.

ISBN-13: 978-0-7278-8976-8 (cased)
ISBN-13: 978-1-78029-697-5 (trade paper)
ISBN-13: 978-1-4483-0422-6 (e-book)

All Severn House titles are printed on acid-free paper.

Severn House Publishers support the Forest Stewardship Council™ [FSC™],
the leading international forest certification organisation.
All our titles that are printed on FSC certified paper carry the FSC logo.

Typeset by Palimpsest Book Production Ltd.,
Falkirk, Stirlingshire, Scotland.
Printed and bound in Great Britain by
TJ International, Padstow, Cornwall.

To those who fought so we'd all have the vote.
We owe you more than we can ever pay.

ONE

September 1908

A lone seagull swooped, gave its cry and rose to the sky again, wings flapping until it was no more than a dark speck against the clouds. Taking his place at the graveside with the other mourners, Superintendent Tom Harper removed his hat. Dress uniform today, and for once he'd put it on without complaint. Annabelle linked her arm through his and he glanced at her. She was in black, a simple, plain dress and a hat with a veil that almost hid the sorrow in her eyes.

Man that is born of a woman hath but a short time to live, and is full of misery. He cometh up, and is cut down, like a flower; he fleeeth as it were a shadow, and never continueth in one stay.

He'd barely noticed the church service, the hymns and the eulogies. Instead, his own memories of Billy Reed had come, jerky, never quite staying in focus, like a moving picture. The time they'd served together on the force, the rift and then the slow healing that solidified into something warm that was almost friendship again. That had arrived after Billy and his wife Elizabeth moved here to Whitby. How long had he known the man? Well over twenty years; so much slid away into the past, hazy and dimmed and heavy.

And all over in the time it took for a heart to stop beating. From one moment to the next. Billy had only been in his middle fifties. Years ahead of him yet; that was what people always said. But it was true.

The pallbearers lowered the coffin into the earth.

In the midst of life we are in death: of whom may we seek for succour, but of thee, O Lord, who for our sins art justly displeased?

Elizabeth stood on the other side of the grave. Silent, hands clasped tight together, clutching a handkerchief. Her children stood around her, all of them grown now. The two youngest seemed stunned, as if they'd been transported into some strange dream they didn't understand.

The telephone call had come in the evening. Harper had just

arrived home, trying to shake off the thoughts of work and let his mind slow down. Elizabeth's voice was faint and hesitant on the other end of the line.

'It's Billy.' A pause so long he believed he could hear her breathing, trying to gather strength. 'He's dead. A heart attack. It was instant. He wouldn't even have known, they said.'

'My God.' He could scarcely believe it. Billy Reed had seemed so alive the last time they met. Fitter than he'd looked in years. And happy. 'I'm so sorry. Is there anything we can do? He . . . when did it happen?'

'Yesterday. He was on his way home from the police station.' Another hesitation, shorter this time. 'The funeral's on Thursday. I don't know if you can come. I'd have rung sooner, but . . .'

So much to do. He understood. And far more than that: overwhelmed, just trying to cope. To comprehend. To try and imagine a future.

'Of course we'll be there,' he said. How could he have refused?

'What is it?' Annabelle asked as she came through from the kitchen. 'You look like you've just seen a ghost.'

He realized he was standing with the receiver in his hand.

'You'd better sit down,' he told her.

He managed to learn a little more the next day; the police grapevine. Billy had keeled over as he was walking along the street at the end of an absolutely ordinary day. Dead before his body even hit the pavement, according to the report.

So sudden, so final. No chance for goodbyes. How could that be part of any great plan?

A sudden breeze rose, rippling the vicar's white surplice and whipping his words out over the North Sea before it stilled again.

In sure and certain hope of the Resurrection to eternal life, through our Lord Jesus Christ; who shall change our vile body, that it may be like unto his glorious body, according to the mighty working, whereby he is able to subdue all things to himself.

Harper stood, his back straight. He could taste the salt tang on his lips. His mind drifted and dived with the birds over the estuary. He watched without seeing as the family threw clods of dirt into the grave. The empty thud of soil on wood. A life over and folded into the earth.

The grace of our Lord Jesus Christ, and the love of God, and the fellowship of the Holy Ghost, be with us all ever more. Amen.

There were plenty of coppers around, from the men Billy had served with on the local force in Whitby all the way to the chief constable in his medals and braid. Nods and handshakes; Harper was here as a friend, but he'd also come as the representative of Leeds City Police.

Finally they reached Elizabeth. She and Annabelle had been close friends, and still exchanged letters regularly. Now they embraced, and the tears flowed. Soft words that his poor hearing couldn't catch. Then it was his turn and he couldn't find anything to say. How could you sum up all they'd gone through in a sentence or two?

'Billy was a good man. You know we're all going to miss him.' It wasn't enough, it wasn't anything at all, and he realized that. But it was the best he could manage.

Elizabeth nodded, her lips tight. He pressed her hand between his and moved on to let someone else murmur to her. At the entrance to the churchyard he turned and looked back. The grave-diggers were already busy with their shovels.

'Are you sure you don't want to stay a day or two?' he asked Annabelle. 'There's no reason for you to go straight back.'

She shook her head as she pushed the veil off her face. The tracks of tears had run through the powder on her cheeks.

'I just asked Elizabeth. She has the children with her and all the people she knows up here. I'd only be in the way.' She gazed down on the town, the river, the old, crumbling abbey on the headland across the water. 'It's not right. They were doing so well.'

Eleven years in Whitby, he thought. Billy had enjoyed his responsibilities as police inspector here. Elizabeth had her tearoom that bustled in the summer months. They'd made a life for themselves. They'd found somewhere they loved, but they hadn't had enough time to enjoy it properly. To enjoy it *together*. Fifty-five years old.

He yanked the watch from his pocket and studied the time.

'You know I need to get back to Leeds.' With no leave due, he'd begged the day off from the chief constable.

Annabelle glanced up at the darkening sky.

'We'd better get a move on, then. It looks like it's set to bucket down soon.'

They'd come out on the early train, steaming across the moors through a brown autumn landscape. Travelling through the falling leaves to attend a funeral. He'd left Ash in charge at Millgarth. With the inspector around, the place wasn't likely to fall apart in a few hours; he was safe and solid. But Harper was still relieved to be going home. Funerals always left him uneasy. All the solemn endings and gravity. Especially for someone he'd known so long, and the morbid sense that fate could just as easily have picked him. Mortality snapping at his heels.

And there was work to be done in Leeds. Always something needing his attention.

Annabelle, though, had the luxury of time these days. After three terms as a Poor Law Guardian she'd decided to step down at the last election, campaigning for her replacement, a coal merchant's wife from Roseville Road.

'They need some fresh blood in there,' she'd told him with a weary smile. 'Maybe my head's just aching after banging it against a brick wall for so long. All I know is something's telling me to get out. I've done all I can.'

'Then you'd better listen,' he agreed. 'Do you have any idea what you'll do instead?'

Her public house, the Victoria in Sheepscar, almost ran itself these days; Dan the barman looked after everything.

'I don't know yet.' An uncertain look hovered on her face. 'Maybe I'll become a lady of leisure for a while.'

Harper snorted. 'That'll last about five minutes.'

'Something will come along. It always does.'

But it hadn't, not yet, and close to two years had passed since then. She still spoke regularly at meetings for women's suffrage and did bits and pieces at the workhouse, but nothing had really caught her eye. She was in limbo and it didn't suit her. It worried him to see her that way, so undecided about the future.

'Penny for them,' he said as the train pulled out of York. Not long now until they were back in Leeds.

'You'd be wasting your money.' She hesitated. 'I was remembering Billy, that's all. Same as you. How we never know what's going to happen. Or when.'

TWO

The motor car stood on Manor Street. It was the only one in Sheepscar, a Rex Tourist, its coachwork gleaming under the streetlamps. Annabelle's pride, her big splurge after she'd decided to end her time as a Guardian. She hadn't even baulked at the price, simply written a cheque and smiled.

She patted the bonnet as they passed and gave a small sigh of contentment.

The Victoria was half full of evening drinkers as they walked in, and Harper waved away a few loud comments about his appearance with a laugh as they passed through the bar. By the time they'd climbed the steps and opened the door to their rooms he'd already forgotten them. He dropped his gloves on the table.

'Smells like Mary kept some food warm in the oven for us.' She smiled. 'Go and change while I dish up. You always look uncomfortable in a uniform.'

Later, in bed, he couldn't turn off his thoughts. A river of them arrived, a flood that wouldn't cease. Images of Billy, the sound of his voice, from anger to sorrow to laughter. He lay in the darkness letting them flow over him and hoping they'd wash him clean. The friendship, the resentment that kept them at a distance all those years, and finally the reconciliation.

'You're quiet this morning, Da,' Mary said.

'Am I?' He smiled. 'I'm remembering, that's all. About Billy.'

Harper looked at his daughter then away again. Sixteen years old. How had all that time passed so quickly? She was a young woman now, a life ahead of her, and with her mother's looks, thank God; better than taking after him.

'You'd better get a move on,' Annabelle called from the kitchen. 'Or you'll be late for work.'

'Yes, Mam.' She took a final gulp of tea, closed her book and put it in her bag.

Most of her friends from gone straight to the mills or become maids after primary school. Not Mary. She'd attended Leeds Girls' High. A scholarship to pay the fees, but they'd had to cover all the other expenses. Still, they were luckier than most; they had the money, and he'd never begrudged spending it on education. At fourteen, leaving certificate in hand, she'd spent a year at a secretarial school, learning typing and shorthand. Now she was working for a solicitor in Park Square.

'It's only for a while,' she'd said to them one evening, just a week after she started the job. Her voice was earnest and intent as she explained her plan. 'I need experience in an office.'

'That's fine, but what do you want to do after that?' Harper asked.

'Open my own secretarial school,' she told him, as if it was the most obvious thing in the world. 'I don't want to spend my life working for a man.'

He remembered her at five years old, so serious as she announced that one day she'd run her own business. It looked like the wish had never gone away.

'It's a good idea,' Annabelle agreed, 'but where will you find the money?'

'From my wages.' She stared at her mother. 'And I'll borrow the rest from you. Everything legal, with interest, of course.'

'Will you now?' She raised an eyebrow. 'I tell you what. You come up with a proper plan, costs for everything, and then we'll see.'

Mary had taken her time, but she'd done exactly that. Annabelle studied it and made her a bargain. Once their daughter turned eighteen, she'd finance the school. The business would be in Annabelle's name until the girl came of age at twenty-one, but Mary would run everything. They'd even agreed the repayment schedule. The pair of them constantly astonished him, and scared him more than a little. So efficient, so matter of fact.

A peck on the cheek from his daughter brought him back to reality.

'I'll be late tonight, Mam,' Mary called. 'Meeting.' And then she dashed off for the tram.

Harper glanced at Annabelle. A meeting. They both knew what that meant. The Women's Social and Political Union. The suffragettes.

'Don't look so surprised,' Annabelle had told him when Mary

announced that she'd joined after the big rally of women's groups in July on Woodhouse Moor. She'd gone with Annabelle. Unlike her mother, a member of the Suffragist Society for years, she'd been attracted by the energy and fire of the suffragettes. Two groups with similar aims, but completely different ideas about achieving them. 'After all, she's heard me going on about the vote and rights since she was a baby. I was a Poor Law Guardian for years. It was bound to rub off. Or would you rather she was docile?'

'Fat chance of that happening in this family,' he said.

Still, it worried him to see his daughter involved with Mrs Pankhurst's women. They were more aggressive than the suffragists. They seemed to relish confrontation. He had a bad feeling about that. So far she'd only attended meetings, but . . .

He glanced at the clock.

'I need to make myself scarce, too. Early meeting for the division commanders with the chief constable. What do you have planned today?'

'A man from Tetley's Brewery is stopping by. Probably wants me to start selling their beer.'

Harper kissed her. 'You can tell me all about it later.'

He was the last to arrive, settling into his chair as the buzz of idle conversation faded.

'Gentlemen,' Chief Constable Crossley began, 'I've received the inspector general's report on the king's visit in July.' He began to smile. 'You'll be pleased to hear we were given full marks.'

Harper felt the wave of relief. Still, it was no more than they deserved. They'd spent months planning every detail and it had gone off without a problem. Only twelve arrests, most of them drunk and disorderly. Sixteen hundred officers brought in from other forces. The biggest operation they'd ever undertaken.

The chief had had overall command. But he'd been a member of the monarch's party, escorting King Edward and Queen Alexandra around Leeds. It had fallen to Harper to direct everything. That made sense; all the places they were visiting – Central Station, the town hall, the university – came under A Division. His responsibility.

'Well done, every one of you.' The good humour left Crossley's face. 'Before we start patting ourselves on the back, though, there's something else.' He picked up a letter. 'This is from Downing Street. As I trust you're aware, Mr Asquith became prime minister earlier this year. He's planning to speak at a meeting in Leeds on October tenth.' He sighed. 'Not exactly a great deal of notice, and more work for us, I know. And I'll remind you that he's local. Born in Morley, educated at Fulneck, so we're going to have to put on a very good show.'

It was the very last thing they needed. First the king and now this. Quite a year. And only two weeks to plan.

'Where's he going to be speaking, sir?' Harper asked.

'The Coliseum on Cookridge Street. It's going to be a public meeting.' A small pause. 'I'm told it holds three and a half thousand people.'

He heard the groans. Even more police required to keep order.

'I know we're being stretched,' Crossley said. 'I'm sorry, but it's out of my hands. We need to start work on this immediately. I've asked for more details. As soon as we have them, we can come up with a proper plan. In the meantime, go through your numbers and tell me how many men you can readily spare that night. October tenth is a Saturday, and we all know what that means.'

Payday, Harper thought. Men out drinking, enjoying themselves, fighting. The cells were always full by Sunday morning. The prime minister on top of that? It was going to be bedlam.

Another half-hour and they were done, putting on their coats and starting to file out.

'Tom, can I have a quick word?' Crossley asked. Once they were alone, the chief reached into a drawer and brought out a large envelope.

'Sir?'

'This is for you. A certificate of appreciation for your work in July. From the king himself. I made sure he knew whose manor he was on.'

'Thank you, sir.' Harper tore open the flap and took out a piece of parchment. Thick black ink on heavy vellum, Edward's signature at the bottom. It looked impressive. It *felt* impressive. He had to read it twice to be certain it was real. Then he beamed. 'I'll have that framed.'

'You deserve it. You took care of everything and did a bloody good job. We're going to have our work cut out next month, though.'

'I agree, sir.'

'I'm landing you with it again, I'm afraid. At least you have the experience now. Two things I didn't tell the others. The meeting is going to be men only.' He frowned. 'You know that's going to stir up trouble with the suffragettes.'

'Of course.'

'Remember what they did when Earl Grey spoke here.'

They'd shouted him down. It could have been worse. No violence, just loud voices. They could cope with the suffragettes. After all, they'd caused no trouble at the by-election earlier that year, and the huge rally on Woodhouse Moor during the summer had gone by without any problems.

'I've also had word that some unemployed men are planning a demonstration on Victoria Square outside the town hall the same evening. Now, that one worries me.'

'How good is the rumour, sir?'

'It's pretty solid. I'm told that it's going to be led by Alf Kitson.'

Harper groaned. He knew about Kitson. A clever, sly operator. An anarchist who loved confrontation. More misery.

'You'll need to start organizing your men immediately. I want this to go off as smoothly as the king's visit.'

But there'd be no bunting hanging from the windows for Asquith, no decorated trams, no sense of joy. That was reserved for royalty. And it all had to happen in his bloody division.

A dreary day for walking through Leeds. Misting drizzle mixed with sharp squalls of rain. But it was late September, what could anyone expect? Harper shook out his mackintosh and hung it on the peg in his office at Millgarth police station, waiting as his squad filed in for their morning meeting.

'How was the funeral, sir?' Detective Inspector Ash asked. Sergeants Walsh and Sissons took the chairs, Detective Constable Galt stood with his back against the wall and Ash filled the doorway, leaning against the jamb.

Billy's funeral. It felt like ancient history now.

'How are any of them?' he answered. There didn't seem to be more to say. Every last farewell was bleak. 'I have some good news for you. We're not going to be bored for the next few weeks.'

Flashes of interest, until he told them they would be policing Asquith's visit.

'I'll be in charge, moving around where I'm needed, and I'll handle things when the prime minister arrives at Central Station. Ash, you're in control outside the Coliseum. Walsh, you'll have the easy duty inside the building. Sissons, I want you keeping a very close eye on this demonstration in Victoria Square.'

'What about me, sir?' Galt asked. He was still young, just twenty-four, promoted to plain clothes two years before. Eager, sharp, maybe a little too cynical about the job. But he always did his duty and much more besides. He was learning, coming along.

'You'll be my runner, delivering messages to the others and bringing reports.' He saw the man's face fall; he'd hoped for something more substantial. That couldn't be helped. 'We'll have plenty of uniforms, and you'll all need to work with them. Go out and take a look at everything. I'd like rough plans and ideas on my desk in the morning.'

He put on his spectacles and picked up the pile of letters waiting on his desk. There'd been jokes when he started to wear them, but they helped. Each year the pile of paperwork seemed to grow; most of the time he felt chained to this desk.

A postcard lay on top, a hand-coloured view of Table Mountain in South Africa. From Fowler. He'd been the detective sergeant in Harper's squad until he volunteered as an intelligence officer at the start of the Boer War. Now he was settled as an inspector with Cape Town police, married with a child and another on the way. One happy ending, at least. He set it aside and went through the rest. The usual complaints and accusations. He dropped most of them in the bin by his feet.

The last, though, stayed in his hands. He read it through twice, then steepled his fingers under his chin. Finally he marched out to the front desk.

No more Sergeant Tollman out there. The old order had changed with the century. For the last eight years it had been Sergeant Mason, an affable, sharp man in his fifties, with three decades of solid police service behind him. But he'd never possess Tollman's long connection to Millgarth. All that memory had gone, the encyclopaedia of knowledge about faces and names, who'd been arrested when and for what.

'Fourteen years ago a child was reported missing,' Harper said. 'A boy named Andrew Sharp. He was two and a half years old.'

'All right, sir,' Mason answered warily.

'His family lived in one of the courts where County Arcade stands now.'

'If you say so, sir.' He could see the doubt on the man's face, wondering where this was leading.

'I'd like the report on his disappearance and the action taken.'

'I'll hunt it down for you.'

Harper smiled. 'Thank you.'

As he passed through the detectives' room, Ash was cramming his old bowler hat on to his head.

'You'd better stay a while. I'm going to need you.'

Back in his office, he read the letter once more. Franked at the Central Post Office, no signature. With its wide curls and loops it was a woman's writing, no doubt of that. But a shaky hand, unsteady and awkward, with some of the words misspelled.

> I am dieing now. Before I meet my maker I need to get something off my chest. Fourteen years ago a man was paid to steal a child. His name was Andrew. He lived in Harmony Yard and he was two and one half years of age. The one who was paid the money is also dead now. But I know that he received money to do it from a family named Cranbrook who are rich. He told me that unce. It has prayed on me that it was wrong to take the little boy from his family. I hope you can do something about it.

A missing child. It would have been important news, something to stir the whole city, to start them searching. It would have been all over the papers, and then the shock if the boy had never been found. But he had no memory of it. Nothing at all. As if it had never happened.

Fourteen years ago he'd been a detective inspector. Harmony Yard was on his patch, he'd have been assigned the case. Yet he'd never heard of this before. No matter how deep he delved in his mind, he couldn't recollect any mention of the disappearance.

Half an hour later Mason knocked on the door and placed a grubby folder on his desk. Tiny fragments of cobweb from the record room clung to his uniform.

'Sorry it took me a while, sir. Turns out it was fifteen years ago, not fourteen. I had to do some digging.'

'Good work, Sergeant.'

'I don't suppose you fancy a cuppa, sir? I'm just going to make one, wash out all that dust in my throat.'

'You don't need to ask, do you?' Harper grinned. 'When have I ever said no?'

Just two sheets of paper in the file. A prickle of worry rose up his spine. It should have been inches thick, bulging with reports and newspaper clippings. The results of dozens of interviews, all the sightings and their follow-ups. Something was very wrong.

He took out the first page. Handwritten, the blue ink rusted brown with age. From the man on the beat, PC Taylor. Harper took a breath. That was a name he didn't want to see. He'd finally sacked him back in '98. No choice, after repeated offences and fines for drinking on the job and consorting with prostitutes. The final straw had been taking a small bribe. Never a good man, never thorough. A stain on the force.

Taylor had been called to Harmony Yard on December 11, 1893. A report of a missing child. He'd talked to the mother, Mrs Alexandra Sharp. According to her, the child must have wandered out of her room and into the yard during the afternoon. By the time she noticed, he was nowhere to be found. She'd asked the neighbours. They'd searched but hadn't found him.

The woman had four other children, aged from six down to nine months. The father, Brian Sharp, had vanished just after the last one was born. Taylor had talked to other families in the yard and looked around the area. No sign of Andrew.

The second sheet was the report from Linton, the duty sergeant for the district, written that evening. Further searching and questioning of residents. No leads, no one could recall seeing the boy that day. The mother was vague. Empty gin bottles in the room and everything slovenly. The three older children seemed uninterested. A note at the bottom to return in the morning and begin a broader search in daylight.

And that was all. Unless the rest of the papers had been misplaced, there had never been a follow-up. Not even a whisper.

'Ash,' he called, 'come in here.'

Harper showed him the letter first. When the inspector finished it and raised questioning eyes, he passed over the thin file. A minute and he'd read it all. Ash looked up, face set. He and his wife had adopted a girl who'd been abducted and abused. She was grown now, married with a family of her own. He saw the man's expression turn grim.

'Do you know a sergeant called Linton? I don't remember him,' he asked Mason when the man returned, balancing a mug and two biscuits.

'Knew of him, sir. I believe he worked out of here for a very short while before he transferred to D Division. Died two years back. Cancer.'

'I see. Thank you.'

Once they were alone again, Ash said, 'I never heard a damned thing about this. Did you, sir?'

'No.' A simple, hard answer.

'A missing kiddie . . . I don't understand. We should have had every man on it. Those are the orders.'

Harper felt the man's anger building. 'Yet there was nothing at all. I want to know why.'

'So do I.'

'Cranbrook,' Harper said.

'I can only think of one, sir. He owns that boot factory on Meanwood Road.'

Boots were big business. He'd have money.

'What else do we have on, apart from preparation for this visit?'

'Not that much, sir. Just the usual burglaries and assaults. Harmony Yard.' Ash rolled the name around his tongue. 'I know someone who lived there. I'll track him down. And I'll set the men on this.'

That was what he needed to hear. He had a squad of men who could think on their feet, and they'd keep digging until they found out what had happened all those years before.

'I want answers. This didn't just fall between the cracks. It was pushed. I'm going to be involved, too.' He needed to prepare for the prime minister's visit. He knew that. But he also had to discover the truth about this and see how they could have gone so completely wrong.

'Of course, sir.' Ash stood and gave a smile.

Harper thought as he spoke. 'We can't do a damned thing about Linton now. But I want Walsh to find Taylor. Get him in here, drag him if you have to. I'm going to give him the grilling of his life. You talk to your friend from Harmony Court and see if he can point you at anyone else who lived there. Galt can dig into things from the other end and see if the Cranbrooks have any children. If so, I want to know about them.'

'Yes, sir. What about Sissons?'

'He likes going through records. Let's see if he can identify whoever wrote this letter. I want him to look up the records of everyone convicted of child-selling in the last fifteen years, then see how many are still alive.'

Ash grinned. 'You know him, sir. He'll be happy as a pig in muck if he can bury himself in paper.'

THREE

The train was quicker than the tram. Harper stepped out at Kirkstall station and started walking back along the road towards Amen Corner and Lindley Place, on top of the embankment that overlooked the railway line.

The weather slapped against his face, a chilly autumnal blow that promised rain later in the day. Still, it cleared the air; even down here by the factories and the forges it smelled fresher.

The house was a through terrace on a short street. The tiny garden at the front was neatly kept, windows shining in the light. He raised his hand and brought it down on a polished brass knocker.

Harper could hear wheezing as an old man shuffled down the hall, but when the door opened, Tollman looked exactly the same as he always had behind his desk at Millgarth. Portly, smiling and jovial, a thick moustache covering his upper lip as he grinned. He might have been gone from the force for seven years now, but Harper hoped his memory hadn't dimmed.

'Well, this is a pleasant surprise, sir. Come on in, please.'

Through to the scullery, of course, and the ritual of placing the kettle on the range.

'The wife's nipped off to the shops.' He winked. 'Gives her a chance to gossip and get away from me.'

'Are you enjoying retirement?'

A frown clouded Tollman's face before he answered. 'I miss

the job, if I'm being honest, sir. I enjoyed working. Using this.' He tapped his skull.

'Then you might be glad I'm here.' He brought out the folder. 'Something to test your mettle.'

The man took his time reading. When he finished, he stood and made the tea, warming the pot before spooning in the leaves and adding the boiling water.

'I'll leave it to mash,' he said and sat down again and tapped his fingertips on the file. A smattering of dark liver spots showed on the back of his hand. 'I have a very faint memory of this, sir. I'm certain I mentioned it to Superintendent Kendall – you were just an inspector at the time, of course.'

'Yes.'

'I definitely recall Taylor and Linton, though. Giving Adam Taylor the boot was one of the best things you did for the division, if you don't mind me saying, sir.'

'He had it coming.'

'He'd been riding his luck for a long time. It doesn't surprise me he'd neglect something like this. And Linton . . .' He pressed his lips together. 'He wasn't with us long. Came from C Division, I think. Started out bright enough, but that faded quickly. Seems to me his wife was very poorly around that time. I didn't really see him after he transferred from Millgarth. And then he had . . .'

'Yes.' The word people danced around. Cancer. But he needed to get to the real question, the one that had brought him out here. 'Why didn't we do anything on this?'

'I've no idea, sir,' Tollman said. 'None at all.'

He poured the tea into two mugs, lifted the window sash and brought in a jug of milk from the ledge.

'We failed them, didn't we?' Tollman said as he sat down again. 'All of us. Yes. We did.' Simple, brutal, true.

'Why, though? Taylor and Linton must have known the procedure with a missing child. Why didn't anything happen?'

'I don't know, sir.' He could hear the man's frustration and sorrow. 'Linton was supposed to inform the uniformed inspector, who should have alerted Superintendent Kendall. He'd have brought in the detectives.'

Every copper knew how it worked. *Every* copper. It was drummed into them as recruits. But it hadn't happened. Harper's hands started to curl into fists and he straightened them again. The more he thought about it, the more certain he became that Taylor must have been on the take. Linton, too.

'Who was their inspector?'

'Halford.' Tollman went quiet for a minute, frowning and biting his lip. 'He was off ill for a while. It might have been around that time, now I think about it. He retired before I did, if you recall. Moved up to some village in the Dales, I think.'

'No one took over while he was poorly?'

'No, we were short.' His eyes were shining with the beginning of tears. 'I'm sorry, sir.'

'It's not your fault. But I'm going to put Taylor through the wringer when we find him.' Him and Linton, both corrupt. What other explanation could there be for the way a missing child had been ignored? 'What can you tell me about Mrs Sharp? Did she have a record?'

'Bound over to keep the peace a couple of times. Drunk when arrested.' The words came immediately, drawn from the huge store of knowledge in his head. 'Charged with prostitution once, I believe.'

No worse than many others. He needed to find her, to hear her side of things.

Now Harper had the background he'd come to discover, he sat back and sipped his tea. 'What have you been doing with yourself since you stopped working?'

'This and that. Some of us cleared a bit of land at the end of the road,' Tollman said. 'Good for growing a few spuds and onions . . .'

Alexandra Sharp. Her children were all grown now. The youngest would be fifteen. They could be anywhere in Leeds, anywhere at all.

As he passed the ruins of Kirkstall Abbey the wind along the river threatened to lift his hat, and he clamped it firmly in place with his hand.

First things first, Harper thought as he walked back into town. The note could be malicious. But it felt right. It felt *real*. And one fact was shamefully certain: the force had done nothing to find the missing child. What had Mrs Sharp gone through, day after day, year after year, as she agonized over what had become of her son? How many nightmares, how long searching every face on the streets?

He was never going to learn the answer to those questions.

'Found it, sir,' the clerk at the town hall said. 'She died in February, 1894. Exposure, it says here. Would you like me to copy out the certificate for you?'

'Yes,' Harper answered. He heard the emptiness in his voice. 'Thank you.'

Back in his office, he read the details, then sent Sergeant Mason back down to the records to dig out the police report. It was spare, a death that warranted no more than half a page.

The body had been discovered by a man on his way to work. He'd spotted it through the broken window of an empty house on Somerset Street. Barely two hundred yards from where Harper was sitting now. The constable on the beat had arrived, confirmed she was dead and hurried back to Millgarth to call out the police surgeon. It had been a bitter day, the report noted, with the temperature below freezing. All she'd been wearing was a thin cotton dress, not even a shawl to wrap around herself. An empty gin bottle lay on the floor at her side.

February the eleventh, two months to the day after Andrew had disappeared.

The constable had gone to Harmony Court. No relatives that anyone knew. He'd taken the children up to the workhouse. Someone would look after them there.

Nothing more than that. Just the bare, sad facts.

Harper stared at the wall for a long time, then picked up the telephone and asked the operator to put him through to the Victoria. Annabelle answered after five rings.

'Do the people at the workhouse still speak to you since you stepped down as a Guardian?' he asked.

'One or two of them, maybe.' She sounded amused. 'Why?'

'I might need your help with something.'

'Really?' He could hear the sudden interest in her voice. 'Then you'd better tell me all about it.'

'I found the chap I knew from Harmony Court,' Ash said. 'According to him—'

'Mrs Sharp died fourteen years ago.' He held up the report. 'I read about it.'

'Broken heart as much as anything, he reckoned. She'd always been a drinker, but it grew worse after her son vanished. Taylor wouldn't lift a finger to help her.' He looked down at the floor. 'Wouldn't give them the time of day. Threatened to come down like a hundredweight of bricks if they complained.'

A local bobby's warning carried heft. Harper shook his head. 'Someone must have been paying him.'

'I've been looking, sir,' Walsh said. 'All we had was the address he was at when you sacked him, and he hasn't lived there in years. No luck yet.'

'Then let's dig him out soon.' Harper slapped his palm down on the desk and the sound echoed around the office. He was being unfair, taking his frustration out on his men; they were doing all they could. More quietly, he continued: 'I want him in that interview room and I want some honest answers out of his mouth.' He turned to Galt. 'What can you tell us about the Cranbrooks?'

'We know he has the boot factory.' The man gave a quick, nervous smile. 'They live in Far Headingley, big house, pretty much what you'd expect, sir. And they have a son named Andrew.'

That was enough to change the atmosphere in the room. They all looked at Galt.

'Carry on,' Harper said. 'I can see you have more than that.'

'The boy goes to Leeds Grammar School. I haven't had a chance to establish much more than that yet. But . . .' He let the moment hang, looking from one face to another to another and seeing their anticipation. 'There's no record of an Andrew Cranbrook being born in Leeds.'

Harper felt a jolt. But he was going to keep a rein on things.

'Remember,' he said, 'by itself that doesn't prove anything.'

'I know, sir,' Galt replied quickly. 'I've written to Somerset House. They have all the records for England, they'll be able to tell me more.'

'Good work. Keep plugging away.'

'There's something else, too,' Galt added. 'The Cranbrooks have another child. A daughter. She's a year younger than Andrew.'

'And?'

'Her name's Marie. I haven't been able to come up with a local birth certificate for her, either.'

Only the ticking of the clock interrupted the silence.

'I see,' Harper said finally.

'I've queried Somerset House on both of them, sir.'

'Right, there's nothing we can do about that until we hear back. When Mrs Sharp died, her children went to the workhouse. I'm finding out about them. We'll meet here tomorrow. And don't forget the plans for the prime minister's visit. I still want your ideas in the morning.'

Annabelle was waiting upstairs at the Victoria, with her long, heavy coat buttoned and a hat tied around her head with a scarf.

'Are we going somewhere?' Harper asked as he placed his envelope on the sideboard.

'You wanted to know about the Sharp children,' she replied. 'We're going to find out. The records are up at the children's home on Street Lane.' She studied his face. 'What is it? You've got that twinkle in your eye.'

'Nothing.'

He let his eyes stray to the envelope, and she picked it up and opened it. Her mouth widened.

'My God, Tom. This is signed by the king.'

He shrugged, as if it was nothing. But inside he was glowing. 'Someone probably put it in front of him and said, "Sign here."'

'I don't care. It's still your name and his.'

He'd been close enough to touch the king at times during his visit. But they'd never exchanged a word. Thousands had been out to greet him, it had been a celebration, cheering and flags everywhere. Yet Harper couldn't see him as the monarch. In his mind, that was still Victoria, the woman who'd already been queen for years when he was born. She'd been dead for seven years now, but her shadow hung over the country, a constant, lingering presence. The public house where he lived was named for her. Somehow she'd become more than flesh and blood: part of the very fabric of Britain.

'We can frame it if you like.'

Annabelle snorted and prodded him with her elbow. 'Just you try and stop me. Don't be daft, of course we're going to frame it. Pride of place over the mantel for that.' She shook her head in amazement. 'My husband with a certificate from the king. Who'd have thought it?'

'Probably half the force received them.'

'No, they didn't, and you know it, Tom Harper.' She gathered up her gloves. 'Come on, we'd better be on our way.'

As she climbed into the Rex and settled behind the steering wheel, he wrapped his hands around the crank. It took strength and effort. More than that, it needed skill and timing. Once the engine caught, the handle whipped back; if you weren't quick, you could end up with a broken wrist.

By the time they reached the end of Manor Street the children were crowding around, shouting, gawking, eyes wide with excitement. Always the same. A motor car was as rare as diamonds around here. Anywhere, really; they were still a novelty.

Annabelle pulled on to Roundhay Road, passing carts that plodded along, utterly focused on her driving, handling the machine with confidence.

As soon as she bought the vehicle, she'd paid a mechanic to teach her how to maintain it. She could retard and advance a spark and all manner of other things, speaking a language that was completely foreign to him.

Whereas he often felt like a man overtaken by time, Annabelle was comfortable with the modern world; she seemed to relish every advance. She'd even used the vehicle to campaign for her successor on the Board of Guardians, drawing a crowd wherever they drove in Sheepscar. It had worked; the woman won by a landslide.

They seemed to go through Harehills in a flash, the buildings blurring together, then past the parade of shops at Oakwood and along Connaught Road. All around, new streets were rising from the ground, big, solid houses that would become homes for the prosperous, but there was still so much green out here, so much emptiness. The city centre felt more than just three miles away.

'What happened with the brewery man?' he asked.

The corners of her mouth drooped for a second, then her expression tightened.

'Long story. I'll tell you later. We're almost there.'

She pulled up outside a group of new buildings on Street Lane and turned off the engine. The only sounds were birds and the ticking of the motor as it cooled. Beyond them, everything was farmland. The northern edge of Leeds. How long before that changed? he wondered.

He watched, amused, as the staff bustled around to answer any request from Mrs Harper. Those nine years as a Guardian gave her authority and respect. But all they had were the addresses where the Sharp children had gone once they left the home or the workhouse.

'I'm sorry it's not more,' Annabelle said as she turned the car and began the drive back to Sheepscar.

'It's somewhere to begin.' He pulled the watch from his pocket. 'Can you drop me off at Millgarth? I still have a few things to do.'

She laughed. 'You like having a driver, don't you?'

'Well, if you're ever looking for a new career . . . go on, we have time now. What did the Tetley's man have to say for himself this morning?'

Her face changed. All the pleasure fled.

'I'll tell you tonight. At home.'

Strange, he thought; exactly what kind of deal had Tetley's been offering?

A note from Walsh was waiting on his desk. Taylor was working as a bookie's runner for Harry Matthews, collecting the cash and the betting slips. He'd been there since he was kicked off the force. Married, living in Hunslet.

But no one had seen him for the last two days. The sergeant had gone to visit Matthews. All he'd managed to learn was that Taylor had finished his day normally, turned everything in, then said he had to take a trip and would be away for a little while.

Taylor's wife claimed to have no idea where he'd gone. He'd come home from work, packed a small valise and told her that something had come up; he'd be back soon. That was the last she'd seen of him. No word since then. She desperately tried to hide it, but she was frantic.

Harper put the paper aside. Gone. Almost as if he'd known the storm was about to break. How, though? How could he have known an anonymous letter was going to the police? Tomorrow they'd begin hunting for him. At least Taylor never had much imagination; he was bound to still be somewhere in Leeds.

He'd just wiped his pen nib when Sissons bustled in, brushing dust from the shoulders of his suit jacket and wearing a satisfied smile.

'You look like a man who's had some success.'

'It's been a long day, sir, but I believe we have something. I came up with half a dozen names from the records, then I checked for death certificates. Two strong possibilities.' He reached into his briefcase and dug out a pair of files. 'See what you think of those.'

Mark Reynolds and Willie Bradley.

He remembered them both. Evil, the pair of them, and better off dead. With a sigh, he settled down to read.

By the time he finished, he felt as if he needed to wash his hands. Child-snatchers, child-sellers. Plenty of time inside, in solitary confinement for their own safety. That hadn't stopped Bradley losing an eye in an attack.

He'd died in 1900, stabbed in Gott's Park, his murderer never found. Reynolds had lasted until 1907, killed by a tumour in his brain. Both of them had been married. What type of woman could love a man like that? he asked himself. But he was going to find out. Their wives were still alive. He needed to find out if either one of them had penned the anonymous letter. One more task for the morning. No rest for the wicked. And even less for those who tried to stop the wickedness.

'That's excellent work. Time for you to go home, Sergeant,' he said. 'We're all going to be busy tomorrow.'

Enough for tonight. It was dark outside, filled with the sounds of Friday evening. Just another half day of work on Saturday and men were already celebrating. The pubs would be full; later the cells would be jammed. Every week the same thing, a ritual, as far back as he could recall.

FOUR

How many suppers had she kept warm in the oven for him over the years? Dozens, more likely hundreds. But it came with the job. Annabelle sat with a cup of tea as he ate.

'You've heard Asquith is coming to speak?' Harper said.

She nodded. 'Miss Ford told me. Only men allowed in, that's the rumour.'

'It's true,' he said as he pushed the empty plate away and wiped his mouth with the serviette. 'We're expecting trouble.'

'Hardly surprising. Women aren't going to miss a chance like that,' she said with a sly smile.

'Suffragists as well as suffragettes?'

She put a hand over her heart in mock surprise. 'Why, Superintendent, are you asking me for information? No, we're not going to be involved. Shouting a few slogans isn't going to change the prime minister's mind. We'll leave that to the suffragettes.'

'It's been one of those years. First the king, now this . . .' He sighed.

She smiled. 'Just as well you never wanted a dull life, isn't it?' Annabelle's grin faded and her expression turned serious. 'I was thinking, Tom, when you go to see the Sharp children, how would you feel about me coming with you?'

'It's police business,' he told her. 'You know that.'

'Yes, but two of those children are girls. It might help to have a woman there. Think about it. Maybe they'd talk more easily. It's not like you have any female coppers.'

It wasn't a bad idea. Those years as a Guardian had given her experience in drawing people out and learning the truth. And she was right; the girls might find a woman's presence comforting.

'All right,' he agreed. 'I'll have someone find their current addresses in the morning and we can go tomorrow afternoon.' He watched the smile bloom on her face. 'You were going to tell me about this visit from the Tetley's man. Have they made you a good offer to sell their beer?'

'In a manner of speaking.' She felt the side of the teapot and poured herself another cup. Playing for time, he thought, drawing out a few more seconds before she had to say anything. 'They want to buy the Victoria.'

'What? Buy the pub?' He could scarcely believe it. She'd never sell. Everyone knew that. The only way she'd leave this place would be feet first in a coffin. 'How much did they offer?'

She told him and he let out a low whistle.

'That's a fortune.'

Annabelle nodded. Her voice was empty. 'I know. They said they'd want me to stay on as landlady for a while.' She snorted. 'On a wage. Cash in an envelope every Saturday.'

'You're not going to do it, are you?'

'I've been here twenty-five years. Sheepscar . . . it's in my blood. Cut me open and it'll be written through me, like a stick of rock. I know them all, on every street. I've represented them.' She looked at him and shook her head. 'My first husband left me this pub to keep me secure.' A gentle smile. 'You know all that. God knows, I've said it often enough.'

'I do.'

'But . . . I have to tell you, Tom, the offer floored me. Not just because it came out of the blue. The size of it. We could live handsomely on that. I could start another business if I wanted.'

'Do you want to?' he asked.

'I don't know,' she answered after a moment. 'Truth is I'm not really sure what I want these days.'

'I can't see you as an employee here,' Harper said.

'No,' she agreed. 'I'd never do that. It wouldn't feel right. Just . . .' She shrugged.

'Then what are you going to do?'

'I told him I wanted to think about it. That he'd taken me off-guard.' Annabelle raised her eyebrows. 'That was certainly true enough.'

'It's up to you, you know that. Your pub, your decision. We're doing fine here, aren't we?'

'We make money. And a damn sight more of it than most in Sheepscar.'

'Well, then, there's no pressure, is there?' Harper stroked the back of her hand. 'You can take your time.'

'I suppose so.' She gathered up the empty dishes. 'But it's impossible not to think about that kind of brass.'

The plans were waiting on his desk. Little more than quick sketches, but he hadn't expected details. It gave him a chance to judge how many men he might need to keep order during the prime minister's visit. A quick calculation: too damn many of them.

The railway station and the Coliseum would be the main problems. Both of them were vulnerable. And he needed to keep the demonstration of unemployed men at a distance. They'd be angry; Kitson would have them stirred up and ready for violence. Plenty of uniformed constables needed to keep them in check. At the moment the suffragettes were the least of his worries.

The squad filed in for their morning meeting.

'We've a good load to keep us on our toes today,' Harper said brightly. 'Taylor did a disappearing act two days ago. Curiously, it was just after our anonymous letter writer put pen to paper.'

'Hardly sounds like a coincidence to me, sir,' Ash said.

'It doesn't, does it?' Harper said with a smile. 'I want a notice out to everyone on the beat. Make sure they're alert for him. I want him down here as soon as they find him. He was working for Harry Matthews. And Sissons has come up with two possible names for the person who penned our love note. We're going to talk to them both.'

'What do you want me to do, sir?' Ash said.

'I have the addresses where the Sharp children went after the children's home. Find out where they are now.'

A short nod. He knew the man would have the information on his desk by dinner time.

'You've made a very good start on your plans for the prime minister's visit. You've given me the bones. By Monday I'd like a little more flesh on them, if you can. We need to be prepared for every type of trouble. Believe me, it's probably going to happen.'

Outside Hettie Bradley's door on Bayswater Terrace, Harper glanced at each end of the street. Nobody lurking, nobody watching them.

'Ready?' he asked.

'Yes, sir,' Sissons said.

She was a large woman, with a hawk nose and curiously bulging eyes, her body tightly held in by the dirty apron tied around her waist. Her cheeks were red, the veins bright and broken on her nose. In the days when she'd been single, Harper had arrested her twice, for shoplifting and soliciting. Both times she'd cursed him up and down for doing his job. Unless she'd changed over the years, Hettie wasn't the type to have a conscience. And certainly not someone to do any favours for the police.

'What do you want?' She folded her arms and stared.

'A word. About your husband.'

'He's dead. Has been for a long time. Out of your reach.'

'Would you rather do this inside?' Harper asked. 'Or do you want to put on a show for the neighbours?'

Reluctantly, she let them in. The room was dirty, half the surfaces filmed with grease. Sissons touched a tabletop, grimaced and turned to look at the superintendent. The men remained standing.

Wheezing, the woman lowered herself on to a chair. 'What's our Willie supposed to have done from the other side of the grave?'

'I've no idea. I'm interested in what he did when he was alive. A child who disappeared at the end of 1893.'

'What about it?'

'That was the type of thing he liked to do, wasn't it, Hettie? Grab a child and sell them to a family who had good money to pay.'

'No.' There was anger in her eyes. 'That's what you lot always said. But he never did owt like that.'

'We had the evidence and the jury convicted him,' Harper told her. 'Twice.'

'You made it all up. Planted things.'

'The children pointed him out when they saw him.'

'Because you told them what to say.'

He wasn't going to get anything here. And definitely not the truth.

'I'm sorry we took your time. Oh,' he added, as if the idea had just come to him, 'would you mind if I took a look at that shopping list on the chair arm?'

The question took her by surprise. Before she could answer, he picked it up. The handwriting was nothing like the letter.

'Thank you.'

As they walked down the street, Harper glanced back. Hettie Bradley stood on the doorstep, glaring after them. Just as well looks couldn't kill, he thought; there'd be two corpses on the street.

'I'm not sure why you needed me, sir,' Sissons said. 'You handled her well enough.'

'You found the name. And you have a good mind; you might think of something that didn't occur to me.'

'Do you think we can ever prove Andrew Cranbrook is Andrew Sharp?' Sissons asked as they walked over to York Road.

Harper didn't reply. He simply didn't know. But he had to keep trying to discover what really happened to the boy. That was what the police were supposed to do. Dig until they discovered the facts, the only things that didn't lie. As they crossed the high bridge at South Accommodation Road, going into Hunslet, he glanced down at the river. Dirty as ever. Black and foul and full of death.

'I have another job for you,' he said. 'Do you know Alf Kitson?'

'The man who'll be leading the unemployed men on their protest when Mr Asquith visits. You want me to keep them under control.'

'Right now I'd like you to find out about him. I want chapter and verse.'

'Very good, sir.'

'Know your enemy. And believe me, that's what he intends to be.'

As soon as Harper saw Charlotte Reynolds, he knew. She was the one. She stood there, a woman dying inch by inch, so little left of her. Every scrap of excess had been shaved away by illness. One glance at him and she turned away, leaving the door hanging open for them to follow.

The room was neat enough, the air stifling with the overripe scent of decay. Her hair was thin, not much more than carefully brushed wisps with white scalp showing through. As she sat, Harper noticed that her stockings were rolled down around her skeletal ankles.

She had the calm, resigned air of someone who knew the end was close. He'd seen it before. Not serenity, just the exhaustion and the hopelessness of fighting any longer. Her face was worn; even the colour of her eyes seemed faded.

'Why?' Harper asked.

Her lips moved to a half-smile. 'I didn't think you'd ever find me.'

He glanced at Sissons. 'Why don't you go and make some tea? Mrs Reynolds looks as if she could use a cup.'

Once the sergeant had gone, Harper said, 'We were lucky. That and a bit of detective work.' He cocked his head and asked again: 'Why?'

'Conscience. I wanted to clear it before I go.' She shifted on the chair, trying to find a comfortable position. 'It was time.'

'Who paid your husband to snatch Andrew Sharp?'

She shook her head. 'Was that the boy's name? I didn't know. I didn't want Mark to tell me. But it was fifty pounds, and that was a fortune to us. I can't say I liked it, it seemed wrong even then. I know, he'd done it before. When you're desperate, though . . . Mark wasn't working. He hadn't had a job in months. Ever since then I've wondered about that lad and his family.'

'His mother died two months later.' There was no reason to spare her the truth.

'Poor woman.' She lowered her head. 'I'm sorry.'

'What about the policeman on the beat there?' Harper asked. 'Was he in on it, too?'

A nod. 'That was what Mark told me. He said it would all go like clockwork, the wheels were greased. I don't remember the copper's name. I think it began with a T . . .'

He squatted by the chair. 'What else can you tell me?' Harper's voice was low and urgent. 'Please, it's important.'

She looked at him. Her skin was so pale that he could see the delicate tracery of veins underneath. 'I didn't *want* to know who was behind it. Would you like to carry that weight around with you every day of your life?' Tears were beginning to form in her eyes. 'We didn't have anything. Nothing at all. Couldn't even pay the rent. He couldn't turn down money like that, could he? Not when it gave us a roof and put food on the table.'

All the reasons, the way she must have justified it to herself again and again over the years. She was crying now. Harper took out his handkerchief and handed it to her. In a curious way, he even understood. Who could afford morals when life was so brutal? No, Mark Reynolds should never have done it. But when the money offered the only way to eat and give them a bed, who would say no?

'We think there might have been someone else taken a year or so later. A girl.'

'It wasn't him.' Her voice was certain as stone. He believed her. 'After that little lad, I told him he was done with all that. He managed to find hisself a job and we lived honest until the Lord took him. But that boy, I don't know . . . it was always there between us, like we had a ghost in the house.'

'Is there anything else? Anything at all.'

He knew there was. He could sense it in her. Something remained, something she hadn't told him yet. But the moment was broken as Sissons returned with three mugs. Charlotte Reynolds retreated into herself, cupping the mug in both hands and keeping her head bowed over it. Still, he'd received his confirmation. Andrew Sharp had been snatched, and Taylor had been involved.

'Who knew you'd written to me?' Harper asked after a long silence.

'Just my daughter. She comes in every day, looks after my shopping and my cooking. I asked her to pop it in the post for me. She wanted to know why I was writing to the police, so I told her. I reckoned that if I was going to be honest with you, I should be with my own flesh and blood, too.'

'What's her name?' he asked gently.

'Roberta. Roberta Larner. She only lives two streets away.'

From the corner of his eye, Harper saw Sissons stiffen.

Five more minutes and he pulled out his pocket watch, making a pretence of checking. 'Thank you for your time. And for the letter.'

Rain had arrived again, a light, chilling drizzle that fell grey with soot. Harper pulled up the collar of his overcoat and tugged down the brim of his hat. 'Taylor was on the take,' he said as they began the walk back to Millgarth. 'Reynolds was paid fifty pounds to handle the snatch. I wonder what Taylor was paid to keep a lid on things.'

'Plenty of money,' Sissons agreed.

'Now we need to discover who organized it.' At least they were making progress. 'Larner. You looked like you recognized the name.'

'John Larner. It's come up a few times, sir. We've never had him in, but it rang a bell. Mostly to do with cons and a bit of bookmaking. Always on the fringes.'

'Bookmaking?' Taylor had been a bookie's runner. 'Take a look at what we have, then bring him to Millgarth and we'll see what he has to say.'

'Very good, sir. Do you think she gave us much else?'

'No. There was hardly anything there,' Harper said. 'Hardly anything at all. For now, anyway.'

FIVE

The note waited on his desk, written in Ash's careful copperplate: current addresses for the other Sharp children. From the workhouse, the eldest boy had been sent to Canada. A new life working on a prairie farm. The others stayed; both the girls were servants, and the youngest lad was an apprentice engineer, lodging in Hunslet.

'Do you still want to help?' he asked Annabelle on the telephone.

'Don't be daft,' she told him. 'Of course I do.'

'I have those addresses.'

'Give me a quarter of an hour and I'll pick you up.'

She was as good as her word, following his directions down into Hunslet and parking on Bloomer Street. By the time they stepped down on to the cobbles, a crowd of children had gathered.

Another neighbourhood that never saw a motor car. Back-to-back houses in the shadow of Larchfield Works and the Union Foundry, where every breath was filled with smoke and hot fragments of iron.

Harper knocked on the door of number fifteen. A minute later they were in the scullery as a young man scrubbed his hands in the sink. But it didn't matter how hard he tried, he'd never get rid of the dirt; it came with the job. It was with you for life.

'I haven't done owt, you know.' He tried to sound at ease, but his voice trilled with fear.

'I know that.' Harper smiled, trying to put him at ease. 'I'm hoping you can help me.'

Annabelle sat, quietly watching.

'How do you mean?' James Sharp looked very young, his skin smooth and his hair short, just the first dark fluff of a moustache over his top lip. Fifteen and beginning to fill out from his work, but still slim and small, with a pinched, suspicious expression.

'You had a brother called Andrew.'

That surprised him. Slowly, he dried himself on the towel. 'That were a long time ago,' he said. 'He disappeared.'

'I know.'

His eyes were quizzical. 'Then why are you asking? I was only a baby then. It's not as if I really *knew* about it. Everyone was so sad. Then my mam . . .'

'Do you remember *him* at all?' Annabelle asked quietly.

'Sometimes I think I do.' Harper studied the lad's face, filing it in his memory. When he finally saw Andrew, maybe he'd spot a resemblance. 'Not what he looked like or owt like that. He was just there, and then he was gone. People were looking round and frantic. Like I said, I was still in nappies then.' He paused and frowned and took a breath. 'Then my mam died and we all went in the workhouse. But my brothers and sisters talked about it all. Maybe that's why I think I remember him.' He shrugged. The workhouse was where his life had been. Everything before . . . how could he even begin to imagine what it must have been like for the lad?

'Your brother and sisters,' Annabelle continued. 'Are you close?'

'Not really. I see Jenny and Margaret at Christmas. They sent Davy to Canada. He wrote a letter after he arrived, from somewhere called Manitoba, but that was it.' He fell silent for a moment. 'That were ten year ago now.'

Time to change the subject, Harper thought, before James lost himself in reflections.

'How long until you finish your apprenticeship?'

'Two more years. It's all right. Be better once I'm earning decent money.' He looked around the room. 'The digs are fine.'

'Is there anything at all about Andrew that you can recall?'

But there wasn't. Hardly surprising; James hadn't even been a year old when his brother was taken.

'Why are you asking about him now?'

'There have been a few questions come up, that's all. He might still be alive.'

'Andrew? Alive?' He said it with complete disbelief. 'How?'

'It's possible. We don't know yet.'

James Sharp scratched at a cut on the back of his hand. 'Fancy that.'

'It wasn't a complete waste of time,' Harper said as Annabelle drove up Hunslet Lane. 'At least it gave me the chance to see him. The next stop is Bramhope. Jenny Sharp, she's almost twenty.'

'You're putting plenty of work into this.'

'We owe them something,' he told her. 'We never did anything at the time. At least one copper was bent. They deserve some truth.'

'And what will you do if you find it?' she asked him. 'Those children have grown up since it happened, Tom. It's all distant to them. You heard that lad. They have their own lives now.'

'I don't know,' he admitted. 'But I have to find out.'

'For them or for yourself?'

'I'm not sure. Maybe both,' he answered after a while. As they passed through Headingley, she accelerated. Harper looked out at the large houses. The Cranbrooks lived in one of those. Sometime, if he ever had enough evidence, he'd go and talk to them.

'Have you had any more thoughts about the offer from the brewery?' he asked.

'I've been trying to ignore it,' Annabelle answered. 'Just let it lie fallow for a while. They've waited this long to ask; they can be patient for my answer.'

The houses became fields. The way the scene changed so abruptly always took him by surprise, the sharp divide between city and country. His world was Leeds, with its bricks and cobblestones and air thick enough to cut with a pocketknife. It seemed like a huge place, sprawling more every day and consuming everything around. But it wasn't. Even with its suburbs it was compact. No more than a few minutes in the motor car and he was out in this. Drystone walls, cattle and sheep, and all that clear, sweet air. Hard to believe anything like it existed when he was cooped up in his office at Millgarth.

Bramhope stood more than halfway to Otley, planted firmly in the country. Just a small village, the face it showed to the world neat and tidy. The house was easy enough to find, standing back from the main street of the village, its name carved in crisp letters on the gateposts. People stopped to stare as they passed. Not just a motor car, but a woman at the wheel. Almost a scandal.

She swept down the drive, parking the Rex outside the front door before untying the scarf around her hat. No need to ring the bell. By the time they reached the step, a confused young maid was already waiting for them.

'Can I help you, miss?' she asked. 'Sir?'

'I'm Detective Superintendent Harper. This is my wife. We'd like to speak to the gentleman of the house.'

He saw panic flare in the girl's eyes. 'He's not here, sir.'

'The mistress, then.'

She bobbed a nervous curtsey and led them through the hall with its polished, gleaming parquet floor, past a staircase lined with framed watercolours, and through to a parlour where a fire beat away the autumn chill. The ashtrays were clean, but the sweet smell of cigars lingered in the air. A woman sat, placing her knitting in her lap as they entered. She was in her forties, with dark hair and a ready smile.

'Detective Superintendent and Mrs Harper, ma'am,' the maid said, and left.

'I'm Mrs Adams. Won't you take a seat? I don't believe we've done anything to warrant a police visit.' Her eyes were curious as she stared at him. 'Have we?'

'Of course not,' Harper replied. 'I'm hoping for a word with one of your maids. Jenny Sharp.' That was enough to make her raise an eyebrow. 'Please don't worry, she's not in trouble. It's about another member of her family, that's all. Something that happened a long time ago.'

'I see.' She spoke the words quietly, considering what to say next. 'I have to tell you, Jenny's a very satisfactory girl. She's thorough, always neat, works well. We're pleased with her here.'

A county accent. Northern, not Leeds, and with money behind it. Mrs Adams and her husband obviously lived a comfortable life. Prosperous, from the size of the house, but just this side of properly rich.

'Might I ask your role, Mrs Harper?'

'I was a Poor Law Guardian,' Annabelle replied. Absolutely true, but still a deliberately ambiguous statement. Let the woman think it related to something at the workhouse; there was certainly a grain of truth to it.

'Very well,' the woman decided. 'Jenny has a room in the attic. I think that's probably a good place for you to talk, don't you?'

Harper nodded. Out of the way, out of sight. It would work very well.

Jenny Sharp was mousy, with the same dark eyes and pinched features as her younger brother, her brown hair pinned under a cap. Close to twenty, but still thin and bony. She wore a long black dress and spotless apron, sitting perched on the edge of the bed, holding herself stiffly, hands curled together in an attempt to hide their roughness. Her eyes darted worriedly. Harper glanced at his wife.

'I'm Mrs Harper,' Annabelle said. 'I used to be on the Board of Guardians.' She gestured with her hand. 'This is my husband. He's a copper, but don't let that put you off. He's all right, really.'

Wary and unsure, the girl nodded.

'I was a servant myself. A long time back, now. When I was

about your age, in fact. Not in a place as grand as this, mind. In a pub.'

Jenny stayed silent, unsure whether to speak.

'I ended up marrying the owner,' Annabelle continued. 'My first husband. But I know what your job's like. Never ends, does it?'

'No, missus.'

'You might as well call me Annabelle. Everyone does.' She grinned. 'Tell me something, Jenny, do you remember your mother?'

'Yes,' the girl said with astonishment. 'Of course I do.'

'I know what happened to her. I can't imagine what it must have been like.' A long pause. 'You had a little brother, too, didn't you? The one who disappeared.'

Another nod. 'Andrew.' Her eyes darkened with suspicion. 'Why? What's happened?'

'The police are looking at it all again,' Annabelle told her. She nodded at Harper. 'My husband's in charge of it.'

'Why?' Jenny asked again, turning to look at him. 'Do you know something? How?'

'We've had some information,' Harper said.

'What?' She stared at him, disbelieving. 'But he's dead. That's what everyone said.'

'Maybe not. He might be alive after all. That's what we're trying to find out.'

'He can't . . . not after all . . . How? I mean . . .' The words defeated her. A very different reaction to James, he thought. But she was older. She'd remember Andrew.

'It would help to know whatever you can tell us about him,' Annabelle said.

'He . . . he was only small.' She turned to face Harper. 'Do you really think it's him?'

'Honestly, we don't know. But my wife's right: anything you can recall might help us find out.'

'Is he well? Does he remember us?' The questions poured out of her.

'I haven't talked to him.' He tried to weigh his reply carefully, not to carry too much hope. 'As far as I know, he's fine. We can't talk to him until we know more. We're not even certain it's him. I'm sorry, I realize this must sound strange, Miss Sharp. But please, trust us. We have to do it this way.'

She was insistent. 'If it is Andrew, what will you do then?'

'We'll tell you, and your brothers and sister. You'll be able to meet him if he wants.'

He couldn't guess at her thoughts. A jumble, probably, swirling out of control. Memories, regrets, God only knew what else. Simply the thought that the brother she'd always imagined dead might be alive. It must be overwhelming. Finally she took a breath and raised her head.

'He was a lovely little boy. I often had to look after him because I was the oldest girl and my mam . . . she was never well. Andrew had very dark eyes. Someone said he looked a lot like my pa, but I can't really remember him because he left when I was small. People used to stop and tell me how bonny Andrew was.' The recollection made her smile for a second.

'What happened when he disappeared?' Annabelle asked. She reached out and took one of Jenny's hands. For a moment the girl began to pull away, then stopped.

'We used to play out in front of the house, in Harmony Yard. There wasn't anywhere in our room. All the children round there did the same. It was always safe. My mam was sleeping. I went out to look for Andrew and he wasn't there.' A single tear trickled down her cheek and she quickly rubbed it away. 'We searched everywhere. Us, the neighbours. I always thought it was my fault because I wasn't watching him. But we couldn't find him and someone went for that bobby.'

'Taylor,' Harper said.

'He was worse than useless.' Her voice turned bitter. 'I could see that even then. And the sergeant who came was just the same. They didn't care because we weren't worth anything.'

'I know,' he said. 'I'm sorry.'

She'd been four when it happened. What she possessed were the remnants of a child's mind and a lifetime of guilt pressing down on her soul. For her brother vanishing, the way it led to her mother's death and all of them ending up in the workhouse. More than anyone should have to shoulder. Finally, Harper thanked her and stood.

'Will you let me know, please?' Jenny Sharp asked. 'Even if it's not Andrew, will you still tell me?'

'Of course we will,' Harper told her. 'I promise. As soon as we know.'

* * *

'Did you see her face when we left?' she asked.

'Yes.' The girl would be living on nerves until she heard. They owed her that. They owed her much, much more. They owed Jenny Sharp her childhood.

'Where now?'

James and Jenny looked like brother and sister. Margaret Sharp could have been from a different family. Almost seventeen, she was already edging towards plumpness, with fair, curly hair and large red cheeks. She was a maid-of-all-work in a terraced villa on Hawthorn Vale in Chapel Allerton, with a room off the kitchen in the cellar.

'Why do you want to know?' she asked when Annabelle spoke Andrew's name. 'That was what started it all. After he went, my mam died and that was it.'

'I know—' Harper began, but she continued.

'If it hadn't been for him we'd have all stayed together. Sometimes I wish he'd never been born at all. She might still have been alive then.'

And that was all. She didn't want to talk about Andrew, refused to even think about him. The resentment and bitterness had been building for most of her life. Who could blame her? Everything had been torn away and left her here. Like her sister, any hope of childhood had vanished with the boy.

'I'm sorry we upset you, Miss Sharp,' he said as he picked up his hat. 'Thank you for your time.'

Not much to say on the way down Chapeltown Road. He could feel her words pushing down on his shoulders. The anger and the sorrow.

'Home?' Annabelle said quietly. She hadn't spoken a word since they'd left the house.

'No.' He sighed. 'I'd better go back to Millgarth. Too much to do.'

'I went to see Harry Matthews,' Ash said. Gambling was only legal at racetracks. But it happened everywhere, impossible to stop. People needed the hope that a flutter on the horses gave them. It was easier for the police to tolerate the bookies, to keep some kind of control. 'I thought I might have more luck than Walsh. Harry and me have known each other a long while. I arrested him back when I was still in uniform. A proper knock-down, drag-out fight. He did six months for it.'

'Any luck?'

'He seems genuinely baffled about why Taylor left. For once I'm inclined to believe him. Didn't give any warning that he was going, Matthews claims. Taylor just came back from his rounds and announced he had to leave for a few days. No explanation at all.'

Exactly the same as he'd said before. 'Not been on the fiddle?'

'No more than the rest of them. Harry expects all his runners to take a bit, says he starts to worry if they don't because they're up to something else. But he wasn't happy at being left in the lurch that way.'

'So we're no closer to finding him.'

'Not yet.' Ash chuckled. 'You know, I was even threatened while I was there.'

'What? By Harry?' Harper asked in surprise. Matthews knew better than that.

'No, the man who opened the door. Cocky little fellow I've never seen before. Harry sent him off with his tail between his legs. Name of Larner.'

Harper straightened on his chair. 'John Larner?'

Ash's mouth tightened. 'That's right, sir. How did you know?'

'He's the son-in-law of the woman who wrote our anonymous note. His wife was the only other person who knew about it. Well, I think we know who tipped Taylor the wink. I told Sissons to find him and bring him in.'

Ash beamed. 'I'll be happy to help with that, sir. He can see what the inside of a police station is like.'

'Remember, the important thing is to find Taylor. Any sign of him yet?'

Harper stared at the rest of his squad as they shook their heads.

'There's not much more we can do tonight. Tomorrow I want to run through the plans for Mr Asquith's visit. We'll meet outside the Coliseum . . . let's say nine, as it's Sunday. You can enjoy a lie-in and breakfast at home for once.'

Almost midnight by the bedside clock. The ringing of the telephone wouldn't stop, dragging him from sleep and a dream that evaporated as he opened his eyes.

'Harper.'

'I'm sorry to bother you, sir.' Galt's voice, tentative at the other end of the line. Harper pressed the receiver closer to his ear to make out the words. 'But we've found Taylor.'

'Very good.' The room was cold, the fire was dead. He shivered in his pyjamas. Outside, rain dripped down the windows. 'Where is he?'

'That's the problem, sir. He's dead. Pulled out of the river an hour ago.'

Harper ran a hand through his hair. Dead? Damnation.

'You'd better send a vehicle for me. Ten minutes.'

SIX

Galt looked cold and sodden in the faint gleam from the bulls-eye lanterns. The rain eased for a moment and he looked up at the sky hopefully.

'Don't get your hopes up, it'll be back in a second,' Harper told him. 'It's set in for the night.' As he stopped speaking, the downpour returned, as heavy as before. 'Just be glad you're not out on the beat.'

They were standing under a corrugated iron overhang in a large, empty yard. A tarpaulin covered the body. Harper had drawn back one end as soon as he arrived. Taylor. No doubt about it. He remembered the face.

'Where was he found?'

'Over there.' He pointed towards the river. 'A stone juts out into the water and his jacket had snagged on it. The warehouse watchman saw a shape—'

'What was a watchman doing out there on a night like this?'

'Part of his rounds, sir. When he saw something bobbing, he realized what it was and ran off for a constable. The copper who came identified him; he used to serve with Taylor.'

'Any marks you could see? Wounds?'

'Nothing obvious, sir. Just what you'd expect from being in the water.'

'You'd better send him to the morgue. Dr Lumb can do his post-mortem in the morning.'

Impossible to tell where the body had gone into the river; with all the rain, it was flowing high and fast.

He should have stayed at home, tucked himself back under the warm blanket and let Galt handle everything. But he'd let curiosity overcome sense, for all the good it did him. How the hell were they ever going to discover the truth about Andrew Sharp now?

'I'll leave this with you. Report on my desk in the morning, please.' It wasn't too late to go home to the Victoria and enjoy a few more hours of sleep. The privilege of rank.

'Yes, sir.'

The rain had blown off to the east, but Cookridge Street was filled with puddles. A low grey morning sky hung over the city; it would turn damp again later. The town hall clock struck nine as Harper and his men stood outside the Coliseum.

'The cobbles, sir,' Ash said. He reached down, dug his fingers between a pair of setts and started to lift one. 'These need cementing in place or we might as well stand here and offer people ammunition.'

'I'll tell the council,' Harper said and turned to stare at the building. It was large, wide, with ornate scrolling on the stone, so grand in its design it looked more like a church than a theatre, waiting for a sermon on this Sunday morning.

'What about inside?' he asked Walsh.

'They'll have plenty of stewards on the door, sir. Check everyone to make sure women don't try to enter disguised as men. We'll need a couple of uniforms to back them up. More around the auditorium and some men in plain clothes in the crowd.'

'How many?'

'We should be able to easily get by with a total of ten, sir. They're not expecting any problems from the people allowed in.'

'Are you sure?' Harper asked. 'It's the prime minister; we don't want to be pinching pennies.'

'I think we'll be fine, sir.'

'What about out here? How many?'

'Sixty,' Ash replied without hesitation. 'We need some covering both sides of the road as Mr Asquith arrives, and a concentration outside the building. I'd like to block off the top of the street and have a barricade at the end of Vernon Street here.'

'Why?'

'We're going to have trouble, sir. We all know it. This way we'll be in a better position to handle it.'

'I'll see what the chief has to say.' It seemed like a sensible idea, but the order to block off streets needed to come from the top.

In front of the town hall, Harper turned to Sissons. 'Tell me your plans.'

'We're going to have those unemployed men with their demonstration here. I want to have coppers around, but not interfering unless they start to move towards the Coliseum. If they do that, we'll need to come down hard on them.'

'Good.' There was no sense in being heavy-handed unless it was necessary. 'What kind of force will you need?'

'Forty should be enough, unless there's trouble. It depends how many turn out to demonstrate, too.'

'I'd suggest at least fifty. Big lads, too. Just in case.'

Sissons nodded. 'Very good, sir.'

'What are you going to do if there *is* trouble?' Harper asked.

'Like I said: we fight like hell, sir.' He grinned.

'You'd best be prepared. Those words are probably going to be truer than you think. Right,' he told them. 'Your numbers all seem sensible. But I'm also going to recommend a reserve force. We'll keep them out of sight and call them up if we need them. Do any of you have any other ideas?'

The mortuary under Hunslet police station was Sabbath quiet. The only sound was Dr Lumb humming softly to himself as he worked on Taylor's body.

'I could have been on the golf course or in the garden this morning,' he said.

'You don't play golf and you don't like to garden,' Harper answered. 'You told me that once.'

The doctor barked out a short laugh. 'That's the problem in working with the police. They hold everything you say against you.'

'Comes with the job. You're working on a former constable now. Have you found out what killed him?'

'I can tell you that he didn't drown, if that's what you're wondering, Superintendent. He was already dead when he went in the water. Take a look at this.' He indicated a cut at the top of the corpse's stomach. 'A knife. Long enough to pierce his heart, so probably twelve inches. And an inch and a half wide.'

'It sounds like something a butcher would use.'

'Or a carving knife you can buy anywhere.' He lowered his head to peer at the wound. 'Single edge. I'd say almost certainly a carving knife. Someone might be using to it cut their Sunday joint right this minute.'

That was a gruesome thought. 'How long ago did it happen?'

'I'd say he was killed two nights ago. Friday. Please don't ask me to be more exact than that, it's impossible.'

Taylor had lived for a few days after he disappeared. And someone had found him.

'I'll let you finish. You might still have time for eighteen holes this afternoon.'

'I'll settle for a good dinner and a snooze in front of the fire. The report will be with you tomorrow.'

It was easy to find the house. Black crepe paper edged the front window. A home in mourning on a street of back-to-backs, their bricks all darkened by soot from the factories that surrounded them. No different from Sheepscar. No different from so many other places in Leeds.

He knocked on the door and waited. The woman who turned the latch surprised him. Loss made her face haggard, but Dotty Taylor was still beautiful, in her early forties, a striking figure in her widows' weeds.

'I'm Detective Superintendent Harper,' he said. 'I—'

She looked at him, her eyes hard, dark as jet. 'You're a copper, so I suppose you want to come in.' He followed, waiting as she sat in a chair by the fireplace, an air of grim dignity around her.

'I'm sorry about your husband.'

'Are you?' Her stare seemed to bore into him. 'Are you really?'

'Yes,' he told her. 'I am.'

'Then you can tell me: did he fall in the river or did someone kill him?'

'Why do you think anyone would do that?'

'Because he took off the other night like the devil was after him. Wouldn't tell me where or why.' She levelled the stare at him again. 'What would you think? I've known him too long not to tell when he's lying.'

'He was murdered,' Harper said. He expected tears, but there was nothing besides a slight nod and the tightening of her mouth. 'I know it's a bad time—'

'There's no good time to have coppers round. Harper.' She spoke the name slowly. 'I know who you are now. I should. He said it often enough when he'd had a few drinks. Hated you, Adam did. You took away the best job he had.'

He wasn't going to debate the issue with her. 'I want to find the man who killed him.'

'Do you? Do you really, luv?' The bitterness spilled over in her voice. 'It's not because of who he was, that's for damned sure.'

'It's my job, Mrs Taylor.'

'Then get on with it and leave a widow in peace. I had one of your lot here two days ago. But I'll warn you right now – if I found out who did for him, you'll be coming after me for murder.'

'It's our job to catch him.' He tried to keep his tone even, but with enough force to make her listen; she had gone somewhere he couldn't reach. 'How long were you married?'

'Four years,' she answered after a moment. 'I worked in one of the shops on the round he does for Harry Matthews. He promised he'd make an honest woman of me.' She gave a sad little laugh and held up her left hand to show a thin band on the third finger. 'He did that, right enough. Gold-plated, mind, not even solid all the way through. But that was Adam for you. Life on the cheap.' She sighed. 'Death even cheaper.'

'You loved him.'

'Course I did.' Her eyes flashed. 'Why, dun't your wife love you, Mr Policeman?'

'She does,' he replied quietly. 'Do you have any idea who did it, Mrs Taylor?'

The woman shook her head. 'I told you. I wish I did.'

'Had he been in any arguments or quarrels with anyone lately?'

'Adam?' She snorted. 'He could get into a fight with a lamppost when he'd been drinking. And he'd have forgotten it the next morning.' She took a breath. 'Tell me summat. Why did you sack him?'

He hesitated. 'You won't like any answer I give.'

She snorted. 'Probably not. I don't like the world at the moment, luv. If it all went away, I wouldn't miss a thing.' The woman brushed a strand of hair off her face and stared at him. 'Go on, you sent him packing from the force. Tell me why.'

'Because he drank on duty, he went off with prostitutes, he bullied the people on his beat and he was probably on the take.'

Harper expected her to flare up and defend him. Instead she nodded wearily.

'That sounds like Adam. He told me he'd had his wild times. But he'd calmed down by the time I met him.' Her mouth tightened. 'You might not believe me, but it's true. He wasn't perfect, but he was better.' A wisp of a smile. 'Said I kept him in line.'

'We'll do everything we can to catch whoever killed him.'

'I won't hold me breath.'

'Why did it happen?' Harper asked. 'Do you have *any* idea at all?'

'I don't know.' She shouted the words. They seemed to hammer against the walls and batter his ears. 'I don't know,' she repeated more quietly.

'He didn't say anything when he left?'

She shook her head. 'Just that something had happened and he'd be back in a few days. Packed a little bag and took himself off.'

'Did you ask him what it was?'

Dotty Taylor gave him a withering look. 'Course I did. I'm not stupid. I begged him. He just told me it would all be fine, gave me a kiss and went.' The hardness on her face started to crumble. She reached into her sleeve for a handkerchief and started to wipe her eyes, not caring if he saw.

Her pain was fresh. The Sharp children had lived with theirs for years. But they'd all carry it for a lifetime.

She didn't know anything that would help the police. He let himself out and left her to weep.

Two men lingered at the end of the street. Loud suits and flat caps pulled down to shade their eyes. They stirred as he began to walk, shifting apart so he'd have to go between them as he turned the corner.

Hard men with large fists and stony, expressionless faces.

But he wasn't going to change his route for them. He was a policeman; this was his city. You never showed fear. Once that began, they'd already won.

The men fell in beside him as he passed. He could smell their stale sweat and the threat that rolled off them.

'Good chat with Mrs Taylor, was it?' The taller one had a voice like gravel. His hands swung easily by his sides.

'Not any business of yours,' Harper said.

'Keep out of Adam Taylor's death. Just a word of advice. Round here we take care of things ourselves.'

'Not in Leeds, you don't.'

The punch came from behind, the silent man. Sudden, short, fast, to the kidney. The blow sent pain spiralling through his body. For a second he felt paralysed. Gasping, trying to breathe, feeling like a hand was squeezing his heart.

He heard the voice again. It seemed to arrive from miles away.

'Stay away from Dotty. I'll not say it twice. This is our business.'

Then the sound of hobnails on flagstones as they walked casually away.

'I've had Larner kicking his heels—' Walsh began, then he stopped. 'Christ. Are you all right, sir?'

Harper could feel the chill sweat on his face as he tried to keep his breathing steady and controlled. He knew how pale he looked. Very gently, he lowered himself onto a chair, wincing as it touched his back. The pain shot through him.

He closed his eyes, trying to will it away. When he opened them again, Walsh was offering a mug of tea.

'Drink that, sir. You look like you need it.'

He sipped gratefully. His body ached; he was exhausted. It had taken almost an hour to walk back to Millgarth, biting his lip with every step, making sure he placed each foot carefully so the agony wouldn't shoot through his body.

'What happened? Do you need a doctor?'

Harper swallowed and shook his head. He'd taken a kidney punch before; he knew what to expect. Plenty of pain for a little while, passing blood for a day or so.

'I was in Hunslet, so I went to see Taylor's widow.' He paused, catching his breath for a moment. 'When I left, two men suggested we should leave the investigation to them.' He moved on the seat and gasped at the pain. 'The one who hit me must have been a professional. Just one blow.'

'I'll talk to the constable on the beat there. He'll have some names.'

'Yes.' He knew he ought to stand, go into his office. But he was sitting down here, and it seemed a very long way to travel. Whatever he did, the pain wasn't about to vanish.

Fifteen years before, he'd have been prepared for an attack like that. He'd never have given them the chance. He'd become soft, slow. He'd grown into the illusion that rank made him invulnerable. Bloody stupid. The ache would go in a few days. But he'd need to remember the lesson.

He could see Walsh speaking on the telephone, glancing back over his shoulder as he talked.

For a moment he wished Billy Reed was still here. Not the Whitby inspector but the young detective sergeant he'd known twenty years before. He'd have shaken his head at Harper for not being prepared, then stalked out to take his revenge. Billy was dead, though, God rest him, and those rough-and-tumble days were long gone.

After a few minutes he felt strong enough to push himself up and tread slowly to his office. As he settled on to his chair with a long sigh, Walsh appeared.

'I've just talked to Superintendent Davidson in Hunslet, sir. He'll have men on it right away.'

'Thank you. You started to say something about Larner?'

'Inspector Ash and I brought him in. He's stewing in the interview room. We've had him there for three hours. I was waiting for you to return.'

Not now. He wasn't ready for a conversation like that. 'You two go ahead and talk to him. You know what to ask.'

'Very good, sir.' A flicker of worry crossed his face. 'Is there anything I can get you? Are you sure you don't want a doctor?'

'I'm not an invalid.' He tempered his words with a smile. 'I suppose some aspirin powder might help.'

'I'll have Sergeant Mason take care of it, sir.'

By late afternoon the pain had dulled to a constant ache, only sharp and burning when he turned the wrong way. As the men trooped into his office, he tried to summon a grin.

Ash was the first to speak. 'How are you feeling now, sir?'

'I'll survive.' His eyes met theirs. They all knew; being a copper meant taking a battering sometimes. It came with the badge. You just hoped it wouldn't be too bad.

'They caught that pair who assaulted you, sir.' Ash grinned under his thick moustache. 'Apparently they resisted arrest, so they're a little the worse for wear in the cells.'

Harper felt a wave of dark satisfaction run through him. Let them suffer a little. 'Who are they?'

'One of them is Mrs Taylor's brother. The other one is a friend of his, a former boxer.'

That explained the power behind the punch.

'Have they admitted it?'

'All done and dusted, sir. Up before the beak in the morning.'

They'd each receive the standard sentence; six months for assaulting a police officer. Maybe it would teach them; probably not. But everything had been taken care of quickly and efficiently. He'd heal. Time to think about other things.

'Larner?'

Walsh glanced at Ash before he spoke.

'He admitted he told Taylor about his mother-in-law's letter. He swears he had no idea Taylor had been involved in the snatch.'

'That's probably true,' Ash agreed with a sharp nod. 'Larner would only have been about ten when it happened.'

'Put the fear of God in him and let him go,' Harper ordered, then thought for a second. 'Before you do, get a list from him of every stop Taylor made on his rounds.'

'Very good, sir.'

He was at the top of the stairs when he heard Annabelle shout 'No.' Half of Sheepscar must have heard her. A brief silence, then the slamming of a door. Harper sighed. Not the first time it had happened, and it certainly wouldn't be the last. Mary and her mother were too much alike, too determined, for either of them to ever back down.

Annabelle had her arms folded as she tried to pace away her anger and frustration.

'Did you hear it?'

'Only the tail end. What was it this time?'

'She wants to join this suffragette protest during Asquith's visit.' The fire was still flaring in her eyes. 'It'll be mayhem.'

'It will,' he agreed. 'Complete chaos. Do you want me to go and speak to her?'

At first she didn't respond. Her face was like stone, trying to hold back the tears. Then she had control of herself once more and gave the smallest nod.

'You do that and I'll get your tea from the oven.'

A knock on the door and he slipped into Mary's room. She was curled on the bed, a pillow clutched against her stomach, wearing exactly the same look of anger and sorrow as her mother. Very gingerly, he lowered himself until he was sitting on the edge of the bed.

'You want to go to the demonstration?'

'Yes.' Her voice was tight.

'I'm going to be in charge of everything that night.'

She raised her head to peer at him. 'Then you can keep it all safe.'

He shook his head and smiled at her. 'I wish I could. It's not going to be as easy as that.' He stroked her hair, pushing a strand away from her face. 'There's going to be trouble.'

'Not from—'

He cut her off. 'From a number of places. My coppers are going to be on edge. If things get out of hand, people will be hurt. It's going to be dangerous. I'm not lying to you.'

'But—'

'I mean it; it'll be bad,' he insisted. 'Your mother's looking out for you, that's all. She's seen for herself what things like this can be like.'

'I'll be careful. I *told* her.' She hammered a fist down on the pillow.

'Things happen and you can't control them. Believe me. How do you think I ended up with these scars?'

'I won't cause any problems. That's not why I'm going.'

'Of course you want to be there. It makes sense. You want to protest; you want to be heard.' He needed an argument that would convince her. Her head, at least. In her heart she was already outside the Coliseum. 'But events . . . they can change so quickly. If they do, you won't have the chance.' He paused. Time to try another tack. 'Let's say you go—'

'Yes.' Her face brightened.

'Let's say you do, and somehow you're arrested. It doesn't matter what it's for, it could be something trivial. You work for a lawyer. You'll lose that job. They won't keep you on.'

That was enough to silence her for a few seconds.

'Then I'll find another.'

'Employers check.' He paused to let that sink in. 'If you've been arrested, they won't want to hire you. Nobody wants an employee who might cause trouble. Please, I'm telling you the truth. Think about it.'

His meal was waiting, dried out but warm and filling.

'What did you say?' Annabelle asked.

'A few things she hadn't considered.'

'Sissons telephoned while you were on your way home. He told me what happened to you.'

He chuckled. 'You've got him well trained, haven't you?'

She ignored the comment. 'How do you feel now?'

'I've been worse.' His back was stiff, aching. Sore around the kidney, the skin tender when he touched it.

'You ought to see a doctor.'

'It'll be fine,' he said. 'Gone in a few days.'

'You're not a young man any more, Tom. And don't try that "fine" malarkey with me. I saw the way you were holding yourself when you came in.'

He could never fool her. 'I felt about eighty years old this afternoon. But it's passing. Honestly.'

'I worry about you.' She turned her head to glance at the closed door to Mary's room. 'And her.'

'She's growing up.'

'I know,' Annabelle said ruefully. 'That's the problem.'

SEVEN

'I've had men searching both banks of the river for the weapon that killed Taylor, sir,' Galt said. 'They've gone as far upstream as Holbeck.'

'I don't suppose they've come up with anything?' Harper asked. His back ached, sore when he moved, the bruise vivid greens and purples on his skin.

'All that rain on Saturday night would have washed away any

blood. And it's easy to toss a knife in the river straight after a body, isn't it?'

'Never mind, we had to try. Have you had any reply from Somerset House on the Cranbrook children?'

Galt shook his head. 'Still waiting, sir.'

'Larner gave us all the stops on Taylor's round before I let him go,' Walsh said. 'I dropped by a few of them yesterday. Everyone was shocked to hear about him.'

'Was he well liked?' From his memory of the man, that would be hard to believe.

'No one came out and said anything bad,' the sergeant replied with care. 'I have the impression he was tolerated more than loved.'

'Visit all the others today. I'm not expecting much, but you might turn up some little gem.'

Ash gave a small cough. 'I went over to Hunslet and had a quiet word with Dotty Taylor's brother and his friend. I have to say, sir, they certainly looked a little the worse for wear.'

He wasn't going to shed any tears over that pair, not when he could still feel the pain in his back. If you beat a copper, you knew what was waiting when you were caught.

'What did they have to say for themselves?'

'They have no idea who might have killed Adam Taylor.'

Harper took off his spectacles and rubbed his cheeks. 'Then it seems we're back to square one. We know Taylor took off after Larner told him about the letter. He must have been scared we'd put two and two together and come after him.' He raised his head and looked at the others. 'My guess is he went to see whoever arranged the snatch. That person killed him and tossed him in the river. Any other theories?'

They were silent as he gazed around the faces. It made perfect sense. But there was still a hole at the centre of it all – the name of the person Taylor had gone to see.

'Sissons, you looked into those child-snatching cases. Go back and see if you can find any other names in there. People who don't seem to fit.'

'Yes, sir.'

One by one they left, until only Ash was waiting by the door.

'How are you feeling this morning, sir?'

'Stiff,' Harper replied. 'A bit fragile. And very stupid. I should never have given him the chance to hit me.'

'Happens to us all, sir.' He brought something from his pocket and placed it on the desk. 'I thought you might find this useful, seeing as you're out and about on this one.'

A cosh, covered in shiny braided leather. Harper raised his eyebrows.

'I took it off a bully boy a few months ago. It's just been lying in my desk. Always pays to be prepared, sir.'

He sat down to write his reports for the chief constable. A short one on the Taylor murder and a longer, detailed plan for the prime minister's visit. By the time he surfaced it was almost twelve.

Harper sat back. As he stretched, he felt a sharp twinge where he'd been punched. The cosh still lay on the desk. He slipped it into his jacket. Ash was right; it wouldn't hurt to have some protection. Just in time, too. Chief Constable Crossley strode into the detectives' room, a triumphant smile on his face.

'I was hoping to catch you, Tom. I've been in the magistrates' court. Those two who assaulted you each received six months.'

'Couldn't happen to two nicer men.'

Crossley rubbed his hands together. 'Do you feel up to a spot of luncheon to celebrate? Not hurting too badly?'

'If you're paying, sir, I'll gladly come. I have these for you, too.'

Crossley riffled through the reports and nodded in satisfaction.

'Very good. It looks like we'll be prepared for Mr Asquith.'

It was the first time he'd been in the Kardomah on Briggate; it had only opened a month before. Decent food, and cheap. The waitress took their empty plates and they sat back with cups of coffee. No business while they were eating; that was the chief's rule. Now, though, they could begin. Crossley cut the tip of a cigar and lit it with a match.

'Tell me about this case of yours.'

A hubbub of conversation filled the cafe. Men talked and ate, every table full, the staff bustling around. It was all background. His hearing wasn't good enough to pick out words; the noise made it difficult enough to hear the chief.

'I know Cranbrook,' Crossley said when he'd finished. 'Always seemed honest and forthright to me.'

'I'm not jumping to any conclusions, sir. I certainly don't have enough to talk to him yet. We still have to hear from Somerset House.'

'Seems to me you'll know more when you discover who killed Taylor.'

'We will.' Find him and they'd be able to connect some dots.

'Just let me know what you intend to do. Now, what about you? You're feeling fine? Be truthful with me.'

'Getting there, sir,' Harper answered with a smile.

'Good, good.' He finished his coffee and studied the tip of his cigar. 'These plans for Asquith's visit. I want to be certain we have enough men for any eventuality. If you think of anything more, don't be afraid to add it. I'd rather be cautious and prepared. The last thing we need is trouble.'

'I agree, sir.' He thought about Mary and her desire to be there with the suffragettes. 'Definitely.'

Galt was on his feet as soon as Harper entered, following him to his office with a letter in his hand.

'Let me guess – you've heard about the Cranbrook babies.'

'Yes, sir.' His face was eager. 'Arrived in the post an hour ago.'

'Go on,' Harper said. 'You're bursting to tell me.'

'They don't have birth certificates for either Andrew or Marie Cranbrook. We have to go and talk to the family now, don't we, sir?'

Did they? He wanted something solid, something they couldn't try to deny.

'Not yet. It's still too flimsy. They could tell us the children were born abroad. Anything at all. What we need is to find the person who arranged the sale. Once we have testimony on that, *then* we'll go and confront Cranbrook.'

Galt's face fell. But there was a time when a letter like that would have sent him haring after the family, too. They were hiding something; he knew it in his bones. Time had taught him a few things, though. Never go up against the rich until you'd built a trap around them. It was fifteen years since Andrew Sharp had been taken. A few more weeks would make no difference at all.

He spent the rest of the afternoon going back over the plan he'd given to the chief. Assessing it for weaknesses, trying to picture how things might happen and the ways the police would react. A few small changes, but it seemed sound, flexible enough to shift tack as the situation demanded. Tomorrow he'd send over this revised version and then hope to God his ideas were right.

'Back still sore?' Annabelle asked.

'I've spent most of the day sitting down. That and being treated to luncheon at the Kardomah.'

'Nice work if you can get it. Now, if you'd said it hurt, I was going to offer to rub in some liniment.'

'In that case, it aches like the devil.'

'Get on with you,' she laughed, but pushed up her sleeves anyway.

The liquid was pungent, warm on his skin as she worked it in slowly.

'This offer from Tetley's,' Annabelle began. 'I'm still going over it in my mind. They sent me a letter today, confirming it all in writing. Seeing that figure, Tom . . . I don't know. I had my mind dead set against it. Now . . .' Her words vanished as her fingers moved over his back.

'How would you feel, giving up this place?'

'Scared,' she said. 'I belong here. You know that. Sheepscar is my home. I was the Guardian for this ward. I'd feel like I was abandoning them if we upped sticks and moved away.'

'But—' He winced as she pressed down on the bruise. 'Eventually you'd sell up at some point, anyway. It's not like we have to go far. There are good houses on Spencer Place. That's hardly a quarter of a mile away.'

'Oh, in my head, I know all that,' she agreed. 'But you've seen those places. Big villas, and the people walk round with their noses stuck in the air. That's not me. It's a different world.'

He understood. The street might be only a stone's throw away, but it was a different world from the overcrowded back-to-back houses down the road in Sheepscar. On the cusp of genteel Chapeltown and the plush part of Harehills.

'We could afford it,' he said. The heat of the liniment felt soothing as it worked its way into his muscles.

'That's not the point and you know it. I've never thought about us anywhere but in this place.'

'And now you have to.'

'About the possibility of it, anyway,' she answered after a small pause. 'But what I wonder is who I'd be if we weren't here. I think I'd feel lost. If we move somewhere everyone has money, I'll think they're all looking down on me.'

'You'd be able to buy and sell most of them,' he pointed out. 'You already can.'

Her fingers pressed deeper into his skin. 'It's not that. It's who we are. The way we speak.'

Common people. Not good enough. At least on the force most of the senior officers had started out on the beat. They had backgrounds the same as the men they commanded. Like his.

But that wasn't all she meant. Any move meant a fresh start in a new place, with unknown neighbours. Even if it was only a few hundred yards, it was still a different community. Around here they all knew Annabelle. They accepted the fact that her husband was a copper, that she had cash in the bank. Elsewhere . . . who could tell? Maybe she didn't embrace change quite as eagerly as he'd imagined.

'You'll know when you've reached a decision,' he told her.

'I suppose so.' She lifted her hands and flexed her fingers. 'That's you done,' she said as she stood. 'One way to make sure you listen to me.'

'I would have done anyway.'

'I know.' She sighed. 'Did the rub help?'

He stretched. Movement felt a little easier. 'Yes.'

'Anything interesting from the remainder of Taylor's round?' he asked Walsh.

The sergeant gave a small shrug. 'Nothing at all, sir. A few liked him, the rest tolerated him. No one's come out and said anything ill of the dead.'

'The only thing missing is his killer,' Harper said with a rueful smile. 'The people who can help us are already dead or don't seem to know. Mrs Reynolds admits her husband was responsible for snatching Andrew Sharp, but says he had nothing to do with the girl. I believe her, at least on that. That means we're looking for someone else.' His gaze moved from one set of eyes to another and another and rested on Sissons. 'Did you come up with the names of anyone else arranging sales of children?'

'Two possibilities, sir. But they're both very faint ones.'

'Never mind. Look into them.'

EIGHT

'You don't look as peaky this morning, sir,' Ash said.

'Almost back to normal,' Harper agreed. His hand brushed against his overcoat pocket, feeling the reassurance of the cosh. For a second he imagined Billy Reed looking down and slowly shaking his head. Never mind; better late than never.

They were sitting on the top deck of a motor bus rumbling along Woodhouse Lane. Just past the new university they alighted at the edge of Woodhouse Moor, then walked down Raglan Road, off into the streets that looked down over the Meanwood Valley.

The smoke and stink from the tanneries and factories rose up the hillside. Identical, anonymous streets of back-to-back houses. Away from the moor, there wasn't a tree or a splash of colour to be seen. Someone's washing hung from a line high across the cobbles, already turning grey from the soot in the air.

'Just along here, sir,' Ash said as they turned the corner. 'Seven houses down. I think you'll find this chap interesting. I met him a year or so ago. He's the criminal version of Tollman, all sorts of history at his fingertips.'

'Reliable information?'

'Top quality. Worth every penny. We know who took Andrew Sharp, but not where the girl came from.'

'It's probably fair to think she was snatched, too.'

'That's what I believe, sir. He might be able to give us a lead on whoever was responsible.'

A black door, donkeystoned front step. Harper stood aside as the inspector rapped on the wood.

'Hello, Clara, is he around? I've brought my boss to meet him.'

The scullery was steamy, with a pan simmering on the range, and a man sitting in his shirtsleeves at the table, reading the paper. Thick grey hair like wire swept up from his skull, and the lines were so deep on his face that they could have been carved there with a chisel.

'Mr Ash,' he said, taking a Capstan cigarette from a packet.

'What brings you here?'

There was a teasing hint of something under the Leeds accent, as if he'd been born in another country and moved here when he was young.

'Same as always, Heinrich. Information. This is Superintendent Harper. I thought it was time I introduced the two of you.'

A cautious nod from the man. 'Sit down.' He shouted something in German and the woman bustled around, filling the kettle and putting it on the stove. Silence reigned through the ritual as the woman made tea and placed the pot and mugs on the oilcloth covering the table. A look from Heinrich and she scuttled off again.

He lit his cigarette and smiled, showing teeth stained a dull, deep brown. 'Now, what do you need?'

'People who've arranged the sale of snatched children in the last fifteen years,' Ash said.

The man pursed his lips. 'Not too many of them.' He squinted. 'Why fifteen years?'

'That's the time I want to cover,' Ash told him.

'Five,' Heinrich said after a few seconds, then paused. 'No, six. But one of those is dead. One I haven't heard of in years.'

'Names?' Harper asked.

The man's eyes brightened. 'How much?'

'Five shillings.'

Heinrich shook his head. 'This is a serious crime. You need the information, so you've come to me.'

'Ten shillings,' Harper offered.

'Better. Two of them are women, I don't know where they live now. Annie Mercer. She's vicious. Started out in baby farming.' He stared at them. 'You know what that is, of course?'

Harper nodded. Taking in children from women who couldn't afford to raise them properly. The mothers paid, imagining they'd be brought up in a good home, but most of the kiddies ended up dead.

'And Brenda Woolcott. She wasn't too young fifteen years ago. I don't know if she's still alive. I never heard she'd died.'

'Those are the women,' Ash said. 'What about the men?'

'Jed McMillan, Charlie Wainwright, and Mickey Todd.'

'Mickey's been crippled for the last three years,' Ash said. 'Can't even speak.'

Heinrich shrugged. 'You wanted names. I'm not a doctor.'

'Do you know anything about Wainwright and McMillan?'

'Just what they're called and what they do.' He tapped his skull. 'All up here.'

'For that price, I hope he's telling the truth,' Harper said once they were back on the street. 'He never even poured us that cuppa.'

'He never does. Just lets it sit there and mash. God only knows why.' Ash smiled. 'His little way. But like I said, sir, his information has always been gold. Once we're back at Millgarth I'll find addresses for them.'

'You and Walsh and Galt can handle it.'

'Very good, sir.'

Marie Cranbrook. Just like Andrew, she had no birth certificate, no information at all. It was time to discover who she really was. He talked to Sergeant Mason, seeing him grimace as he began to understand the task.

'Use a couple of bright bobbies to search. They'll probably be glad to take the weight off their feet for a couple of hours.'

That was enough to make him smile. 'I have just the pair you need, sir. Leave it with me. Do you fancy a cup of tea? I'm about to make one.'

Harper thought of the untouched pot on Heinrich's table, steam coming from the spout. 'I'd love one.'

A little after three o'clock a tentative knock on the door made him raise his head from the pile of reports on his desk. The young constable standing there looked uncertain, nervous before a senior officer.

'Come on in,' Harper said.

The man stood at attention, helmet gathered under his arm, staring straight ahead, exactly the way he'd been taught.

'PC Doyle, sir, 736. I work out of Wortley. My superintendent said I should come down and see you.'

Curious, Harper thought. What did he need at Millgarth?

'Do you walk a beat?'

'Yes, sir.'

'Then you could probably do with a sit down for a few minutes.'

Doyle looked astonished at the suggestion, as if it upset the natural order of life.

'I'd rather stand if you don't mind, sir.'

'Whatever you prefer, Mr Doyle. Now, what brings you down here?'

'I've been off poorly for the last three days,' he began. 'Bad chest. When I came back, I heard about Taylor. That you'd found his body.'

'Go on.' He watched the young man with interest. Doyle still sounded wary, but grew a little more comfortable as he found his stride.

'I saw him the day he died, sir. The Friday.'

'Where?' Harper asked sharply. 'When?'

'On the canal towpath, out towards Armley. It must have been about six in the evening.'

'Give me all the details, Constable. Everything you can remember.'

'Part of my beat takes me along there, sir. Taylor was walking with another man. They were talking. He glanced at me, then looked away again.'

'How did you know it was him?'

Doyle gave his first smile. 'I grew up in Bond's Court. I don't know if you knew it, sir; they knocked it down to build County Arcade. He was the bobby there until, well, you know.' Until he was sacked, the man meant. 'A couple of times he gave me a clout for being cheeky when I was a nipper. I knew who he was, even if he didn't recognize me.'

Life, Harper thought. Everything came around. 'Do you remember a child being taken from Harmony Court in 1893?'

Doyle frowned. 'Not really. I'd only have been five years old then. I don't think I'd have noticed. Why, sir?'

'It doesn't matter.' If Doyle had known Andrew Sharp, the coincidence would have been too great. 'Go on. Did you know the man with Taylor?'

'No, sir. I've never seen him before. He was tall, though, close on six feet. Brown cap, worn overcoat, a thin reddish moustache. In his forties, I'd say.' A slight pause. 'He looked worried, as if something was bothering him.'

'That's a good memory, Constable.'

'Thank you, sir.' He blushed, the colour rising up his neck and cheeks. 'Taylor was carrying a small leather valise.'

That fitted with what his wife had said.

'Which way were they going?'

'Towards town. Taylor didn't look happy, either, sir. Glum, I suppose you'd say,' he added. 'His shoulders were certainly slumped.'

'You're very observant.'

'Only because I knew him, sir. I was curious.'

'Is there anything else you remember?'

'I'm afraid not. We passed each other and that was it. I didn't think much about it.'

And why would he? 'Write up a report for me, please. And thank you for coming to tell me.'

Doyle beamed. 'I'll do that, sir.' A salute and he marched out, boots thumping on the floor.

Another fragment of information. And the description of a man seen with Taylor was valuable. Piece by tiny piece, things were edging along. Not quickly enough, of course. But it never was.

His thoughts were disturbed by Sergeant Mason with a small pile of folders, every one of them bulging.

'That's what you requested, sir. Girls under five years old who were reported missing from 1894 to '96 and never found.'

'How many of them?'

'Six, sir.' He frowned and breathed deep. 'Too many, isn't it?'

'It is,' Harper agreed sadly. 'Far too many.'

It was the third one he read. It had to be her. Vanished from Armley in July, 1895, not quite two years old. He had a very faint memory of the case. At least this time there'd been an outcry, a proper search, not like Andrew Sharp. But the result had been the same; no trace ever found of her. After a month, the operation had ended.

The dates fitted. What made him certain was the girl's name: Marie. Marie Davis. The younger of two children. Her father worked at Armley Mills.

He knew it inside, as certain as breathing. The Cranbrooks had been bringing up two children who didn't belong to them. Children taken from home.

Now, how the hell could he prove it?

Outside, daylight was rapidly fading, the streetlamps glowing in the gloom. A drizzle had begun, darkening the streets with fine drops.

'Read the file, tell me what you think,' he said as he passed it around. 'And we have a sighting on Taylor late Friday afternoon.' Harper gave the description of the man seen with him. 'Does that ring any bells?'

No; it would be too much to hope that it did.

'A pity,' he said, then smiled. 'Well, gentlemen, what do you have? Sissons?'

'The two baby-sellers I saw both deny they had anything to do with selling a girl. I even said they wouldn't be prosecuted if they told me the truth, but that didn't shift them.' He moved on the seat, stretching out a long pair of legs. 'Both claim they had no idea who might have done it.' He shrugged. 'Sorry, sir, but it's a dead end.'

He hadn't expected much more. Few were ever likely to admit a crime like that unless they were caught in the act.

'Ash?'

'I followed up on the information we were given, sir.' A finger laid along on his nose, no name mentioned, keeping his snouts secret. 'Managed to find addresses on three of them. Another one is dead, and no trace of the fifth. We'll go and see them in the morning.'

'Sir?' Galt said. He had the Marie Davis folder open on his lap. 'We have to go and talk to the Cranbrooks now, don't we? There's this, and the letter about Andrew Sharp, and no birth certificates for the children they claim are theirs.'

Harper shook his head. 'I told you earlier. We need to know who sold both the children. I want evidence and I want it watertight.' He saw the frustration appear on the man's face. 'Find me something they can't deny and we'll confront them.'

'With your permission, sir, I'd like to dig deeper into the Cranbrooks.' Anger bubbled up in his voice.

'As long as you do it very carefully, so they don't know it's happening.' Galt started to open his mouth. Harper cut him off. 'I mean it. Discreet.'

'Yes, sir.'

'We need to find this man who was seen with Taylor. I know it's hardly a detailed description, but start asking around. There's a fair chance he's the murderer. Even if he's not, he'll be able to tell us more. Someone must know who he is. Between everything, we're all going to be busy tomorrow, so you'd better make sure you're tucked up early with your cocoa tonight.'

NINE

'Mr Galt. I'd like a word, please,' Harper said after dismissing the men. It was a raw morning, a touch of very early frost on the roofs, breath clouding the air as men walked on the streets. For once, Leeds smelled clear and sharp.

The detective constable stood, staring down at the floorboards while the others left. As soon as they were alone, he said, 'I'm sorry sir, I know I've been going on too much about pursuing the Cranbrooks.'

'I was wondering why. Do you know them?'

He blinked in surprise. 'No, sir. I'd never heard of them before all this. It's just . . . my brother died when he was two. Not snatched or anything like that,' he added hastily. 'Something that settled in his lungs.'

'I'm sorry,' Harper said. 'How old were you?'

'Six.' The man was silent for a long time. 'My parents were never the same after that. I think they blamed themselves. And the rest of us felt it, too, as if we were guilty of something, even if we didn't know what.' Another gap, just the sound of movement around Millgarth, feet, the hum of conversation. 'My mother took her life two years after that. The balance of her mind was disturbed, according to the coroner.' He gave a twisted, pained smile. 'I looked it up a few years ago. My father couldn't look after us all and work. Not with four children. My aunt took a couple of us in. They couldn't have little ones of their own, so they doted on us.'

'But you couldn't forget.'

Galt shook his head. 'No, sir. I think that's why this one hit me so hard. Everything it caused, and those children shipped off to the workhouse.'

It could so easily have been him. That was what he meant. He felt it in every fibre.

'Tell me something. Be honest. Do you think you're the best man to investigate the Cranbrooks? You're coming into this already judging them.'

'I believe I can stay balanced, sir.'

'Believe isn't good enough,' Harper said. 'You don't have any choice in the matter. You *have* to be.'

'Yes, sir. Of course.'

'I'm depending on you to do your job fairly.'

'I will, sir.'

After two years of working with the man, he knew Galt was telling the truth. But he'd still examine the results with a critical eye.

'Then I'll leave you to get on with it.'

Relief spread across the young man's face. 'Thank you.'

'Who are we going to see?' he asked Ash as the tram rattled out along Kirkstall Lane.

'Annie Mercer first. Next stop for us, in fact, sir.'

The wind swept along the valley, brisk and chilly, a few drops of rain beginning to fall. He let Ash lead the way to a terraced street that rose up the hill towards Burley Road.

'Mrs Mercer?'

She looked to be in her late thirties, but frazzled well beyond her years. Wiry hair with thick streaks of grey and worn skin.

'Miss,' she corrected them.

'Annie Mercer?' Ash asked. She shook her head.

'That's my mam. She's poorly, has been for a long time.'

'This is Inspector Ash. I'm Superintendent Harper. We're with Leeds City Police.' He showed his identification card. 'We'd like to talk to her.'

'You can try, I suppose,' the woman said doubtfully. 'But her mind's all over the place. Sometimes she's clear, mostly she's confused.'

'What about today?'

'It's a bad day.' A weighted pause. 'More and more of them are like that now. It's why I'm here. Leave her alone and she'd be wandering all over the neighbourhood.'

'What do you know about your mother's past?' Harper asked.

'Enough.' Her face hardened. 'I've told her, God won't let you into heaven with what you did.'

'We're looking into something that happened fifteen years ago.'

She shook her head. 'I can't help you. I was married then, living in Oldham.' She raised her eyes towards the bedroom. 'And *she* won't be able to tell you. Not today, any road.'

'A pity,' Ash said as they returned to the tram stop. A fine drizzle had started, misting and annoying.

'That's the problem with a case that's so old. The people are all falling apart.'

'Or dead.'

'Where next?'

'Bramley, sir. Brenda Woolcott. Maybe we'll have more luck there.'

But when they knocked on the door there was only the hollow sound of an empty house. The woman next door appeared on the doorstep, a triumphant smile cracking a shrewish face.

'You the rent men?'

'No,' Ash told her.

'Bailiffs?'

'Police,' Harper said.

'You're too late. She did a flit on Saturday night. Everything out of here on a handcart as soon as it was dark.'

From the corner of his eye, Harper could see the inspector looking at him. Saturday. The night Taylor's body was found in the river.

'Do you have any idea where she went?'

'No, and I'd not tell the likes of you if I did.' She turned, slamming the door behind her.

'Sounds like Brenda is the one to look for,' Harper said. He gazed up and down the street. Not a soul to be seen, as if they knew the police were around. 'Let's find the beat bobby and see what he can tell us.'

'I know the house you mean, sir,' Constable Ackland said, 'and I can picture the woman who lives there. But I've never had any dealings with her.'

He was a slow, lumbering beast of a man, with a thick neck and heavy head. Well over six and a half feet tall in his uniform and helmet as he stood in front of the small parade of shops where they'd found him.

'She's gone,' Harper said. 'Done a flit.'

'I'm afraid I wouldn't know anything about that, sir. Not heard a word.'

'We're looking for her,' Ash told him. 'Who might know where she's gone?'

Ackland pressed his lips together and thought. 'I'm not right sure about that, sir. Like I say, I never spoke to her. Never any need.'

'Then ask some questions, Constable,' Harper ordered. 'Find out. This is your beat; you should know who to talk to. You should know everything that's going on.'

'Yes, sir.' His face took on a wounded look. 'I will.'

'We're taking on anyone these days,' Ash said as they walked to the tram stop. 'His job is to know every soul around here and every piece of gossip.'

'It's not our division,' Harper reminded him. 'The timing of when she vanished, though . . .'

'Very suspicious, I'd say. We've certainly unearthed something here, sir.'

No doubt about that. The question was how deeply buried had it been?

'Mrs Davis? My name's Superintendent Harper with Leeds City Police. May I come in for a moment?'

It was a rundown house on the edge of the Bank, just a few hundred yards from Millgarth. Paint had flaked away from the window frames, mortar leaked between bricks. The entire street looked as if it might crumble at any moment. A sense of desperation hung over everything. It was the type of place that would make anyone want to escape.

Sergeant Mason had found the address, tracing the family through the years as their fortunes grew worse. The woman who faced him now looked as if she'd long since given up on life.

'We haven't done anything.' Her voice was weary, defeated by the years.

'I know that. I'm looking at an old case,' Harper said. 'Marie.'

For a second something flashed in her eyes, then died, so brief it might never have existed.

'Yes, you'd best come in, then.'

A single room with an empty hearth, a stone sink under the window, a staircase up to the bedroom. A faded rag rug lay in front of the fireplace, a pair of chairs looked as if they'd been carried from house to house as the family's fate declined.

The woman stood, arms folded over a thin chest. 'Why are you looking into that again?' There was no hope in her voice; it had all been squeezed away. 'The only thing we want is to try and forget it.'

But she couldn't. He could see that written plainly on her face. She'd never wipe the horror of her daughter's disappearance from her mind.

'Sometimes we go back over old cases.' He wasn't about to say more than that. Not when he had no evidence beyond the feeling in his chest.

The woman didn't want to talk about it. She'd learned to live with the nightmares, the blame; she didn't want to tear open the scars and start all over again.

'Do you have a photograph of Marie?'

Mrs Davis shook her head. 'Burned it three years to the day after she was taken. By then I knew she was never coming back.'

'Your husband—'

'He kept looking for her, even after your lot had given up. I made him stop before he went round the bend. Now he works and drinks. I know he still looks at faces, every girl about the right age, and he wonders. But she's dead. She has to be.'

'Your other child . . .'

'Grown and gone.' A flat, final statement. 'I don't know what you think you can find, but Marie's dead. I can feel it in here.' She placed the flat of her hand against her chest. 'She died a long time ago and you're never going to catch whoever did it. No one is.'

'I'm sorry if I upset you.'

'You didn't. I know my Marie will be waiting up there for me when I die. I gave up on seeing her in this life a long time ago.'

'Da,' Mary said, 'I've been thinking about what you said the other night.'

As soon as he'd walked through the door, Annabelle had sent him out again to buy fish and chips for their supper. Without a word, Mary joined him.

'About what?'

'If I demonstrate against Mr Asquith and end up arrested.'

'I'm glad I made you think, at least.' He glanced at her. 'Is this one of those talks when we need to take the long way?'

'No,' she replied. Then: 'Yes. I don't know.'

Her hands swung by her side, and she moved with the easy, fluid grace of youth.

'Let's go down here,' he said, and turned along Enfield Street. 'A police record is a serious thing.'

'I know that.' Of course she did; she had a copper for a father. 'But—'

'No buts,' Harper told her. 'I told you what would happen and I was telling you the truth. I see it every day.'

'But,' she began again, 'if we don't protest and make ourselves heard, how will women ever have the vote? Nothing's worked so far, has it?'

He could hardly disagree with that. Down in Parliament, their ears were closed.

'That's one to take up with your mother. She knows more about it than I ever will.' He smiled. 'I'm just a policeman. I enforce the laws. I don't make them.'

Maybe that would be enough. Sidestepping the question. Not a chance, though.

'What do you do when the laws are wrong, though?' She sounded so earnest that he knew he owed her an honest reply.

'My duty.'

'You've let people go sometimes,' Mary insisted. 'I know you have. I've heard you talking to my mam.'

Dear God, this was going to be a very long trek.

'What did she want?' Annabelle asked when they settled in bed. She was snuggled in the crook of his arm, head resting against his collar bone.

'She still wants to go on that demonstration. She was trying to batter me with logic.'

Annabelle raised her head. 'I hope you didn't give in.'

'No.' He smiled into the darkness. 'I told her that if she wants to discuss the finer points of suffrage and protest, she should talk to you.'

'She'll be bending my ear again.'

'Probably. I don't think a simple no is going to work this time.' Her hair tickled his face. He reached across and smoothed it down. 'Have you made up your mind about the offer from Tetley's?'

'Not yet.' Two small words, but they carried so much. Frustration, history, possibilities.

'Tell me where we stand on everything.'

The morning meeting. A ritual that kept him up to date on every investigation. But for now there was only one case that had their attention.

'We don't have any more information on Brenda Woolcott, sir,' Ash said. 'The best I've been able to find out is that she's in her late fifties and quite nondescript. The local shops in Bramley could barely remember her.'

'That's not going to help. If she decides to change her name, we'll have an impossible job finding her.' Harper glanced at the other men. 'Tracing her is vital. We have good information that she sold children, and she went missing the night Taylor's body was found . . .' He gave a grim smile. 'Curious, isn't it? She might well be the one who snatched and sold Marie Davis. If she is, we have two separate cases. Just what we need.' He ran a hand through his hair. 'How's the search coming for this man with the red moustache?'

'Sissons and I have been working on that,' Walsh said. 'We've turned up a few possibilities. Eight so far. Four of them have records and we have photographs of them from their arrests.'

'That's a good start.'

'I wish it were, sir. I went to show them to Constable Doyle, but he swears it wasn't any of them. We found one of those others, but it's not him, either. Still three to go.'

'It's worth listening to Doyle. He's observant. Still, check the rest of them today, just in case.'

'Yes, sir.'

A thought came to Harper. 'We need to go and see Taylor's widow again. If she'll talk to you, she might know this man's name.'

Walsh grinned. 'Good idea, sir.'

'I do have them sometimes. Just not often enough.' He turned to Galt. 'The Cranbrooks. What else have you learned?'

'It's slow going, sir. Have to be very careful who I ask and what I say.'

'Yes, you do,' Harper agreed. 'What do we know?'

Galt took out his notebook. 'He's one of these self-made men.

Goes on about it in every interview with the newspapers. Grew up in Kirkstall, apprenticed to a cobbler. Had his own workshop by the time he was twenty-three and built it up from there.'

'How old is he now?'

'Fifty-four. Married when he was forty. He has contracts with a few governments across the empire to supply boots for their armies. From what people say, he's coining it in.'

'At least that's something none of us will ever need to worry about.'

It was enough to make them all laugh.

'He likes to stress his humble beginnings. Very proud of that, is Cranbrook.' Galt raised an eyebrow.

'What are you trying to say?' Harper asked.

'Andrew Sharp and Marie Davis both came from poor families. I wondered if that connects to the humble beginnings idea.'

Harper considered the idea for a moment. Far too deep for him.

'Let's put that aside for now. Focus on who he knows. If Cranbrook did buy those children, he'd have needed some criminal contacts.'

Galt grimaced. 'That's quite a few years ago, sir.'

'Doesn't matter. People wouldn't forget someone as important as him. I want you to investigate that aspect.'

'Yes, sir.' He scribbled down a note.

'Have a look at his wife, too. We're making progress,' Harper said, even though it felt like a lie. 'Let's keep at it.'

The endless grind of papers to be read, papers to be filed, letters to be written. He needed a secretary with a typewriter, someone who could write everything down in shorthand and bring him the finished piece to sign.

But this was the police. It would happen eventually, just not for a long time yet. Until then, he was condemned to pen and paper and cramped fingers.

By eleven, he'd had enough. He needed to be outside the four walls for a while, to cleanse the jumble of words from his brain.

Rain was falling, heavy enough to clear all but the hardiest from the open market and send him hurrying into the main hall. A penny's worth of lemon drops, sharp enough to make his mouth pucker, and a wander round. The place was full of women, the poor and the rich pressed together as they moved along the aisles. The cries of the men trying to sell their goods filled the air, competing against each other. A cheap set of crockery, lamb chops, some fresh oysters. Everything a family could want, all under one big glass roof. The building was a marvel of engineering, just four years old, still new enough to seem fresh. The paint was bright on the ironwork, the flagstone floors even. It smelt of the future in a way the old market never managed. New, yet completely redolent of Leeds.

An hour refreshed him, a sandwich and a cup of tea from a stall. He was anonymous in the crowd, just another man in a hat and coat. No responsibilities here, no weight pushing down on his shoulders. By the time he returned to Millgarth he felt ready to take on the world once more.

TEN

He'd scarcely had the chance to take off his coat and sit down before Galt was tapping at his office door.

'I've come up with something you ought to know about, sir.' He looked concerned, nibbling at his lower lip.

'About the Cranbrooks?' Harper asked.

'Mrs Cranbrook.' He opened his notebook. 'She was born Sarah Mathis, grew up in Wortley. Her father was a wood turner, worked on and off, when he wasn't picking pockets. I checked; we arrested him sixteen times.'

'Sixteen?' He raised his eyebrows and chuckled. 'Not particularly successful, was he?'

Galt didn't smile. 'Sarah left school when she was ten, went to work in the mill, then down at the big Pygmalion store in town. She seems to have left there under a cloud.'

'Go on.' Scandal in the past. Well, the Cranbrooks would hardly be the first family to have that.

'Nothing official, but hints in the file that she was stealing, mainly clothing. Enough to dismiss her.' He paused. 'It becomes very interesting after that. Arrested for soliciting in the Dark Arches under the railway station. One pound fine, bound over to keep the peace for six months. The usual.'

'Well, well,' Harper said.

'From there she seems to have stuck to the straight and narrow.' He raised an eyebrow. 'Several years of work. She was twenty-five when she married Cranbrook.'

'How long ago was this?'

He consulted the notebook again. 'Back in '88. Cranbrook was just building his factory then. Had his first order for army boots. He must have been on a promise of something bigger.'

Five years before Andrew Sharp was taken. Quite long enough for the couple to discover they couldn't have children. And Mrs Cranbrook could well have had a few murky connections of her own.

'How did they meet?' he asked. 'Have you managed to find out?'

Galt shook his head. 'Haven't had a chance, sir. And you wanted me to tread carefully.'

'If you can come up with something, fine. If not, we have plenty to work with there.'

'Yes, sir.'

'Lawrence Armstrong,' Walsh announced. 'The man with the red moustache. Mrs Taylor knew right off the bat who he was.'

'Armstrong's often in Armley, so that would fit with PC Doyle seeing him with Taylor by the canal,' Sissons added. 'We've put out the word. Should have him by tomorrow.'

'Excellent.' Finally they were moving forward. It was a start. Interview Armstrong and they'd know more. They might even have their killer. The man could be the key to everything. 'What else?'

Nothing.

'We'll call it a night. Back bright and early tomorrow.'

He knew they'd be all out during the evening, in the pubs, asking questions; that was what a detective did, he'd spent years at it himself. But the main business of the day was over.

'How's the kidney, sir?' Ash asked as they strolled out of Millgarth together.

'Much better.' To his surprise, he'd barely thought about it all day. Not even a twinge of pain. Maybe Annabelle's liniment had done the trick. 'Almost as good as new.' He gave a small grimace. 'Mind you, these days I'm not sure how wonderful that is.'

There was plenty to think about as the tram bumped its way

along North Street. Armstrong, Brenda Woolcott, then Mrs Cranbrook. She certainly didn't have an unblemished past. The same was true for many other women; the big difference was that most of them didn't end up marrying rich men.

And then to the heart of the matter. Where this had begun. What about Andrew Sharp and Marie Davis? He felt absolutely certain they were the Cranbrook children. He might never find proof, but he *knew*. But what good would the truth do? How much would it cost them all if it came out? The only family Andrew and Marie had really known was the Cranbrooks. They probably couldn't even remember a time before that. That knowledge would rip their worlds apart. And it would destroy the Cranbrooks.

Truth was important, but in the end, what would it achieve?

Harper didn't have an answer. He'd face the question if it happened. Before that, they still had a murderer to catch.

'Armstrong. Anything yet?'

Walsh shook his head.

'He's the only lead we have in Taylor's killing,' Harper said. 'I want him in the interview room today. All of you on it.'

'Even me, sir?' Galt asked. 'Put the Cranbrook family research aside?'

Harper nodded. 'For now. Sissons, you make sure everyone knows what's going on and divide the tasks.'

Alone, he stood by the window. Another grey day as autumn tightened its grip. Low clouds, the constant taste of soot and smoke in the mouth. People coughed, the winter bronchitis arriving early as they moved up and down the street, galloping busily about their lives. All with their private joys and worries, all the thoughts they kept locked inside, unspoken.

Sometimes, a head turned to glance up at the police station then quickly look away again. The place had that effect. People needed law, they wanted justice, but they were also terrified that it might reach out and touch them.

Harper settled to the papers waiting for him. Dreary routine. He'd been doing this for more than a decade, but it never seemed to grow easier. Still, the work had to be done, and it was his responsibility. Buckle down and complete it. Forms and reports waited for no man, even a superintendent.

By late in the afternoon, he'd finished, sitting back to the satisfaction of a clear desk. The door to the detectives' room crashed open, banging against the wall. Galt and Walsh wrestled a man through and pushed him down on to a chair.

'Who do we have here?' Harper was on his feet, watching, ready in case the man tried to spring up.

'Lawrence Armstrong, sir.' Galt was panting. Blood was smeared around a cut on his cheek. 'He wasn't too happy at wanting to join us.'

'Where did you find him?'

'Turns out he was only over on Meadow Lane,' Walsh said. 'He screamed blue murder the whole way here.'

'Well, well.' Harper circled the man. 'Welcome, Mr Armstrong.'

He had a wild, feral smell, as if he'd spent too long out of doors without washing. Maybe in his late thirties, it was impossible to be certain from his scrawny, undernourished body, lank, dark hair, and heavy stubble. His eyes were wary, his gaze darting around the room like an animal desperately searching for a way to escape. He looked at the men surrounding him, hissed and tried to spit. It ran slowly down his chin.

'Has he said much?'

'Nothing that makes sense,' Walsh replied.

Harper grabbed Armstrong's jaw and tilted the man's head until they were staring at each other.

'Adam Taylor.' He spoke the name quietly, calmly. After a moment, it seemed to register with Armstrong. His expression turned solemn, then exploded with rage.

'Devil,' Armstrong roared. 'Devil.' He lunged forward with a scream. Fingernails raked down Harper's neck and he felt a warm trickle of blood. He brought up his hand, clamping it on Armstrong's throat and pushing him away. Galt and Walsh grabbed the man and forced him down, cuffing his wrists. He began to moan, an odd, unearthly sound that grew louder and louder until it felt as if it filled the room.

'For God's sake, take him down to the cells,' Harper shouted. 'See he's fed, and make sure someone watches him so he doesn't hurt himself. I want him observed every single moment.'

Armstrong resisted. He shouted and cursed and let himself fall to the floor. It took two more hefty coppers to carry him away.

'Was he that way when you found him?' he asked the men when they returned. He dabbed at the scratch with his handkerchief, feeling his heartbeat slowly return to normal. It had been like trying to subdue a wild beast.

A glance between the two of them, then Galt said: 'Nowhere near as bad as that, sir. He was muttering. A proper conversation, answering himself and everything.'

'On Meadow Lane, you said?'

'Yes sir, he was just the other side of the river, walking along. People were moving out of his way.'

Harper was thinking. Armstrong's stink hung in the air.

'Who told you where to find him?'

'A charity,' Walsh answered. 'They've known him for a while. Feed him, give him a bed sometimes, clean him up. They know where he likes to go.'

'Does that mean he's often this way?'

'That's what they told us, sir. He has times when he makes more sense, evidently, but . . .' He shrugged.

What more was there to say? Like this, Armstrong could easily have killed Taylor. He might not even remember he'd done it. A thrust from a knife, a push into the river; it was so simple.

'How did he and Taylor know each other? Do we have any idea?' They seemed unlikely friends.

'No, sir. All Mrs Taylor said was that her husband already knew Armstrong before she met him.'

They needed to hold the man until he was lucid again. But who knew when that might be?

'Go back and talk to that charity,' he said. 'Find out what you can about him from them. They might be able to direct you to someone else.'

'Very good, sir.'

'Ring Armley, too. Have them send Doyle down here, see if he can identify Armstrong as the man he saw with Adam Taylor.'

He'd try questioning him again in the morning. Maybe a night's sleep and some solid food would calm him. If it didn't, the only alternative was the asylum. And they'd be right back where they began. Nowhere.

So much for making progress. No matter which way he turned on this case, a brick wall stood in front of him.

Maybe things would seem brighter tomorrow. Probably not, but he needed to give himself a little hope. And he needed to think about the prime minister's visit. It was coming closer and closer. It was going to be a test.

Annabelle was too quiet. Not a word while they ate. Just the two of them at home, Mary off to the music hall at the Palace with some of her friends.

'Come on,' he said as she poured the tea. 'Tell me.'

'This.' She took the letter from the pocket of her skirt. It was folded into a small square, compressed. Harper looked at her as he opened it up. 'Came in the second post.'

Written in pencil. A rough hand, a scrawl.

> Go on, sell up and get out of here, you bitch. You've made your money from us. That was all you ever wanted. Acting like Lady Bountiful with that guardian talk while you flaunted what you had and pushed our faces in the muck. Get out of here and we'll be well rid of you.

Poisoned pens. There was always one hateful person. No point in asking how they'd heard about the offer on the pub; gossip always drifted on the wind.

'I can't tell you to pay it no mind.'

'No.' She stirred her tea, watching it swirl in the cup. 'Why?' She raised her head to look at him. 'Why would someone feel like that about me?'

'Jealousy, anger . . . could be anything. But it's not true. You know it's not.'

'It made me think. The motor car and everything . . .'

'Don't,' he told her. 'You've done nothing wrong.'

'I tried to *help* them, Tom. That's why I did nine years as a Guardian. I was proud to represent the people round here, to stand up for them.'

He took her hand and squeezed it lightly. 'Some people are always going to be that way. Spite, that's all it is. Human nature.'

'Maybe.'

'They still come to you with their problems, don't they?' He'd seen them, the women who stopped her on the way to the shops. Wanting to talk, asking for advice.

'Yes,' she agreed slowly.

'And you help them. How many in Sheepscar want votes for women now?'

'I don't know. A few, maybe.'

'More than that,' Harper said with a smile. 'A lot of it is due to you.'

She shook her head. 'The credit goes to Isabella Ford and the women with her. They do all the hard work. All the organizing.'

'You do your share for them, too.' She'd been involved in the suffrage movement for fifteen years; she'd done more than enough.

'I get up and open my yap, that's all.' She took the letter from his hands, re-folded it into a tiny square and placed it back in her pocket. 'Do you really think everything she wrote is wrong?'

'Yes,' he answered without any hesitation. 'There are hundreds round here who'd agree with me. They're grateful for what you've done.'

She looked up and he could see tears glistening in her eyes.

'I don't need them to be grateful, Tom. I was doing my job, that's all. What they elected me to do, nothing more than that. I just don't want them to hate me.'

'Armstrong,' he asked. 'Is he making any more sense this morning?'

'No, sir,' Galt said. 'He had to be restrained twice during the night. He's a danger to himself.'

Harper ran a hand through his hair. 'You'd better tell High Royds we have a patient for them.' He slapped his hand down on the desk. 'Dammit. As soon as we think we're about to find answers, we discover we're nowhere.'

'The useful thing is that Doyle came and took a look at him. He says Armstrong is definitely the man he saw by the canal with Taylor.'

For all the good that did. He stared at his squad.

'I'm open to any suggestions. Anything at all. Maybe Armstrong murdered Taylor, but I wouldn't fancy our chances of a confession that'll hold water in court.' His gaze moved slowly from one face to the next. 'Gentlemen?'

'We should find out about Armstrong's past, sir,' Ash said. 'It might tell us something about his connection to Taylor.'

'You work on that.' A thought sprang into his head. 'While you're talking to that charity, ask if they're missing a carving knife from their kitchen. Walsh, I want you and Galt digging deep into

Taylor's background. Go back before the children disappeared. See if you can find out who he knew then. Anything you can.'

'Tall order, sir.'

'I know,' Harper agreed with a sigh. 'What the hell else can we do? Let's see if we can tease something out of all that. A few names would be a godsend.'

'If they're still alive, sir,' Galt said.

He gave a rueful laugh. 'Let's hope so. I'm not intending to interview by seance.'

'Where do you want me, sir?' Sissons asked.

'Right here. I asked you to find out about Alf Kitson. You can tell me what you've learned.'

Sissons opened his briefcase and removed a folder. 'All in here, sir.'

Harper took the file and placed it on the desk. 'Very good. Those are the facts. Now tell me the rest. You've talked to people. What did they make of him? Is he liked? Feared?'

'A bit of both, sir. He's affiliated with the Leeds Permanent Committee on Unemployment.'

'Affiliated?'

'Very loose ties, sir. Alf Kitson's more or less an anarchist.'

A prime minister and an anarchist together. An explosive mix.

'Much of a record?'

'Fines, bound over to keep the peace. He's never been to jail,' Sissons answered with a wry smile. 'His commitment to the cause doesn't seem to extend quite that far.'

That was a helpful little nugget. The man was scared of prison time.

'It doesn't stop him organizing things like demonstrating against Mr Asquith or getting into political scraps,' the sergeant continued. 'And he seems to have something about him. People turn out for his meetings.'

'There's hardly a shortage of unemployed men in Leeds,' Harper said.

'True enough, sir. But he knows how to stir them up. A very eloquent speaker, by all accounts.'

'Where can I find him?'

'He lives in Beeston. Part of something called the Beeston Brotherhood. Bunch of idealists. They have a cooperative making stockings. Are you going to see him, sir?'

Harper smiled. 'Can't hurt to have a word, can it? I don't imagine I'll change his mind, but who knows, maybe we can avoid some violence. God loves a trier.'

Sissons shook his head. 'With the prime minister here, he'll be determined to make a splash. That's what everyone told me.'

'If he tries, we'll give as good as we get. But I'd like to dissuade him if I can.'

'He drinks at the Drysalters Arms, down where Elland Road and Crow Foot Lane meet. It's all written in the notes, sir.'

'Thank you. I want you to talk to High Royds. Arrange Armstrong's transfer. Warn them he can be violent.' His fingertips stroked the small cuts on his neck.

'Yes, sir.' The office door closed behind him.

Alone, Harper stared out of the window. Things were beginning to move. But where would they end?

ELEVEN

Leeds was his home. He'd been born here, not a quarter of a mile from Millgarth, and he'd die here. He had no desire to be anywhere else. Harper knew the city in his bones. He felt it breathe. It was a part of him.

He wanted to be out there, doing more. But right now, he'd simply be a spare part. Most of his contacts had died or moved away or found themselves a safer way to live. His time working the streets every day had passed.

He'd been the superintendent here for thirteen years, almost half the time he'd been a copper. He was proud of it. But inch by inch, rank brought isolation. He'd lost his quickness, his nose for trouble and danger. The punch the other day had proved that. When he and Billy worked together—

The thought brought him up short. Billy was gone. For a moment he felt empty, as if a part of him had fled too. Maybe it had. They'd been a good team. But it felt like the type of story he'd read to Mary when she was small. Once upon a time . . . all history. Nothing more than flesh decomposing in the soil now.

Harper shook his head. There was no point in thoughts like that.

They didn't do a damned bit of good, simply made him maudlin. And they certainly wouldn't help find Adam Taylor's killer.

He picked up the folder Sissons had left and read through the information.

There was certainly one thing he *could* do.

'Have a car ready for me in ten minutes,' he told Sergeant Mason.

A quick spruce-up, washing his hands and combing his hair. There was still a bruise over his kidney, tender when he pressed it, but otherwise he was back to normal. Still, those scratches on his throat, covered in gentian violet to help them heal, gave him a menacing air, Harper thought. Perfect.

'Drop me here and wait,' he told the driver, and the car pulled to the side of the road.

He was a good quarter of a mile from the pub. But he'd do better arriving on foot. A vehicle parked outside would be too grand, and would reek of privilege. The wind whipped along Elland Road. Still plenty of farmland out here, fields that spread up the hillsides, separated by drystone walls. A few sheep out grazing. He glanced over his shoulder, seeing the haze that rested over Leeds, then drew in a deep breath. Fresh air.

The pub was small. It looked as if it might have been a farmhouse once, a few walls demolished inside to create a single, large room. Flagstones on the floor, a fug of tobacco clinging just below the ceiling.

He ordered a half of bitter. Melbourne Ales, decent enough. He was aware of the people watching him. Not too many strangers would come into a place like this, especially ones wearing a collar and tie and a good overcoat.

'Alf Kitson around?' he asked the landlord.

Without a word, the man nodded towards the table in the corner. A man with broad shoulders sat there, looking at a newspaper. Not reading, Harper thought. He'd be watching everything that was going on. The superintendent picked up his drink and wandered over.

'So you're Alf Kitson.'

The man stared at him. Clear eyes, clean-shaven, dark hair neatly parted and pomaded. A thick woollen working man's suit, no collar on his shirt.

'And you're a policeman.'

He didn't look worried. Amused, more like. Harper gestured at the chair. After a moment, the man nodded.

'Superintendent Harper.'

'Head of A Division,' Kitson recited, 'and you're going to be in charge when Asquith visits.'

'That's right.'

'Thought you'd come and see how the other half lives?'

'If you know so much about me, you'll know that's a stupid question,' Harper told him. No sense in pussyfooting around.

'All right.' He pulled out a crushed packet of five Woodbines, straightened one and lit it. 'So what do you want?'

'A peaceful demonstration.'

'Why?' Kitson asked.

'That way you can make your point and we all go home happy. Nobody ends up hurt.'

Even as he spoke, the man was shaking his head. 'Tell me, Superintendent, do you know how many unemployed there are in Leeds?'

'Too many.'

'Very good, very quick. But you don't know.' Kitson frowned. 'Neither do I, exactly. No one does, expect it's always too bloody many. Ask your wife, she's seen it.'

The man had done his homework; *know your enemy* cut both ways.

'And if there's violence when the prime minister visits, how will that help? Will it give anyone a job?'

'It'll let him know we're sick and tired of it all. Every single day we're lied to by the politicians, we're treated like we're nothing. It's about time he saw that we've had enough.' There was the fire of belief in his voice, unwavering certainty in his eyes. He wasn't about to compromise.

'It's a pity,' Harper said quietly. 'You know what they say – you catch more flies with honey.'

Kitson snorted. 'You haven't read much history, have you, Superintendent? Politeness never achieved anything. Words have their uses, but they only go so far. I want change. You wait and see. There'll be plenty with me who feel the same. The only way is direct action.'

As he walked back to the car a drizzle began, growing heavier as he trudged along Elland Road. Action. Exactly the same as the suffragettes. He needed to be prepared for the worst.

Well, he'd tried.

Ash and Sissons looked like a pair of drowned rats. It had poured all afternoon and was still pelting down like stair rods. Outside, the streetlamps threw reflections into the puddles, and men and women dashed along, hidden by their umbrellas.

'I hope you found something worthwhile for your soaking.'

'We've spent the day going around the shelters and charities, sir.' Ash shook out his mackintosh, throwing a flood of drops across the floor. 'They all know Armstrong, have done for several years.'

'He's harmless most of the time,' Galt continued. 'Keeps himself to himself. Mutters a lot. The only trouble comes when he's afraid or he's been drinking.'

'That's when he can turn violent,' Ash said.

'We already saw that for ourselves.'

'They gave us a few names who might know more, but' – he glanced out of the window at the weather – 'they're all out of sight, keeping out of this. We might come up with more tomorrow.'

'You might as well go home and change into some dry clothes. There's no more to do today.'

By six, Walsh and Sissons hadn't returned. With a final glance, Harper turned off the light.

Annabelle was out, working with a group of women over in Wortley. Burgess meetings, they called them, educating about democracy and the vote, so they'd be ready when it finally came. He'd stood faithfully in the rain, cranking the starter of the Rex until it caught, then watched her drive out of sight along Manor Street.

Mary was gone again, a young woman with a busy life of her own. Only him in the house, the soft hum and rumble from the drinkers downstairs in the bar for company. All that peace and quiet, and he didn't know what to do with himself.

A dry morning. But the air was damp and the sky the colour of old lead, the ground covered with puddles and mud.

'We've got some good news, sir,' Sissons said. He had the smile of a man who'd learned some secrets and was desperate to tell them.

'Thank God for that. We need it.'

As Harper watched, the rain began again, just heavy enough to speckle the windows.

'We talked to some men who used to work with Armstrong. He went down the mines as soon as he left school.' Walsh began the story. 'Worked at Middleton Broom Colliery. He seemed to like it, even started to learn the French horn in their brass band. Had a real feel for the music, they said.'

Harper raised an eyebrow, trying to square that with the man who'd howled and groaned and fought in here.

'What happened?'

'When he was nineteen, there was a cave-in on the seam where he was working,' Sissons continued. 'Armstrong and three others were trapped. They were dug out five hours later, nobody hurt, but it seems to have affected him. He went back to work the next day. Started fretting as soon as he was in the cage. Once he was underground, he was shaking and shivering. After a few yards, he couldn't move any further. They had to bring him back up top and he refused to go down again. That was the start of it.'

'You can hardly blame him, can you?' Harper said. 'Underground like that, not knowing if he'd be rescued.' A shudder ripped through him as he tried to imagine the terror of it. 'What did he do afterwards?'

'The colliery found him a job on the surface,' Walsh replied. 'He lasted a few months, then started wandering off. It reached the point where he couldn't stand being confined anywhere. He'd leave for an hour or two at first. Then all day, after that even longer, vanishing for two or three days on the trot. Even gave up his music. Finally they had to let him go.'

'Does he have any family?' Harper asked.

'Three sisters; they're all married to miners. Parents dead. After about a year, he left Middleton altogether, and didn't go back. By then, his sisters knew they couldn't help him.'

'How long ago was this?' Harper asked.

'Back in '96, sir,' Walsh said. 'He was still in Middleton when the children were taken.'

But Taylor was on the beat back in 1896. He must have met Armstrong in Leeds. They seemed unlikely friends, though.

'You've done a very thorough job. Work with the others, let's see if we can find out what he's been up to recently.'

He had a few ideas of his own.

Harper was cautious as he approached Taylor's house, all too aware of what had happened the last time he was here.

The man had been buried the day before, and when she opened the door his widow stood hollow-eyed, thinner, ragged around the edges. The mourning clothes seemed to hang off her. But the accusations still flared in her eyes as she saw his face.

'Can I come in for a minute?'

'The doorstep will be fine.' She crossed her arms and glared up and down the street. 'Go on,' she said, raising her voice, 'ask your questions.'

Harper nodded. He'd come here for answers, if she had any. On the street or inside, it didn't matter to him.

'If that how you want it, that's how we'll do it. You told my men that your husband knew Lawrence Armstrong.'

She snorted. 'Oh aye. Another one who didn't even care enough to show up and pay his respects.'

'He's in High Royds,' Harper told her.

Her expression changed. 'I'm sorry for him, then,' she said grudgingly.

'Were they close?'

She shook her head. 'Not pals or anything like that. A natter if they saw each other, that was about the size of it.' She smiled for a moment. 'Adam would slip him a penny or two or buy him a drink.'

'Did you know him at all?'

'Met him twice when we were out. He wouldn't ever talk when I was there. Didn't even look at me. I think he was scared of women.' Dotty Taylor cocked her head. 'Why do you want to know, any road?'

'He was seen with your husband on the day he died.'

'What?' Her jaw opened wide. 'You think *Lawrence* did it?'

'I don't know.' Harper stared at her. 'We couldn't get any sense out of him. That's why I'm asking you.'

'Lawrence? You've got that wrong. You must have. He'd never hurt anyone. He'd be too frightened. I know you're a copper, but even you should be able to see that.'

Harper pointed to the scratches on his neck. 'He did that.' She gazed with grim satisfaction but said nothing. 'How long ago did they meet?'

She shook her head. 'No idea. Years, I think. Well before I knew Adam, that's for certain. Is that it?'

'Yes,' he replied. 'That's all. Thank you.'

'For what? I didn't tell you owt. It's not like you were coming to tell me who killed him.'

'I will.'

'Maybe.' She said the word as if she didn't believe it would ever happen. 'You know, Adam only had a proper plot and casket because Harry Matthews was generous. He'd have gone into a guinea grave otherwise.'

'I'm sorry.' What else could he say? He raised his hat.

As he turned, she quietly said, 'My brother and his mate were wrong. They shouldn't have tried to do you.'

An apology. He hadn't expected that. 'They're paying for it now.'

'One way or another, the poor always do. You reckon we don't all know that?'

Inch by inch, things were moving forward. But it was like wading through treacle. Maybe Armstrong had killed Taylor, but Harper had the niggling feeling that he was nothing more than a lost innocent. A madman. The person responsible was the one behind the child-snatchings. Protecting himself. They'd find their answers eventually, find a name and build a solid case. Some of those answers, at least. The others, like what to do about Andrew and Marie . . . he'd face that when it came.

'Sorry to bother you, sir,' Sergeant Mason said as soon as he walked through the door at Millgarth. 'But all your men are out.' He frowned and scratched his head. 'Got something that might be of interest to you.'

'What is it?'

'Constable Barley was approached by a woman on his beat. He covers that area behind the Coliseum over to Little Woodhouse.'

The Coliseum? Where Asquith would be speaking. That drew his attention immediately. 'Go on.'

'She read the newspaper article about Taylor being killed and told Barley that she'd seen him on her street Friday evening.

Roaring drunk, she says, and with another man. I thought I'd better tell you.'

'Give me her address.'

Back-to-back houses, street after relentless street of them climbing up the hillside. Children playing in the middle of the road. Their hands and faces were mucky, and they paid him not a scrap of attention as they shouted to each other. Whipping tops, hopscotch for the girls, a ball to kick around for the boys. Half of them should have been in school, but he wasn't a truant officer. Camden Place stood tucked away, just east of Woodhouse Lane; this wasn't a place where anyone would idly stroll.

Harper knocked on the door of number eight. He hoped to God this wasn't a wild goose chase. The way their luck was running, though, it was probably inevitable.

The woman standing in front of him was small, with bright, intelligent eyes and a mobile face. Grey hair, quietly dressed with an apron over her clothes. She assessed him quickly.

'You must be a policeman.'

'Detective Superintendent Harper.'

'Always been able to tell a copper a mile off.' But she was smiling as she spoke. 'Come in.'

The room was neat as a pin, a small fire burning in the grate. A plate of scones stood on the table. From the smell in the air, she'd just finished baking.

'Have a seat,' she said. 'I've just brewed up. You won't say no, will you?'

'Never,' he agreed with a smile. 'Thank you, Mrs—'

'Jones. Emmeline Jones. If you're Harper, your wife must be Annabelle.'

'That's right.'

'I've seen her speak once or twice.' She gave an approving nod. 'She's good, talks some sense.'

'She does.' As he took the cup of tea from her, he said, 'You said you saw Adam Taylor the evening he died.'

'I did.' She perched on the edge of a wooden chair, gathering her skirt around her ankles. 'I had to pop to the shop and there he was, large as life, coming down the street with another man. Loud, they were, too, paying no heed to the world.'

'Loud?' Harper asked. 'How?'

'The way men are when they've been drinking.' She gave a knowing look. 'Enjoying themselves too much.'

'What time was this?'

'Eight?' she replied after a moment. 'Somewhere around there. Early to be in that state, I thought.'

Eight o'clock. That pushed things a little further. 'How did you know it was Taylor?'

'I lived on his beat for a few years and I'm good with faces. Never forget one.'

'Do you remember what happened in Harmony Court fifteen years ago?' Harper asked. 'A boy went missing.'

'I do.' She nodded slowly. 'And his mother died not long after that. Poor thing. I never knew her, but I felt for her.' Mrs Jones raised an eyebrow. 'That was a long time back. History. Almost as ancient as me.'

'I know. You're certain it was Taylor you saw?'

'Positive.' The way she said it left no room for doubt. She was clear, calm; he believed her.

'What about the man with him? Did you know him at all?'

'Never seen him before in my life. It wasn't anyone from round here, I can tell you that much.'

'They were both in the same state?'

She nodded. 'Staggering a bit, but still upright. You know what I mean.'

He did. Any night in Leeds, men would be in that state. But usually not until later in the evening.

'Where did they go?'

'Down towards town. I didn't pay much attention, other than to see it was Taylor. That's why it stuck in my mind when I saw the piece in the paper.'

'Was there anything at all about the other man? Something you remember?'

She thought for a minute. 'He had a bit of a wild look in his eyes, maybe. I'm sorry, that's all.'

'What about a red moustache?'

Mrs Jones narrowed her eyes, picturing it in her head. 'It's possible. I only saw them for a few seconds and the light was dim. But yes . . . I suppose he might have had a moustache.'

'If I were to show you a photograph, would that help?'

'It might,' she said after a moment.

'I'll have one of my men bring it round.' He stood. 'Thank you for coming forward.'

'I can't say that I did much, really. I only told you what I saw.'

'I've asked High Royds to send us a photograph of Armstrong,' Harper said. 'We'll see if it rings any bells with her.' He massaged the bridge of his nose. 'Even if it was him with Taylor, what does that prove?'

'We know where he was a little later in the evening, sir,' Galt said. 'And that he'd had a few drinks. That's some progress.'

'Is it? It doesn't feel like it.'

'You know some cases are like this sir,' Ash told him. 'We've all seen it before. We go round and round in circles, then something will pop and we'll solve it like that.' He snapped his fingers.

He smiled. 'A lovely idea. But we can't just sit on our backsides and hope something happens. Go and stir it all up.'

After the squad filed out Ash lingered at the door, a frown on his face.

'You sound discouraged, sir,' he said quietly.

'Of course I am,' Harper snapped. 'What do you expect? I don't think Armstrong killed Taylor, but I doubt we'll ever know for sure.'

'And there's a very good chance he didn't, sir.' Ash's voice was patient. 'We don't have all the facts yet. Keep a little faith.'

He snorted. 'Do I have any choice?' Maybe the man was right. Maybe not.

TWELVE

Something will pop. He wished he could be that optimistic. All he saw were questions ahead of him. About the only good thing was that the rain had stopped, replaced by thin, angry gusts of wind.

He shrugged on his mackintosh and closed the office door behind him. Perhaps dinner would help. Something hot and filling. At the front desk, Sergeant Mason was on the telephone. He held up a finger and Harper paused.

'Yes. Yes, I'll tell him.'

'What is it?'

'That man we had here. Armstrong. The one we sent out to High Royds. They've just rung.'

'What about him?' He felt a chill creeping up his spine. They wouldn't telephone without an important reason.

'He's hung himself. Too late when they found him.'

He sighed and offered up a short, silent prayer. If there was a God, maybe He'd listen.

Suicide. Who knew what devils in his head had forced him to that? Maybe it was his fault for sending Armstrong to a place where he'd be confined. But what else could he have done? He couldn't have allowed him to go free. The man was a danger to everyone.

Now they'd never learn what happened with him and Taylor. That knowledge had vanished with his last breath.

The news had ripped away his appetite. Instead he walked around town, along Boar Lane and past the railway station, and finally up to Park Square, where he sat, hoping the wind would clear his thoughts and blow away his guilt.

It didn't help. Striding back, he dodged between traffic and people on Commercial Street, feeling as if the city was grinding against him. All this and the prime minister's visit just around the corner.

At Millgarth, a note waited on his desk. An address off Burley Road. Ash's writing.

The house had been prosperous forty years before. Over time it had grown neglected, half the windows broken, mortar powdering between the bricks. Now it was crammed with people, each room rented to a family who could afford nothing better. The smell of boiled cabbage hung thick in the air. He saw a woman's face peer from behind a tattered curtain.

The inspector was standing outside the building with a pair of constables. A black coroner's wagon stood in the street, the horses munching from their nosebags.

'It's John Larner, sir,' Ash said before he could ask. 'You remember him. Worked for Harry Matthews.'

Harper nodded. The man who'd told Taylor about the letter and sent him on the run. It had to be connected. *Had* to be.

'What happened?'

'One of the rooms in the cellar has been locked since yesterday morning. A man here noticed a stink and let the copper on the beat know. Larner was inside, dead.'

'How did he die? Any idea?'

A moment's hesitation. 'Strangled, sir.'

Harper looked up at the house. Dark windows, darker stone.

'Let's find out who owns this place, who'd have keys to the rooms. Talk to everyone living here. You know what to do.'

'Yes, sir.'

'I'll go and see Harry Matthews.' He heard the emptiness in his own voice. 'Armstrong committed suicide at High Royds.'

'Another one.' Ash shook his head. 'One thing's certain, though. He didn't do this. Armstrong was in the cells at Millgarth when it happened.'

Harper grimaced. 'So he probably didn't murder Taylor, either . . .'

'Exactly, sir.'

'John?' Harry Matthews said. His face was pale and his hands had begun to shake. 'That can't be right. It can't.'

'I'm sorry,' Harper said. 'Come on, you'd best sit down.'

The man did as he was told. Immediately, he was on his feet again, pacing around the small room, thrusting his hands into his trouser pockets.

'I told him to make himself scarce for a few days after you lot had him in. That's all I said.' He was rambling, trying to make sense of it all. 'First Adam, now John.' He stopped suddenly, turning his head. 'Does someone have it in for me?'

'For whatever it's worth, I don't believe it has anything to do with you, Harry. It's all connected to something Taylor did a long time ago.'

'Then why John? For God's sake, he was only young.'

'I don't know,' Harper admitted. 'That's why I'm trying to find out. Larner had a wife, didn't he?'

Matthews nodded absently, then his face seemed to fall in on itself. 'Roberta.' He closed his eyes, sighed, and seemed to sway for a moment. 'I'll have to tell her. How can I do that?'

'I'll take care of it. What I need from you is a list of anyone who might want to hurt him.'

'No one. He was a good lad. Mouthy, but they all are at that age. No real harm in him.'

'Sit down, have a think and write me a list of his friends, then,' Harper said. 'It's important. And give me his address.'

Only a few streets away, five minutes' walk, but a small step or two down towards poverty. A back-to-back with a shared, stinking privy that hadn't been emptied in weeks. Somewhere a baby wailed.

This was the part of the job he'd always hated. There was never an easy way to give this kind of news. He paused for a second with his hand on the wood, took a breath and knocked. The young woman who answered stood wide-eyed, her hair clumsily gathered up, a shabby frock over a thin body.

'Mrs Larner?'

She nodded, staring up at him.

'I'm Detective Superintendent Harper with Leeds City Police. May I come in?'

Hurriedly, she stood aside. He already knew what the room would be like. The usual stone sink, fireplace, two wooden chairs beside a scarred table. A few unframed photographs on the mantel.

'John Larner is your husband?'

'Yes,' she replied, looking at him without understanding. 'Course he is. Why?' Her mouth widened. 'You've arrested him, haven't you? What's he done? Where is he?'

The words tumbled out, a river of them, and all he could do was wait until she finished.

'It's not like that. He's not in custody for anything. I'm very sorry, Mrs Larner. He's dead.'

She stood, completely still, all the colour disappearing from her face. Then her eyes rolled up in her head and her knees buckled. He caught her before she reached the floor, her body so light there seemed to be nothing to it, as brittle as a sparrow. He settled her on one of the chairs and knelt by her until she began to stir.

'You said . . .' At first her voice slurred over the words, then caught as the truth blossomed inside her. 'You said John's dead?'

'I'm sorry. I'm afraid he is.'

She covered her face with her hands, as if she could hide from the truth.

She shook her head. 'He can't be. He just can't. You've got to be wrong.'

It took half an hour to learn the little she knew. Larner hadn't been one for telling his wife much. After Harry ordered him to disappear, that was what he'd done. Left a little money on the sink and a note saying he'd be back in a few days. Almost an echo of Adam Taylor. That was the last she'd heard of him. She finished, and an empty silence filled the room.

'Do you want me to take you over to your mother's house?'

'Yes,' she answered, an obedient child's voice. 'Yes, please.'

On the way she leaned heavily against him like an invalid, stumbling a few times, shuffling awkwardly along the pavement, as if each step was her very first.

Charlotte Reynolds was quick to the door. One look and she took her daughter in her arms, muttering soothingly into her hair. The dying and the lost.

'Is he?' she asked, and Harper nodded.

For a moment the woman said nothing, staring off into the grey sky. Then: 'Does it have to do with . . .'

'Yes,' he answered. 'It does.'

She exhaled, and he could see the way the guilt weighed her down. 'If I'd never written that letter they'd both of them still be alive, wouldn't they? It's all my fault.'

'No,' he told her. 'You couldn't know this would ever happen. Nobody could. Don't blame yourself.'

Pointless words. She'd closed the door in his face before he could finish speaking.

'I don't know. How many times do you want me to say it? *I don't bloody know*,' Harry Matthews shouted. 'I haven't the foggiest where he went.'

'Someone does,' Harper told him, 'and it's not his wife.'

'You find them, then. It's your job.'

A few minutes and Matthews had recovered some of his fire. From the smell of him, a drink or two had helped. And now he sounded at the end of his tether.

'Who did he know? Who were his friends?'

Matthews pointed to the list on the table. 'Right there, just like you asked. They're the ones I know. Ask his missus.'

'She's not in any state to answer questions right now. I'm sure you can imagine.'

'Well, that's all I've got for you.'

'Ask. People are more likely to talk to you than to me.'

Matthews stared, pushed his lips together, then nodded. 'Are you sure it's nothing to do with me?'

'Harry, I'm positive.'

Most bookies were like Matthews, simply small businesses serving a neighbourhood. They rarely caused trouble. Hardly any different from the local grocer on the corner. That was why the police tolerated them. Men would always gamble anyway; better the devil you knew.

At least he'd come away with a few names. A place to start.

But why kill John Larner? What had he done, besides tell Taylor about the letter? He was far too young to have been involved with the child-snatching. A cocky lad, but who wasn't at that age when they still felt immortal? The killing made absolutely no sense. It had to be connected to the case somehow, but it wasn't a *part* of it. Those few words in the letter seemed to be the root of everything. Maybe Charlotte Reynolds was right; things might have been better if they'd never been written, if the past had been left alone.

Too late now, though. Much too late.

'Speak to all the names on Harry's list. We need to account for the time between Larner leaving home and the body being found.'

An evening meeting, already full darkness outside, the sounds of the city changing from daytime scramble to the muffled sounds of night.

'It's exactly the same as Taylor, sir,' Sissons said. 'There was a gap of a few days there, too.'

'And we still haven't discovered what happened to *him* in that time.' He glanced at the clock on the wall. 'You should be able to find a few of those people tonight.' He thought for a moment. 'Ask about Adam Taylor, too. Maybe we can find a connection to explore. Have we had any word on that child-seller yet? Brenda Walcott?'

'Not a peep, sir.'

'I want her found, and we're going to drag some truth out of her. We'll have a photograph of Armstrong from High Royds tomorrow. Galt, you take it to Mrs Jones, see if she recognizes him.'

'Yes, sir.'

Chairs scraped over the floor and the men filed out.

'I thought you said something would break,' Harper told Ash.

'I did add patience to that, sir. It will.'

He was sorting through the papers on his desk when the telephone rang.

'I'm glad I caught you, Tom. I know you're under the cosh with these murders, but could you find time to come over in the morning?'

He had to smile. The chief constable's orders were always so politely phrased, as if you'd be doing him the greatest favour by obeying.

'Of course, sir. Anything special?'

'Just a couple of items, that's all. Shall we make it early?'

'Yes, sir.'

After so long, he was used to the way Crossley saw the day. Early meant seven. Dinner meant noon, and late varied between five and six in the afternoon. For a moment he wondered what the man wanted, then the thought slipped away; he'd find out tomorrow.

'You look glum,' Annabelle said.

'Work,' he told her, and that was explanation enough. 'No more letters?'

'No.'

Mary raised her head. 'What letters, Mam?'

'Someone thinks your mother will be betraying everyone round here if she sells the Victoria,' Harper said.

'What? That's pathetic.' She spat the word, and he saw the venom in her eyes. 'You've done everything for them.'

'I've done a little bit here and there. It's why they elected me.'

'You've done a damned sight more than that.'

'Language, young lady,' Annabelle warned. 'You're not with your friends now.'

'It's true, though, isn't it? As far back as I can remember you've been working to help everyone. Why would someone come out with that?'

'Jealousy,' Harper told her.

'Why?' Mary asked in disbelief. 'Because we have a bob or two?'

'Some people are like that.'

'If I find out who sent it—'

'You'll do nothing.' Annabelle's voice came down like a steel rod. 'If that's how they want to think, let them. It's petty, that's all. Jealous, like your da said.'

Mary glared at them and stormed into her room, letting the door slam behind her.

'She's on your side,' Harper said quietly.

'I know.' She gave a sad smile. 'But what good will it do to stir up a feud? Better to ignore it. They'll give up.'

'Have you made up your mind about selling yet?'

She shook her head. 'It feels like the biggest decision I've ever had to make. I need to be sure it's the right one.'

'Whichever way you choose, I'll be right behind you.'

'I know. I just wish I had that kind of confidence in myself.'

The town hall was hushed. No echo of feet on the staircases. Most of the offices wouldn't open until nine. The only light came through the chief constable's door. Harper knocked and waited.

Walking along the Headrow, dead leaves had blown around his feet in their browns and reds. Where had they come from? The only trees in town lay in Park Square. The rest was all dirty brick and stone, not a patch of green to be seen.

'Come in.' Crossley rose, hand extended, always welcoming. 'Sit down. I'd offer you a cup of tea, but there's no one here to make it yet.'

'No need, sir. I had breakfast at home.'

'Good, good.' He nodded approvingly. 'How are you progressing on your murders?'

'Nowhere, sir. Absolutely nowhere.'

That was enough to make the chief look quizzical. 'Nothing at all?'

'As soon as we come up with a lead, it turns to dust.'

'That can happen. Keep at it. Your men have an excellent record. I have every faith in you.'

'Thank you, sir.'

'I wanted you here to discuss the prime minister's visit.' He frowned. 'I've very graciously been given a little more information. He's going to have the home secretary with him, Mr Gladstone. You know what that means.'

Oh yes, he knew. The home secretary had ultimate charge of the police. They'd need to put on a very good show.

'I have a few more details about the itinerary. From the station they'll be going on to the Liberal Club to unveil a portrait of Gladstone's father before they move on to the Coliseum.'

'That's going to complicate matters, sir.'

'I understand that,' Crossley said. 'I've asked, but they're not willing to change.'

'Then we'd better take them up Park Row to the venue,' Harper said. He tried to think, to picture all the streets in his head. 'That way we'll avoid the unemployed protesting outside the town hall. But now we have two senior men from the government . . . it's bound to be even more of a target, sir.'

'I agree entirely. That's what we have, though, and we need to make the best of it. I'd suggest adding some police horses to your needs.'

'Yes, sir.' An excellent idea. The animals would make an effective barrier, and the sheer size of them scared people.

'Mr Gladstone will be spending the night with Lord Airedale at Gledhow Hall. Evidently the family believes he might propose to their daughter. We should have a couple of men stationed in the grounds, just in case there's a problem.'

'He ought to be safe enough out there. But we're certainly going to have trouble in town.'

'I know. I'm relying on you to keep as much order as you can. Contain them.'

'I talked to Alf Kitson. He more or less promised a confrontation.'

'If he starts anything, jump down his throat. We're going to keep control of the evening.'

'I'll do my best, sir.'

Crossley gave a weary smile. 'I know. That's all I ask, Tom. We both realize the whole thing is a disaster waiting to happen. Let's make it as small as possible.' He sighed. 'There's one other thing . . .'

'Sir?' What else could there be? This was bad enough.

'The Cranbrooks. I was over there a couple of days ago. Do you still want to speak to them?'

'Very definitely, sir. But I still want a little more evidence first.'

The chief eyed him carefully. 'How close are you to getting it?'

'Honestly? Nowhere near close enough.'

'When you're ready, be circumspect with them. No accusations, just polite questions.'

'Of course, sir.'

'If it needs to be more than that, come and see me first.'

'Yes, sir. I will.'

He walked from the town hall back to Millgarth, moving against the tide of workers going to their offices. The thoughts swirled through his brain. All these arrangements for the politicians . . . however much they prepared, it was going to be chaos. Unemployed men and suffragettes. The prime minister's visit was going to be a long, vicious night. A lot of coppers would be wearing their bruises for days.

THIRTEEN

'Those are the changes to Mr Asquith's visit,' he told his squad. 'Think about them, consider what alterations you need to your own plans, and tell me. We need to be ready.'

He could see the dismay. The last thing they needed was even more work. But the whole affair was his responsibility. He needed it to go as smoothly as it could. At least keep the fighting to a minimum.

'Go over everything again,' he said. 'Meanwhile, gentlemen, we have a pair of murders to solve. How do we stand? Where was Larner while he disappeared? Who was he with?'

'I've been working my way through that list Harry Matthews gave you, sir,' Ash said. 'One of them claims he had a glimpse of Larner on the day he died, late in the afternoon. He was with a man the friend didn't know. That's it so far. I still have two of them to see.'

'Where was he? Still in Hunslet?'

'In the middle of town.'

'And no idea at all who this other man could be?'

'None, sir. The witness only had a quick glimpse, he was going past on a tram. Larner didn't even see him.'

'Never mind. It's a start, I suppose. Did any of them know Taylor?'

'No, sir. Blank looks all round.'

'I suppose it would have been too much to hope. Keep at it.'

Harper picked up a photograph and looked at Galt. 'Take this over to Mrs Jones. It's Armstrong when he was admitted to High Royds, rest his soul. See if that's who she saw with Taylor.'

'Very good, sir.' He slipped it into his jacket pocket.

'I know you're all as frustrated as I am,' Harper said. 'We take one step forward and we're pushed two steps back again. If you're hoping for a few inspiring words from me, you're out of luck. That's my wife's speciality, and she refuses to teach me the knack.' At least that brought a few smiles. 'Just do your best and we'll find the answers. And let's not forget this started with Andrew Sharp and Marie Davis. We need some truth for them. All right?'

They left. Ash lingered in the doorway for a second. His mouth twitched into a smile and he winked. Good enough.

Now he had to hope. If he was a praying man he'd head off to church and get down on his knees for a while.

The day dragged. The autopsy report on Larner arrived. Strangled the evening before he was found. Contusions on the head, enough to knock him out before the hands closed on his throat. A horrible way to die; about the only blessing was that he'd have been unconscious.

Now they knew how it had happened. But it didn't give them any indication who might have done it.

He sorted through all the papers in the Larner file until he found the one he wanted. The property on Burley Road was owned by someone called Arnold Dawson. According to the city directory, he lived in Chapeltown and had an office on New Briggate.

Harper glanced at the clock. Almost twelve. Time for a spot of dinner and a stroll.

It was a shabby little place, sitting two floors above a newsagent's shop close by the entrance to St John's churchyard. A photographer and an entertainment agency shared the floor below.

Harper knocked on Dawson's door and tried the handle. It turned under his hand and he pushed it open. A single room with a pair of grubby windows looking down on New Briggate. No sign of the man, although a worn leather briefcase sat on the floor beside a wooden chair. Papers were scattered about the desk, and a glass ashtray was filled with cigarette ends.

It was five minutes before the man returned. Even with Harper's poor hearing, the heavy clump of footsteps on the stairs was unmistakable, the smell of fried fish and chips rising ahead of him.

The man stopped as he entered the room. 'Who are you?'

Harper showed his identification.

'Ah,' Dawson said, and his face sagged. 'The body.' He settled on to his chair and unwrapped the newspaper around his meal. 'No disrespect, Superintendent, but I want to eat them while they're hot.'

'Go right ahead, sir. I might buy some myself after I leave here. You own the house where the dead man was found, is that correct?'

'It is.'

He looked to be around sixty, wearing a suit that had been expensive a long time ago. It had been treated well, but still showed its age. The cuffs of his shirt were frayed, and thin strands of white hair were combed across his scalp. There was an air of neglected vanity about him. He might have been well off once, Harper thought, but that was far in the past. Now he probably had just enough to get by, a widower who needed the routine of an office every day to keep making sense of his life.

'He was found in a locked room. Who might have had the key?'

The man swallowed a mouthful of food before replying. 'The only one I can think of is Charlie Elgin. He's the agent for my properties. Looks after renting them, the maintenance, things like that.'

Harper recalled the condition of the house; Elgin wasn't particularly thorough.

'How many places do you own, sir?'

'Four.' Dawson gave the ghost of a smile. 'I know, it's not an empire, but it keeps me bobbing along.'

'How often do you go and inspect them?'

'I don't,' he replied. 'That's Elgin's job.'

'Have you ever heard of John Larner before?'

He shook his head. 'Never. I checked the records; he hasn't been a tenant of mine. Was it . . . bad?'

'It always is, sir.' Let him think the worst, it might spur him to help. 'I'm going to need the records of people who've rented rooms at the house. How long have you owned it?'

'Sixteen years now.'

'I'll want them going back to when you bought it.'

The man opened his mouth, then simply nodded.

'And I need an address for Mr Elgin.'

'Yes, of course.' He finished the last of his meal, dragging a chip through the grease on the paper before wadding it all up and wiping his hands before he threw it into the bin and lit a cigarette. 'Let me write it down for you. I hope you'll give the family my condolences and tell them how shocked I am.'

'I'll pass that on, sir.'

Harper left, carrying a ledger and a piece of paper. Later he'd go and track down Charlie Elgin. First, though, he'd sit down with his own plate of fish and chips at Youngman's.

Harper walked back to Millgarth with the taste of vinegar still sharp in his mouth. Before he could enter, two constables ran out and across the road, still fumbling their helmets in place.

'What's happening?' he asked Mason.

'Disturbance up on the Bank, sir. Someone tried to attack a woman. An ambulance is on its way for her. Don't know anything more than that at the moment.'

Attacking a woman? They were lawless enough on the Bank, but they usually wouldn't tolerate something like that. It had to possess a deeper meaning.

'Where exactly?'

'Corner of Bread Street, sir.'

Harper placed the ledger on the desk. 'Look after that for me.'

A fast jog and he was there in five minutes. A crowd had gathered, women, a couple of men with no work. Panting hard, Harper pushed his way through them to a copper standing over an unconscious woman on the pavement. Someone had folded an overcoat and placed it under her head.

'What happened?'

'Benson, sir, number 679.' He pointed to the end of the block. 'I'd just come round the corner up there, and I saw a man hitting her. I blew my whistle and started to run. He took off towards York Road. She was like this, already out cold. I thought I'd do best to stop and look after her. Kept blowing my whistle and had two of our lads here within a minute. They've gone searching for him.'

He looked down at the woman. In her fifties, he guessed, plump, hair all grey. Out cold, eyelids not even fluttering. But she was still breathing regularly, a little blood leaking from a gash at the back of her head.

'Do you know her at all?'

'Only seen her twice, sir. She moved here a little while ago. Widow woman, that's what I heard. Haven't even spoken to her.'

A battered wicker shopping bag lay close to her, the purse still inside. Not a robbery, or the man would have grabbed that before he ran.

The ambulance arrived, the horse skittering across the cobbles as the driver pulled hard on the reins. The men lifted her gently on to a stretcher, placing the bag on her stomach.

'Anyone know her name?'

'I think she's called Brenda,' a woman called out.

Brenda? Harper turned and stared at the people around him.

'Do you know her surname?' he shouted. But no response.

As soon as the ambulance pulled away, Harper said to the constable: 'Which house is hers?'

'Number three, sir.'

'We're going to take a look.'

It only took a moment to pick the lock.

'This is so flimsy a child could break in,' Benson muttered. 'Round here, one or two probably have, too.'

It was a weathered back-to-back. Still a few boxes on the floor, waiting to be unpacked. He began riffling through a stack of paper.

'Beg pardon, sir, but what are you searching for?'

'Anything with her name on it. Here we are.' A rates receipt made out to Mrs Brenda Woolcott. He had her. Once she came to, he had questions to ask about snatched children. 'I'm going to need a full statement from you,' he told Benson. 'And as good a description as you can give of the man.'

'I only saw him for a moment, sir, and it was from the other end of the block.'

'I still need everything you can remember. Meanwhile, I want someone outside this place until we've had a chance to go through it properly.'

'Sir?' the constable asked in surprise.

'We've been looking for this woman,' Harper said. 'And it seems we weren't the only ones.'

'I've spoken to the infirmary. Brenda Woolcott is still unconscious. The doctor thinks she must have hit her head on the flagstones and it's caused a bleed on her brain.'

'Does he know when she might come to?' Galt asked.

'He doesn't have a clue,' Harper replied. 'Told me as much, but they'll let us know as soon as there's any change. Sissons, you're good with papers. You and Walsh go through everything in her house. I want to know all about her by tomorrow. Galt, I have a ledger sitting behind Mason's desk. Look at every name in there and see if there are any we've come across in this investigation.'

'Yes, sir.'

'What about me, sir?' Ash asked.

The superintendent smiled. 'You're leading the hunt for the man who attacked Brenda. The description's next to nothing, but a couple of bobbies were on his tail.'

'And Mrs Woolcott herself, sir?'

He shrugged. 'Nothing we can do until she comes round. She's in a room by herself with a constable guarding the door. Let's snap to it.'

This time it was Galt who remained when the others had gone. He brought the photograph of Armstrong from his pocket and placed it on the desk.

'I showed it to Mrs Jones, sir. She's certain it was him.'

At least it was confirmation. They'd tracked Taylor deeper into the evening of his death. But what had happened after that? he wondered. Maybe they'd never know the full truth.

'Find me something useful in that ledger, Mr Galt,' Harper said. He felt weary, empty.

'I'll do my best, sir.'

He was a good lad, eager, too quick off the mark sometimes, but ready to work all the hours God sent and to learn the job inside and out. Happy to undertake whatever was necessary. Nothing was beneath him. Above all, he brought some youth to the squad; they certainly needed that. Harper knew that all the years he'd served showed on his face. Ash's hair was grey, even his moustache. Walsh had filled out. Even Sissons had been tempered and hardened by nine years as a detective. New blood was good.

'I know you will,' he told the young man.

Already evening, the sky dark and lamps twinkling along the street. People clambered on to trams and motor buses to make their way home from work. But his day wasn't done yet. Harper took his seat inside on the tram, next to a cadaver of a man who reeked of stale sweat and bad breath and stared steadfastly ahead.

Harper alighted in Armley, working his way into the back streets. But when he reached the house, it looked like a wasted journey. No lights inside. Still, he banged on the door, sensing the emptiness.

He'd just turned away when a voice called out along the street: 'Are you looking for me?'

Charlie Elgin walked with a limp. He hurried along with a smile on a big, round face, putting out a hand as he approached. Harper shook it, feeling the firm grip and the calluses on the skin.

'What can I do for you?'

Harper introduced himself, seeing the curiosity in the man's eyes.

'Aye, it's a terrible thing, all right.' He took off his cap as he unlocked the door. 'You'd best come in. Going to be parky, I'll need to build a fire.'

Everything was in impeccable shape, the breakfast dishes washed and dry on the draining board, all the furniture polished and dusted within an inch of its life. A very ordered man, someone who liked his world to be just so.

'I don't know what I can tell you,' Elgin continued. 'I wasn't even there, didn't hear about it until well after it happened.'

'He was found in a locked room,' Harper said.

'Aye. That's an odd thing.' He sat in his chair, bending forward to unlace his boots. 'It's not a room we can rent, just a cubby hole, really, so we let the tenants use it to store things if they need to. Keep it unlocked. That way, if anything goes missing, it's not our fault.'

Harper smiled at the way Elgin sounded so possessive about the house, as if he was the one who owned the building.

'Who'd have a key?'

'I've been putting my mind to that.' He pulled a large, heavy keyring from his jacket pocket, selected one and held it up. 'That's the key for the room. I carry it with me and I've never used it in all my time working for Mr Dawson.'

'How long is that?'

'Six year, near enough. I don't know of any other copies. Mind you, that lock would be easy enough to open. To close, too. You would probably do it with a hairpin.'

'All the tenants knew about it?'

'Aye,' Elgin said. 'It's hardly a secret.' He brought out a small clay pipe and a match, tamped down the tobacco and struck a light with his thumb. Simple, compact motions, something he probably did every night when he settled in the chair.

'You've been there often enough,' Harper said. 'Are there any tenants you wouldn't trust?'

'Dozens of them over the years,' he answered with a smile. 'No, most of them are fine. Just trying to get by. It's not the smartest address, is it? Not the worst, either. But there's no one stands out in my mind.'

Harper pushed himself to his feet. 'I'll thank you for your time, then. One last thing: you don't know why John Larner would be at the house, do you?'

'Larner? Was that his name?' Elgin shook his head. 'No, I've never heard it before. I'm sorry for his family.'

One more dead end, not that he'd ever expected much from it. Still, if you didn't ask, you never knew. And it was a detective's job to follow every possibility. That was what his old boss, Superintendent Kendall, had instilled in him when he was starting out in CID. Another one who was dead now; Harper had filled his shoes at Millgarth. Billy, Kendall, so many others . . . very soon the dead in his life would outnumber the living.

The wind whipped across the cemetery. Harper and Ash stood in the lee of an old oak tree, most of its leaves already gone and scattered across the grass. Fifty yards away, six men carried Lawrence Armstrong's coffin to the waiting grave in Middleton.

A small crowd, two or three relatives, along with a handful of miners from when he'd worked at the pit. The colliery brass band stood and played 'Abide With Me' as the casket was lowered.

'I'm not sure why we've come all the way out here, sir,' Ash said. 'It's not as if he was murdered.'

'I just thought someone should,' Harper replied after a long, empty silence. 'I'm the one who sent him to High Royds. If I hadn't, he might still be alive.'

'Guilt won't help.'

'Probably not. But he still deserves something.'

Ash nodded towards the people who stood, the wind pulling at their clothes. 'Looks like he got it.'

'I suppose so.'

He needed to put death from his mind. But how could he do that when every day seemed filled with it? A woman bent, picked up a clump of earth and crumbled it through her fingers into the grave. Harper turned away and began to walk.

'Brenda Woolcott still hadn't regained consciousness when I checked this morning,' he said.

'I have a better description of the man who attacked her, sir. Still far from exact. It's out with the boys on the beat to see if any of them recognize him. I wouldn't put money on it, though.'

'Let's just say she comes to and admits she arranged the taking of Marie Davis,' Harper said. 'We already know that Mark Reynolds was responsible for Andrew Sharp. What do we do then?'

'We visit the Cranbrooks, sir,' Ash replied. 'We have to.'

'Fine, and they admit buying a boy and a girl and raising them as their own, in a house where there's money and comfort.' He stared at the inspector. 'What do we do then? That's the only home Andrew and Marie have ever really had. For all we know, they're a happy, loving family. They've been raised in more comfort than they'd ever have known in their old lives. More chances ahead of them. Yes, it's a crime, but . . .'

'I see what you're saying, sir.' He pursed his lips. 'I can't give you an answer to that.'

'Neither can I. That's the problem.'

FOURTEEN

A note was waiting on his desk, written in Mason's careful hand.

The infirmary telephoned. Mrs Woolcott has regained consciousness.

He exhaled slowly. Hallelujah. Progress at least.

'Don't bother taking your coat off,' Harper called to Ash. 'We're going out again.'

The familiar corridors and smells of the hospital, the sting of carbolic that tried to mask the sick-sweet decay underneath. The air a mix of carefully hushed silences and moans.

Outside the room, the doctor glanced back to be certain the door was closed, took off his spectacles and pinched the bridge of his nose.

'She's awake,' he said, measuring out his words. He looked like a man in desperate need of sleep, with dark, heavy pouches under his eyes. 'Her eyes are open. She hasn't said a word yet, but she appears to be aware of her surroundings. She reacts to touch, she can grip a little.'

'Could we see her?' Harper asked. At least he could ask his questions and see if she responded.

'If you must, Superintendent,' the doctor replied with a sigh. 'But only with a nurse present, and it has to be brief. There's so much we don't understand about head injuries. Mrs Woolcott might make a complete recovery, or . . .' He shrugged. 'We just don't know.'

Some of her hair had been shaved away to examine the wound. Brenda Woolcott lay completely still. Only her eyes moved, following them across the room until they stood by the side of the bed.

'I'm Detective Superintendent Harper and this is Inspector Ash.' His voice was soft; what was it about hospitals that made people speak so quietly, he wondered? 'It's good to see you awake again. Do you remember being attacked?'

She blinked. Once, twice, as she stared at him. No sign that she was going to speak. He tried two more questions and received the same response. In the corner, the nurse coughed. Harper turned and looked at her.

'I'm sorry, Superintendent, but that's all we can allow for now. You can see for yourself, there's no real response.'

'Yes, of course.' He glanced down at the woman in the bed. 'You rest. We'll come back another time.'

'What do you think, sir?' Ash asked as they walked back to the heart of town. A car and a lorry came along Great George Street, roaring past the carts. A horse shied a little in its traces. Beyond the dirty black bulk of the town hall, the two of them cut down Calverley Street by the library to the Headrow.

'I don't know. Was there ever a Mr Woolcott?'

'There was, sir. Not for long, they'd only been married for three years when he died. Nothing suspicious, happened at work. No children. She used to look after the little ones on her street. For a fee, of course.'

'Not a huge step from that to selling them, is it?' Harper said.

'Not at all. It seems we suspected her in a couple of cases, but we never had enough to bring her in. I'd say that flit of hers makes it certain, though.'

'Yes' Something nagged at him. 'Why give her enough warning to vanish, then attack her a few days later, though? Explain that.'

'We'll find out when we catch the man who did it,' Ash said. 'He's a cold bastard, I'll tell you that, sir. With Taylor and Larner, he's already murdered two men and who can tell how Mrs Woolcott will end up. Whatever he's protecting, he's trying to make absolutely sure we don't come close.'

'Do you have a sense of him yet?' He couldn't even form an image in his mind.

Ash frowned and shook his head. 'He's still all shadows. See what today brings, sir.'

A woman was waiting at Millgarth, curly dark hair showing under a broad-brimmed hat.

'Mrs Baines, sir,' Sergeant Mason said. 'She's here to see you.'

This was a surprise. But certainly for the best. He introduced himself and led her through to his office. So this was the woman who'd be leading the suffragette protest against the prime minister. Tall, raw-boned, with a serious, brooding face. Working class. She couldn't hide it and she didn't want to. No airs and graces, no fancy, fashionable clothes. Everything she wore was made to last, sturdy enough to stand plenty of wear and tear.

'What can I do for you, Mrs Baines? I believe you're new in Leeds. I trust you're enjoying the place.'

'I'm not here for pleasure,' she told him. 'I'm the area organizer for the WSPU. The suffragettes, in case you didn't know.'

Her voice was nasal, from the Midlands, he guessed, overlaid with something else he couldn't quite identify. But she spoke clearly enough for his weak hearing to pick out every word.

'I'm aware of that,' he answered with a smile. 'I've heard your name. At a guess, you want to talk about the prime minister's visit.'

'That's right.' She stared him in the eye. 'Him and the home secretary. They tell me you're in charge.'

'I am. We're happy to accommodate a peaceful demonstration.' He nodded at her. 'I trust that's all it will be, Mrs Baines.'

'That depends on the women. And how your policemen act.' She sat on the edge of her chair, back perfectly straight, hands primly gathered in her lap.

'I can control my coppers.'

'I've heard that one before. I was in the Salvation Army, Superintendent. A lieutenant and a police court missionary before I turned to this. I've seen what can happen.'

'Not in Leeds.'

A flicker of a smile. 'It's the same all over. Your wife.'

'What about her?' The quick change of tack took him by surprise.

'I understand she doesn't support us.'

'Really?' he asked. 'I'd hardly say that. She's been speaking out for suffrage for fifteen years.' She was trying to needle him, to work her way under his skin. He wasn't about to let that happen.

'She's with Miss Ford and the National Union.'

'Don't you all have the same goal?'

'We do,' she agreed. 'But their approach hasn't worked too well, has it? We think it's time to be a little more direct.'

The exact thing Kitson had said. The promise of a fight.

'Confrontational?' Harper asked.

Mrs Baines smiled again. 'Your word, not mine. You daughter supports what we do.'

The woman had done her homework. He couldn't fault her on that; she'd arrived prepared.

'She's sixteen, still underage,' Harper replied. 'As I'm sure you know.'

'But she still has her beliefs.' There was a hint of triumph in her voice.

'Of course. She's quite able to make up her own mind.' He wasn't going to be dragged any deeper into that. 'Forgive me, but I'm not sure I see the point of your visit.'

'We'll be seeing each other again soon enough. I thought we should take the measure of one another first.'

The Black Country, he decided. Birmingham. That was where she'd grown up, the vowels marked and rounded. A working woman in a plain coat. Whatever she'd learned had come long after she left school. The same as Annabelle. The same as him.

'My job is to keep order on the night and to make sure the politicians are safe. That *everyone* is safe.'

'And mine is to make sure Mr Asquith knows women want the vote now.'

'I suspect he's already aware of that.'

'Then we'll keep repeating it until something changes.' Not a threat. A simple statement of fact.

'As long as you stick to shouting, we'll all be happy.'

She raised an eyebrow. 'Know our place, you mean?'

He allowed a moment to pass before replying. 'Please don't put words in my mouth, Mrs Baines. Keep everything peaceful, I meant. As I'm sure you realize.'

'I told you, Superintendent, we're not intending to start trouble. But we *will* put our point across to the prime minister, and we'll do it forcefully. Make no mistake about that.'

Start trouble. Forcefully. Telling phrases.

'We both know where we stand, then, Mrs Baines. If I need to contact you . . .?'

'I've nothing to hide. We have a temporary office at Leeds Arts Club.' She gave him the address on Woodhouse Lane.

'Do you know Mr Kitson at all?'

'We've met in passing.' He waited for more, but she held her peace.

As he held the door for her, she asked, 'Will your daughter be joining us on the night?'

'No,' Harper said. 'She's too young. There's time when she's older.'

'I hope by then it won't be necessary. Good day, Superintendent.'

She'd planted her flag and put him on notice. Between the suffragettes and the unemployed, the night of the prime minister's visit was going to be rough.

'We've been through everything in Mrs Woolcott's house, sir,' Walsh said. 'There's nothing to tie her to the Cranbrook girl. Or to any children, for that matter.'

Harper had never really expected to find evidence. But the opportunity had been too good to miss.

He turned to Galt. 'What have you turned up in that ledger?'

'Two interesting names, sir.' The young man grinned like a cat who'd just found a bowl of cream. 'It seems Lawrence Armstrong lived there a few years ago.'

'Really?' Harper asked in surprise. 'When?'

'Back in 1901, sir. Just for a few weeks, then he was turfed out for not paying his rent.'

Seven years ago. A lifetime. But he couldn't have had anything to do with this.

'You said two names.'

'John Davis.'

'Who?' He couldn't think of anyone with that name.

'If you recall, sir, Marie Cranbrook was born Marie Davis, sir. John Davis is her father. His name is in the statement.'

His mind jumped to the woman he'd met, still trying to get over the grief for her daughter. She'd said her husband would never accept that the girl was dead.

'What was he doing there?'

'It was only a short time, about a week. Two years ago.'

'Are you sure it's the same man? It's a common name.'

Galt grinned. 'I went and checked with some of the tenants who lived there at the time. It's him, sir, no doubt about it. Argument with his wife and she told him to leave. He was always going on about the fact that everything had changed after his daughter's disappearance. Seems the pair of them made it up and he toddled off home again.'

'That's excellent work,' Harper told him, seeing the man beam with pleasure.

'There's a tiny bit more, sir. Davis is a labourer, seems to hold a job well enough. But when he was young he spent a year working for a locksmith.'

With a background like that, he'd have no problem seeing to that door.

'Make that outstanding work. Why don't you find Mr Davis and invite him to join us for a little chat?'

'Gladly, sir.' Galt was already on his feet and moving towards the door.

'Be polite, helping with our inquiries, that sort of thing. Let's spring this on him once he's here.'

'Very good, sir.'

'When he comes in, you handle the questioning, Walsh.'

He'd become the best interrogator of them all. Subtle, picking up on every sign, and knowing exactly the right time to pounce. If Davis was hiding something, Walsh would be able to ferret it out.

All the elements were there, but they needed to discover the connections.

He sat back and sighed.

Waiting for answers. Always the hardest thing to do.

Four o'clock. He had time to nip over to the Coliseum and make sure everything was in place. Mrs Baines's visit had made him all too aware of what lay ahead of them.

The council workmen were busy repairing the road, prying up the loose cobbles and cementing them back in place. Harper showed his identification to the foreman.

'All be finished by the end of the day,' the man said. He had a heavy beard, and a clay pipe in his mouth that bobbed up and down as he spoke. 'They'll not be getting any of those up to throw.' He sniffed. 'They ought to be cheering the prime minister, not demonstrating.'

'I've met two who'd disagree with you. And they'd be throwing these at my men, not politicians.'

'They bloody well won't by the time we're done,' the foreman told him. 'You'll need a pickaxe to get one of them up. Owt else you want us to do while we're here?'

'Can you check along Vernon Street and do the same?' They intended to pen the suffragettes there. He didn't picture them hefting stones at the police, but after seeing Jennie Baines, it was better safe than sorry.

The man nodded and strode off, giving orders as he walked.

Harper inspected the area, taking his time before moving down the hill to Victoria Square. So much that could go wrong. Too much.

'I met someone today who knew your name.'

'Who was that?' Annabelle was washing the pots, carefully drying each plate on a tea towel before putting it away. Harper leaned against the range, a mug of tea in his hand. Mary was in her room, dolling herself up for an evening out with her friends.

'A lady named Jennie Baines.'

'Never heard of her.'

'She's the area organizer for the suffragettes.'

'Another new one?' Annabelle turned her head and looked at him. 'Seems like they change them every month.'

'She came in to see me about the demonstration. She was aware that you work with Miss Ford.'

'Anyone local could have told her that. Hardly a state secret, is it?' She wiped her hands.

'And she asked if my daughter would be attending. I told her no.'

'At least she's up to snuff on things. What did you make of her?'

'Formidable,' he replied after a moment. 'Not someone who's likely to back down.'

'That's exactly who you want in a position like that. A woman strong enough to put backbone into everyone.'

Harper chuckled. 'She'll do that, all right.'

'Worried?'

He nodded. 'Yes. I have a very bad feeling about this.'

'Copper's intuition?' She felt the side of the teapot and poured herself another cup.

'Common sense. It's like having a bomb and hoping no one's going to light the fuse while everyone's running around with matches.'

Annabelle raised an eyebrow. 'With phrases like that, you should have been a poet.'

Harper snorted. 'It would probably be easier than this job. Between that and trying to get to the bottom of these stolen children . . .'

'You're sure they were snatched?'

'I am,' he answered after a moment. 'The only thing missing is the proof.'

She said nothing. They'd been married long enough that words weren't always necessary. The silences could be as eloquent as any speeches. He knew she was thinking of Andrew Sharp's sisters and brothers and the lives they were leading. The things that might have been.

A door closed and Mary bustled in, bonny as a picture, adjusting the hat on her head.

'Do you think this brooch goes with the outfit, Mam?'

A cameo at her throat, something she'd picked up in the market on the way home from work.

'Very bonny. Sets it off nicely.'

'I won't be late. We have tickets for the first house and I'll come straight home afterwards.'

A quick kiss on the cheek for each of them and she was gone.

'She's like a whirlwind,' Annabelle said with a wistful smile. 'Were we ever that eager for life, do you think?'

'At her age I was usually too exhausted after work.' He'd left school at nine and rolled barrels at Brunswick Brewery until he was accepted into the police at eighteen. Relentless, physical work.

'So was I. Never mind. Two more years and she'll be running her own business. That'll take up every waking hour.'

'Your business,' he corrected her.

'My *name*,' Annabelle pointed out. 'And only until she's twenty-one. Either way, she'll be the one doing the hard slog.'

He could still scarcely believe that their daughter had such a firm idea of what she wanted from life. But doubt had never been in her vocabulary. Was so much certainty good or bad at her age? he wondered. Still, she'd make it work, he was absolutely certain of that. She had the nous and the determination.

Annabelle's words interrupted his thoughts. 'What are you going to do about these children?'

'Sooner or later I'm going to have to talk to the Cranbrooks. I'm hoping Brenda Woolcott will be able to tell us something when she can speak again. It's not looking good, though. Not with these murders.'

He'd telephoned the infirmary before he came home. Brenda woke, she slept. Her eyes moved, but that was all. Wait and see, they told him. Wait and see.

'I thought you might appreciate a little background on Mrs Baines, sir,' Ash said as he laid a thin folder on the desk.

'I take it you heard about her visit,' Harper said.

'Talk of the station, sir, marching in here bold as brass. I chatted to a few people I know in other forces. There's not a great deal in there, but at least we have something.' His mouth twitched under the moustache.

Two pages in Ash's flowing copperplate. Sarah Jane Baines. Born in 1866 in Birmingham – at least he'd been right on that. Started working in an ordnance factory at eleven, joined the Salvation Army at fourteen, ending up as a lieutenant, dispatched to be an evangelist in a working men's mission in Bolton and a police court missionary for arrested women. Exactly as she'd told him. Temperance. Married, five children. She'd been with the

WSPU since 1905, had become an area organizer early this year, paid two pounds a week. Based in Stockport, travelling around, speaking and setting up new branches of the organization, then moving on again.

She'd given him the truth about herself. A woman who'd achieved a great deal. She'd experienced the raw side of life. It was hard not to admire someone like that.

But the words at the bottom caught his attention: *Believed to have tendencies towards more militant action.* Harper thought about what she'd said to him . . . *we will put our point across to the prime minister, and we'll do it forcefully.* Maybe she was aching for the smallest provocation. And he had no doubt she'd find it.

FIFTEEN

'We have John Davis, sir.' Galt put his head around the door of Harper's office. 'Walsh is speaking to him now.'

'Thank you.'

He paused by the door of the interview room. The sergeant was in full flow; he could hear the voice, but his hearing was too poor to make out the words. There was a short stammering reply, then he turned the handle and entered.

Davis was a big man with ragged grey hair and a weathered face. His cheeks had sunk where teeth had been pulled. Harper glanced at the man's hands. Large, scarred by work. Definitely strong enough to strangle the life from someone.

'My boss,' Walsh said as Harper took the chair in the corner, behind Davis. The man looked over his shoulder, a nervous expression in his eyes. 'How long did you stay in the house, sir?'

'No more'n a week.' He looked down as he spoke, as if the answers lay in his lap. 'Me and the missus, we had an argument. We do that a lot. Sometimes she gets very low and tells me to clear out.' He brightened a little. 'Allus takes me back after a few days, mind, once it's out of her system.'

'Why did you end up there?' Walsh asked. 'It's not close to where you live.'

'The job I had back then were close by.' He shrugged. 'Saw a sign in the newsagent near work. Rooms for rent.'

'Did you hear what happened there? Someone was murdered.'

Davis bobbed his head. 'I saw it in the newspaper. Terrible, that is. Awful.'

'How did you come to know John Larner?'

'Who?' Davis said. But he waited just a fraction of a second too long to reply.

Walsh smiled. 'The man who died.'

'I don't know his name.'

'You should, Mr Davis. You killed him.'

'I never—'

'Strangled him and left the body in the house,' Walsh continued. 'Locked the room and hoped no one would find him for a while.'

'I—' he said, but Walsh kept speaking. This was the time to swoop and he knew it.

'How did you hear about him? Did you think he'd know something about Marie, is that it? And when he didn't, you tried to force it out of him?'

Harper watched. Any moment now, the man would crumble. It was the mention of Marie that tipped things. There was nothing hard about him, no real shell to cover him. The truth would pour out.

Two more minutes and the flood began. A friend of his lived over in Hunslet and placed his bets with Harry Matthews. The gossip had filtered through, first the details behind Adam Taylor's death, then Larner vanishing.

'I thought he had to know summat,' Davis said.

'How did you find him?' Walsh asked. His voice had turned to honey, easing out the rest of the admission.

'I didn't go looking or owt. I was at a pub in town with my mate after work. He saw him, nudged me and said that was who he'd been talking about.'

As simple as that. John Larner's deadly luck. Davis had taken him round a few pubs and bought him drinks until closing time. After the pubs shut, it was easy to lure him into the alley and start asking questions.

Of course, Larner didn't know anything about Marie. He'd never even heard of her. But that wasn't what Davis wanted to hear. After all these years, he believed he'd finally find some truth.

'I thought if I choked him a bit, he'd tell me.'

'You squeezed too hard, didn't you?'

'I must have. We weren't far from the house. I remembered that room . . .'

Walsh didn't say a word. No need now. Davis was pushing ahead under his own steam.

'I thought if I put him in there . . . nobody would know him. No one would remember me. Only took me ten seconds to lock it.' He looked up. 'I'm sorry.'

Davis didn't know anything about Adam Taylor's death. He simply looked bewildered and shook his head. Harper left, giving Walsh a nod of approval.

He would be going down to the cells. He'd plead guilty in court. If he had a good lawyer, all those years of missing his daughter and searching for her in every face he saw might mean life in prison instead of hanging for murder. Whichever way it went, there was no good ending. Just more misery and heartache.

One death solved, but it did nothing to help them find Taylor's killer. A separate case, but still with the letter at its root.

In his office, he reached for the telephone and asked the operator to connect him to the hospital. After five minutes of waiting, the receiver pressed tight against his good ear, the doctor came on the line.

'Mrs Woolcott has improved this morning,' he said with a note of caution.

'What does that mean?' Harper held his breath; maybe she was finally able to speak.

'She can move her hands a little, wiggle her fingers and turn her head. *That* means I'm hopeful she'll eventually regain all her movement. But it will take time, Superintendent. As I'm sure you appreciate.'

'What about speech?'

'She's trying, but all she can manage are a few sounds.'

'Can she understand what's said to her?' Harper asked.

A long pause before the doctor replied.

'Yes. Some of it, anyway. But I couldn't swear to that.'

It was enough. 'I'm coming over to talk to her.'

'I—'

'It's important,' he said as he ended the call.

* * *

The same rooms, the same smells that caught in the back of his throat. Brenda Woolcott looked much better, no doubt about that. She was still lying in bed, but a nurse had given her some attention, brushed her hair. She looked more like a person, less like a helpless patient. The woman turned her head towards him as he entered the room. A slow movement, very slow, an act of will. But the doctor was right. It was progress.

'I'm Detective Superintendent Harper. I came to visit you the other day.' No flash of recognition. 'You were attacked. Can you remember it at all?'

He searched her face. Her eyes narrowed at the words and she seemed to pinch her lips together. Finally, with effort, she moved her head to the left and back. No.

'Do you know who might have done it? Was there anyone who wanted to hurt you?'

Nothing. He might have been talking to the air.

'We know you did a flit from your house in Bramley, Mrs Woolcott. Was it because someone had been to see you?'

This time there was panic on her face. No mistaking it. She struggled, starting to thrash a little in the bed, body jerking. He placed a hand on her shoulder, just a light touch.

'It's fine,' he assured her. 'Absolutely fine. You're safe in here. There's a policeman guarding the door.' He waited until her breathing slowed and her gaze was on him once more.

He had no choice, even if language was beyond her reach. Who could tell if she'd ever be able to speak again, or how long that might take? He needed some answers, no matter how she gave them.

'Mrs Woolcott, we know you arranged the sale of children.' He let the statement hang between them. She stared at him, trapped, afraid. At his mercy. 'I'm going to say two names. Please, tell me if you know them. They were both a long time ago.'

He waited, feeling his heart pound hard in his chest. His palms were slick with sweat as he waited for some kind of response.

Finally, she raised her head slightly and let it fall again.

'Thank you,' he said softly. 'Does the name Adam Taylor mean anything to you?'

Mrs Woolcott stared into his face but her expression remained blank.

'Good,' he told her. 'One more question and I'll leave you to rest. Do you know a family called Cranbrook?'

She took her time, but he was certain she'd reply. Her eyes moved around the room as if she was taking it all in for the first time, before returning to him, examining his face. And then, the tiny movement. Yes.

He squeezed her hand lightly. 'Thank you,' he said again.

Two answers. Not everything he needed, nowhere near. And no Taylor in there; that was interesting. But he had a link to the Cranbrooks, thin as it was. Finally, it was time to pay them a visit.

SIXTEEN

Should he take Galt with him? Harper wondered as he read the file on the Cranbrook family again. The young man had done the work, he'd assembled all the facts and noted them down. But he was still impetuous, liable to go off half-cocked, and this interview would need calm and plenty of tact. Better to have someone with experience.

'I'll need a car and driver at six,' he told Mason. 'Most likely for a couple of hours.'

'Very good, sir.'

On the dot of six o'clock he emerged from Millgarth, Ash beside him, and climbed into the motor car, its engine already idling. A chilly evening, the smoke haze thick over the city, and they wouldn't feel any warmer in here.

He'd never grow used to being driven around like this, to the shuddering sound of the engine. But it would set the right tone to arrive this way, better than a bus and walking down the drive like a pair of pedlars.

The roads were busy with carts and trams and people on their way home from work. They bumped past Woodhouse Moor and out through Headingley. Then they were on a gravel avenue, an imposing house ahead of them.

Cranbrook had done well for himself. The place was no more than a few years old, two broad storeys and attic windows for the servants' rooms. Harper saw a face peek through the glass as they pulled to a halt.

'Ready?' he asked.

'As I'll ever be, sir,' Ash replied.

A servant was waiting at the door, her face showing nothing when they introduced themselves as police. She escorted them to a parlour where a fire burned bright, throwing out welcome heat. On the way, Harper caught a glimpse of a young woman in a dark silk dress climbing the stairs. Marie, he thought. His first sighting of her. She didn't turn her head to look at him.

The room was heavy with furniture, upholstered chairs, a table by the window with a vase of flowers, full bookshelves along one wall. Nothing cheap, but it felt cluttered and awkward.

They waited for twenty minutes. That was nothing unusual; it was barely even rude. Whenever a copper turned up at a rich man's house he needed to be reminded of his place in the social order.

'When they come in,' he told Ash, 'keep your eye on the wife.'

'I will, sir.'

Finally, the sharp click of heels on a tile floor and the door opened. Mrs Cranbrook entered first, her husband behind her, coffee cup still in his hand, cigar between his fingers.

They had the kind of sleekness that money bought. His hair was so clean it seemed to shine, clear skin and good white teeth. Sarah Cranbrook wore her wealth just as easily. Her face was carefully made-up, her gown from an expensive dressmaker, hands soft and pale. She stared at him, and for a moment Harper thought he saw hatred. Gone so fast that he wondered if he'd imagined it.

Robert Cranbrook placed his cup and saucer on the arm of a chair and puffed his cigar back to life. A self-satisfied man, Harper decided, someone who knew that everything around him was the result of his own hard work.

'Superintendent . . .'

'Harper. This is Detective Inspector Ash. I'm sorry to barge in on you, but I wanted to try and catch you both at home.' He laid a small emphasis on 'both'.

'Well, you've found us.' Leeds was right there in his voice. No amount of money was going to erase that, and he probably preferred it that way. The bluff Yorkshire businessman. 'What can we do for you? We're perfectly law-abiding.' He allowed himself a condescending smile.

'We're not here to arrest you. Nothing like that. Just a few questions.'

'Always happy to help the police. It's a civic duty.'

'I'm glad to hear that, sir. Tell me, do you know a woman named Brenda Woolcott?'

Cranbrook put the cigar in his mouth and puffed. Smoke rose around his face.

'No, I don't. As far as I'm aware, I've never even heard the name. What about you, Sarah? You're more likely to know a woman than I am.'

'No,' she answered quickly, staring down at the floor.

'There you are, Superintendent.' Cranbrook smiled. 'We don't know her at all. What's she supposed to have done?'

'She's in the infirmary at the moment, sir. Someone attacked her. She's unable to speak, but slowly recovering.'

The man cocked his head. 'I don't understand. What would something like that have to do with us?'

Good, Harper thought. By starting with Brenda he'd caught the man off-guard.

'She's part of something we're investigating, sir. It might well relate to a murder. If she dies, two murders.'

Cranbrook frowned, then his expression hardened. 'I'll ask you again: what does any of this have to do with us?'

'As I say, sir, your name happened to come up.'

'How?' It wasn't a question; it was a demand. He was someone who'd become too used to people obeying him.

'Just someone we were interviewing.' Harper smiled. He could feel the tension crackle in the air. Cranbrook hadn't so much as looked at his wife since they began talking. She was still staring at the Oriental rug as if she wanted to memorize the pattern. 'Since you've never heard of her, we won't trouble you any more.'

He gathered his hat off the table.

'Why would someone attack this woman?' Mrs Cranbrook asked. She didn't raise her head and kept her voice low. But even with his hearing, he could make out the shakiness underneath her words.

'We believe it has to do with something she was involved in years ago.' He paused. 'She had a business selling stolen infants.' Standing in the open doorway, he turned. 'Thank you for your time.'

The car was heading back towards Leeds. The glow of lights seemed to rise around the city in the distance.

'Cleverly done, if I might say so, sir. Much better than going in with a bludgeon, and a very sweet parting shot.'

'How did she react when I mentioned Brenda's name?'

'Couldn't see too much from where I was standing, but definitely worried. She knew exactly who it was. I reckon the pair of them will be having a sleepless night.'

'We might not have the evidence to accuse them of anything, but at least we've put a cat among the pigeons.' He stared out at the people on the pavement, men straggling into the Skyrack for a drink after work. 'Which of them would you go after?'

'The wife,' Ash replied. No hesitation at all. 'He'll huff and puff till the cows come home, but I could practically feel the guilt oozing off her.'

Not just huff and puff, he'd try to blow the whole bloody house down. Robert Cranbrook would never admit a thing unless he was cornered and the evidence was overwhelming.

'Give it a day or two, then go and talk to her again. Let them have time to stew.'

'My pleasure, sir. Take Galt along, do you think? The lad's earned it.'

Harper considered the idea. 'As long as you make sure he's under strict orders not to say a word.'

'I think I can keep him on a short lead.'

'Do that. Now, let's get to the big question: how are we going to find Taylor's killer?'

A few years before, a priest had told him that they were in much the same business. Both of them looked into people's hearts, he said, and tried to discover the truth. Harper had been sceptical at first. He arrested and looked for justice; a priest forgave. But as time passed, he kept coming back to the words, slowly realizing just how true it was.

And with the Cranbrooks, he'd need to dive very deep into their hearts to begin to understand what they'd done.

Harper stepped down from the tram in Sheepscar. The night was heavy, growing chillier by the hour. The first hint of damp mist in the air, felt rather than seen. He burrowed into his overcoat and crossed the street to the bright lights of the Victoria. Warmer inside, with a fire in the hearth, the press of bodies and conversation filling the air.

Moving through the crowd, saying hello to faces he knew, he spotted Billy Larkin sitting alone in a corner. That was unusual; his local was the White Stag on North Street, and he was always as loyal as the day was long. The man turned his head, raised his glass and gave a small nod.

Harper ordered a pint of mild from Dan the barman, took it over to the table and placed it in front of Larkin.

'I can't recall ever seeing you in here before, Billy. Been barred from the Stag and decided to try somewhere better?'

The man grinned, his laugh coming out like a wheeze. Both his front teeth were missing, leaving a broad, black gap.

'Nothing like that, Mr Harper. Just fancied a change of scene. Reckoned I might run into you.'

'Is that right? Well, it's a fair bet since I live here.'

'Thought you and me might have a little chat.'

Billy had given him good information in the past. Not often, but when he did, it was always solid.

'That's what we're doing.' He sat down. Billy's way was to go all round the houses, from A to B by way of the whole alphabet; it was his little ritual. This was going to be the same. Five minutes later, they were still in the middle of idle talk. Half the pint had gone.

'What's it all about?' Harper asked quietly. 'It's good to see you, but I've had a long day and I'd like to get up to my family. There's a hot meal waiting for me.'

Larkin bobbed his head up and down and gave another of his wide smiles. 'You should have said. Don't want to keep a man from his food.'

'I'm glad to hear it.'

'You've been looking into someone's murder.'

'Come on, Billy. That's hardly news.'

Larkin continued as if he hadn't heard Harper's comment. 'Adam Taylor's murder. Used to be one of your lot, didn't he?'

'A long time ago. I was the one who dismissed him.'

'He kept bad company once upon a time.'

'Did he? Anyone in particular?'

'I heard he was friendly with Tosh Walker's oldest lad for a while.'

Walker was dead now. The police had torn his empire apart while he was in jail, put an end to his moneylending, the protection rackets and selling the bodies of young girls. He'd been an evil man, but by the time he walked out of the gates of Armley Gaol he was a broken one. Powerless and penniless. Even his family had deserted him. He'd died in '04, body discovered one winter's morning behind a pile of rubbish.

Frank, the oldest of his sons, had tried to follow in his father's footsteps. Petty crime, a robbery or two. But he'd never quite managed his father's ruthlessness or cunning.

'Are you saying Frank murdered him?' Harper asked.

'I'm not saying anything. Just that they were pally back when Taylor was on the beat. You remember Frank was trying to make a name for himself then.'

'What's he doing these days?' He hadn't heard the name in a few years.

'Still around, still thinks he'll end up cock o' the walk like his pa one day. He's mostly in Armley, from what I hear. Has himself a house on Burley Road.' A pause while he drained the rest of the pint. 'I'm not saying he's killed anyone, mind. Not even saying he was involved. I'm just suggesting you might want to take a look at him.'

That was good enough. Something for the men in the morning. Harper pulled coins from his pocket, counted out two shillings and placed them on the table. 'The next one will be waiting behind the bar for you, Billy.'

'That's very decent of you.'

Harper winked. 'Landlady's husband. Doesn't cost me a penny.'

'We ate ages ago,' Annabelle said. 'I kept yours in the oven.'

Again. She didn't need to say it.

'Sorry. Work.'

'Da . . .' Mary began as he ate. The liver was dry and tough, but the onions were silky and smooth, the mashed potato creamy.

'What?' he asked. Whenever she started that way, it always meant a difficult question. He glanced at Annabelle; she shrugged.

'Do you think it's reasonable to do something small that might be against the law if it means there might be some greater good in the end?'

Harper finished his meal before he answered, then took a sip of tea. He wasn't about to go hungry for some hypothetical debate.

'Generally, no,' he replied. He'd bent the rules himself in the past, and she knew it all too well. No black-and-white reply was ever going to satisfy her. 'There's a balance you have to weigh. And it depends on what you mean by something small, as well as the cause. One person's greater good can be someone else's evil.'

He knew better than to try and soft-soap her or lie. His daughter was every bit as sharp as her mother.

'Well.' She hesitated, putting the argument together in her head. 'Let's say it's to help women receive the vote. Would you say that's good?'

'Of course. You know that. The question is: would anyone be hurt by this small act?'

'No,' she said. Her voice wavered at first, then firmer as she repeated herself. 'No.'

'Are you sure?' Harper asked.

'Positive, Da.'

'I still can't give you a simple answer. I don't have any details.' He smiled to take the sting out of his next words. 'And somehow, I don't think you're going to tell me.'

'No.' She blushed.

'Then we're never going to reach a conclusion.'

'I can't, Da.'

'You two should stop,' Annabelle said, 'or we'll be going round and round all night. Come on,' she told Mary. 'You can help me with the pots.'

'What do you think that was all about?' Annabelle asked when they were tucked up under the covers. Outside, mist hung thicker in the air, the cobbles slick and damp.

'Maybe she's heard about something the suffragettes are planning,' Harper said. 'My guess is she's not too happy about it.'

'A warning?'

'Possibly. Or maybe she's trying to square it with her conscience. I don't know.'

He could find out more. Interrogate her. But he didn't want to use his own daughter that way. Someone like Billy Larkin, that was different. If Mary wanted to spill everything, that was fine. Otherwise . . . he'd take precautions. It was all he could do.

'Any more nasty letters?' he asked.

'Nothing. No dirty looks in the shops, no snide remarks,' Annabelle answered. 'Happen she's got it out of her system.'

'She?'

'It's a woman. Pound to a penny, bound to be.'

Morning, and Harper came out of the Victoria into thick fog. He could barely see five feet ahead, the taste bitter and acrid in his throat. It muffled all the sounds; he might have been the only man in Leeds. Here and there faint lights seemed to hang in the mist, shining from windows. Twice he almost bumped into someone going in the other direction.

Two things rattled round his brain as he walked. First of all, Frank Walker. He'd telephone David Hyde, the superintendent in charge at Armley. Find a little background before he turned his squad loose. And then there were the suffragettes. If they were planning something that troubled Mary, he needed to worry. She was sensible, as practical as they came. Still young and idealistic and finding her place in the world, discovering all the moral shades of grey. But that was part of growing up. Still, he believed she'd done exactly what he'd told Annabelle: delivered a warning of sorts, even if Mary herself didn't realize it. And on that one, he'd simply have to play it by ear and be prepared.

SEVENTEEN

He pressed the telephone receiver against his ear as he waited for Hyde to answer. The man had only been superintendent at Armley for six months, barely long enough to develop a feel for the place. He'd come in from Bradford or Halifax, somewhere like that, fifteen years' service under his belt and a reputation for cracking down on crime.

'David?' Harper said. 'It's Tom Harper at A Division. I'm hoping you can give me a little help.'

The line hummed and cut, then came back as he gave Hyde the

name. Why was a telephone conversation in Leeds so difficult, he wondered, when the calls he used to make to Billy Reed in Whitby were crisp and clear?

'Frank Walker,' Hyde said. 'We know him. He's nothing, really, however much he wants to be. I gather his father was a nasty piece of work.'

Harper snorted. 'That doesn't begin to describe him. What would you make of the idea that Frank had murdered someone?' Two if Brenda Woolcott died.

'Never.' There wasn't even a moment's doubt in Hyde's reply. 'He wouldn't dirty his hands like that. He'd get someone to do it for him.'

'Anyone in particular?'

In the quiet he could make out the dim noise of voices, then Hyde returned.

'My sergeant says Walker would probably use someone called Eric Stead for the violent work. Built like a rock and has a temper on him. What do you think he might have done?'

Harper summed up the background.

'I have to say, selling children doesn't sound like Walker to me,' Hyde said. 'But that was long before I came here, so don't take my word as gospel.'

'If I send a couple of my people over, can you point them in the right direction to find Walker and Stead?'

'We'll go along with them for the sheer pleasure of it. I've got a big lad here who's in line for the Yorkshire Police heavyweight title. He'd enjoy the chance to go toe to toe with Stead, and I'd put good money on him winning.'

Harper laughed. 'They'll be there in a while.'

He sent Walsh and Ash over to Armley and set Sissons on digging through records on Walker and Stead, then lifted the telephone receiver again and asked to be connected to the infirmary. Brenda Woolcott was a little stronger, she could be fed and there was more movement in her limbs. But speech was still beyond her.

Harper sat back, staring out of the window as he thought. The fog hung thick over the city. People walked with scarves or handkerchiefs over their mouths and noses. Everything was muted; it almost made the city peaceful. But under it all life still went on, hidden and muffled. Nothing changed.

He picked up the telephone for the third time.

'I've had a faint hint that the suffragettes might be planning something when the prime minister's here,' he told the chief constable.

'Any idea what?'

'No, sir. I was wondering if your sources had given you anything.'

'Nothing at all,' Crossley said. 'I'd have told you. I'll ask again. Is your information good?'

Harper smiled to himself. 'Yes, sir. I believe it is.'

'Then leave it with me.'

'Mrs Baines came in to see me.'

Crossley chuckled. 'You can see why the suffragettes put her in charge here, can't you?'

'She'll keep us on our toes.'

'And she's sharp. Watch out for her, Tom. I'll see if I can discover anything for you.'

Dinnertime and no word from Armley yet. Only Galt remained in the office, working on a report.

'You look like a man who needs some food,' Harper said.

He gave a pained, weary smile. 'I feel like someone who never wants to fill out another piece of paper, sir.'

'Wait until you run a division. It never stops. Get your coat, I'll treat you to your dinner.'

The constable looked a little deflated as Harper opened the door to the café in the market, as if he'd been expecting something more lavish.

'It's hot, it's filling, it's tasty, and the tea's strong enough to march out of here on its own. Just what a copper needs.'

Tripe in milk for Galt, steak and kidney pie for him. 'Tell me, what do you think you do best as a policeman?'

He wanted to make the young man consider.

'I don't know, sir,' Galt replied after a while. 'I believe I'm observant, I can put things together. And I can spot a wrong 'un. Maybe I'm not the best person to judge.'

'All those things are true. And once you get an idea in your head, it's hard to dislodge it.'

'I suppose I can be that way sometimes,' he admitted, reddening. 'Sorry, sir.'

'Don't worry. You just have to learn which ones are worth keeping. If it helps, I was like that at your age, too.'

'I'll try and curb it, sir,' he promised. 'I enjoy being on the squad.'

'You're still with us because you're good. Don't forget that.'

'Thank you, sir.' He ducked his head, but the blush remained on his neck.

Jam roly-poly drenched in custard for pudding, and a second cup of tea. Galt brought out a packet of Woodbines and toyed with it for a moment.

'Go ahead and smoke if you like.' He looked at his watch. 'Time we were back at the station, anyway.'

'What's going to happen with those children?' Galt asked as they strolled along George Street. The fog had thinned a little, but it was hard to believe they were in the middle of the day. In the distance, people looked like ghosts, only taking on form as they drew close. Breathe in and the air tasted of chemicals and soot.

'I don't know.' Harper sighed. 'I wish I did.'

Walsh had the beginnings of a black eye and a grin as wide as the river. Ash was rubbing some alcohol over scraped knuckles.

'You two look like you've been in the wars.'

'Stead, sir,' Walsh said. 'Walker's hard man. He didn't want to come in for questioning.'

'Where is he now?'

'Licking his wounds in the cells, sir. Assaulting a police officer. That constable Superintendent Hyde sent out with us gave him a proper leathering.' He laughed at the memory. 'You'd have enjoyed it. An absolute pleasure to see.'

'What about Frank Walker?'

'Interview room, sir,' Ash replied.

'Did he give you any trouble?'

'Meek as a lamb.'

The file was waiting on his desk. Walker had started out doing jobs for his father, then taken over the family business once Tosh went inside. But Harper and his men had dismantled that empire and left him with nothing. Frank had plenty of minor convictions, but there was nothing to indicate he'd ever sold children. Still, Billy Larkin had been convinced enough to pass on the information. It was worth a few questions.

Frank was the spit and image of his father, in his forties now, with the same hard, angular face and bushy dark hair. The fury in the eyes and the thin, cold mouth that had marked out Tosh.

'You put my dad away.'

'That's right,' Harper said as he sat down. 'One of the best day's work I've ever done.'

'Going to frame me for something now?'

'You? You're not big enough to be worth a lie. No, Mr Walker, you're just here as a concerned citizen of Leeds to help us with some inquiries.'

'I can leave whenever I want?' He sounded suspicious, as if it might all be a trick.

The superintendent waved his hand. 'Be my guest, if that's what you want.' As Walker started to rise, he added, 'Of course, if you go we'll be taking a very close look at your enterprises.'

The man lowered himself back on to the chair. 'I want my lawyer.'

'You're not under arrest. You came in willingly, if you recall.'

A long pause while he considered his options. 'Go on, then. Ask your questions.'

'How good is your memory?'

'What?'

But he knew exactly what Harper meant; it was there on his face, a slyness and cunning.

'What were you doing fifteen years ago?'

'Fifteen years?' He gave a dismissive bark. 'How the hell am I supposed to remember that far back?'

'Try.'

Harper waited. Walker's fingertips drummed on the table.

'I was twenty-eight,' the man said eventually. 'I must have been working.'

'Doing what?'

A shrug. 'This and that.'

'Trying to be like your father.' He opened the file. 'In more ways than one. 1893. You did thirty days for handling stolen property, another week for affray.'

'If that's what it says.'

'It's the things you got away with that interest me. Ever heard of a man called Adam Taylor? He used to be a policeman.'

Walker pursed his lips. 'Doesn't mean anything to me. Should it?'

'You need to look at the papers. He was killed a few days ago.'

Walker ran his tongue over his lips. His expression was impossible to read.

'What? You think I did it?'

Harper smiled. 'I never said that, did I, Frank? I only asked if you'd heard of him.'

'And I told you I haven't.'

'We were talking about 1893.'

'You were. I told you I don't remember. Is that it?' He rose from his chair again.

'Selling children.'

Walker stopped, turned. His mouth hung wide. 'You what?'

'Someone snatched and sold two children around that time.'

A hard, furious stare. 'Not me.'

'Just like your father. He did that, remember? Let men use them. Ended up in prison for it.'

'You're bloody mad.' Walker turned away again. At the door he looked back and shook his head, then marched off.

Harper sat staring at the wall until he heard a tap on the jamb and Ash filled the doorway.

'Not successful, sir?'

'Not even good enough to be called a draw.' He sighed and ran a hand through his hair. 'My fault. I went at it badly.'

'What did we have besides a tip?'

'Nothing. That's the problem. We don't have a scrap of evidence anywhere in this case. Walker knows it, Cranbrook knows it.'

'And us, unfortunately,' Ash added.

'If we find Taylor's killer, we'll find the person behind the stolen children. When are you going to see Mrs Cranbrook?'

'Day after tomorrow, I thought, sir. We'll give it time to weigh on her heart.'

'Ask Galt to check if she ever had any connection to Frank Walker. You never know.'

But even as he spoke, he heard how desperate it sounded.

'We can try, sir.'

Harper raised an eyebrow. 'You think that's what it's doing? Weighing on her heart?'

'I couldn't tell you, sir. It's something my Nancy read. But it seems apt.'

'Maybe it does at that. Tell the men I want them in my office at five.'

'We found Larner's killer. That's one thing solved. But,' he added, holding up one finger, 'we've still got the square root of nothing on Adam Taylor's murder. And we have Mr Asquith's visit looming. We need to be properly prepared for that. We need to start drilling the constables so they'll be ready.'

'Where are we supposed to find the time, sir?' Walsh asked. The bruise around his eye had developed into a full shiner now, greens and blacks and purples staining his skin. A thin sheen of sweat coated his forehead and he winced as he shifted on the chair.

'I wish I could tell you.' He knew exactly what the chief would say: the prime minister took precedence. Crossley would ask two questions: how was their investigation progressing? Were they close to any arrests? And once he heard the answers, he'd give a look, as if the path ahead was obvious.

Maybe that was what they needed to do, keep all this simmering on the back burner until the visit was over. It was only for a few days, and they were getting nowhere. A little longer would make no difference to Andrew and Marie.

That was what his head told him. But his heart didn't want to listen.

The evening was damp and chilly, the fog still lurking in clumps and swirls, just waiting to return. Harper walked to the tram stop, paused for a moment, then kept on, turning up the Headrow, Calverley Street and behind the town hall to the infirmary.

The constable outside Brenda Woolcott's room stood and saluted as he approached.

'Has she had any visitors?' Harper asked.

'No, sir, just the nurses and the doctor.'

Inside, everything was hushed, only a soft gas mantle glowing and throwing shadows against the walls. The curtains were drawn against the night. It smelt like every sick room he'd ever known, close and cloying.

Standing by the bed, he could see her watching him, bunching her hands into fists and opening them again.

'Hello, Brenda. Do you remember me? Detective Superintendent Harper.'

A small shake of her head, the movements still difficult.

'I was here yesterday. I asked you about some things from a long time ago. Two children, and a family called Cranbrook.'

He saw the glimmer of memory in her eyes. Her gaze darted around, as if she was looking for a way out. She began to move her arms.

'No need to worry,' he said and stroked the back of her hand. The flesh was warm, as white as a china cup, the veins showing blue through her skin. 'Honestly. I don't want to punish you. I just came to see you again, that's all.'

He stayed for five minutes, talking idly about nothing in particular, the weather, small items he'd seen in the *Post*. Nothing to do with any investigation. Just human contact, everyday things. Finally he moved away from the bed. Her face seemed to have softened a little, all the fear gone.

'I'll try to come back again,' he said. 'You concentrate on getting yourself well.'

A good deed. But who had he really done it for? Her or himself?

'You're quiet, Da,' Mary said. She'd already cleaned her plate right down to the pattern and was working her way through the suet pudding. Young, growing, always hungry. 'You've hardly said a word since you came home.'

'You should be grateful,' he told her. 'Leaves more room for you and your mother to talk.'

He felt Annabelle's gaze. 'You'd better watch your step, Tom Harper, or you'll be snoring on the settee tonight.'

'I don't snore,' he said.

'Da.' Mary rolled her eyes. 'I can hear it in *my* room sometimes.'

'You see?' Annabelle said.

'A conspiracy of women.' He scooped mashed potato on to his fork and started to eat.

'That's exactly what the world needs,' Mary agreed with a broad grin. 'More conspiracies of women. Maybe things would change then.' She scraped the last of the custard from her bowl and pushed her chair away from the table. 'I have a meeting. I won't be late, I promise.'

'Here and gone and eating us out of house and home while she's around. I don't know where she puts it,' Annabelle said. 'It's not like she has an ounce of fat on her. She's right, though, you are very quiet tonight.'

'Work.' He didn't want to say more than that. Better to let it lie fallow. Maybe a seed or two would grow overnight. 'No more letters?'

'Only from the brewery, wondering if I'd made my mind up yet.'

'Have you?'

She shook her head. 'No rush. The answer will come when it's good and ready.'

EIGHTEEN

Another morning of thick, cloaking fog. It clung and choked in the throat, foul and phlegmy in the nostrils. Plenty more of this to come all through the winter. It was impossible to tell if it was day or night.

By the time he reached Millgarth he felt as if he'd swallowed half the stink of Leeds, grateful when Mason appeared with a mug of tea.

'You look like you need it, sir.'

'You're a lifesaver. Don't let anyone tell you different.'

The sergeant grinned. 'I'll let the drunks know that when they're hauled in.'

A telephone call to the infirmary. A quiet night for Brenda Woolcott, but no change in her condition.

The men came in, unwrapping themselves from overcoats and scarves and hats, still coughing and spluttering from the murk outside.

'For the next few days we're going to concentrate on the prime minister's visit,' he told them. Sissons opened his mouth to speak, but Harper lifted his hand. 'It's getting very close now. We're not ignoring everything else, but this is going to be the centre of attention. Remember, it's our heads on the block if this goes badly. The whole country's going to be looking at us. We'd better make sure they don't find fault. Understood?'

Nods of agreement and no objections.

'This afternoon you're going to be spending time with your squads. Take them through every little thing. Go over to the Coliseum. Plenty of them won't be familiar with the area. By the time the prime minister arrives I want them all to know it like the backs of their hands.'

'What about this morning, sir?' Galt asked.

'I'm glad you asked.' Harper smiled. 'I want to look for any connection between Cranbrook and Frank Walker around the time the children disappeared.'

'Tall order after all this time, sir,' Ash said.

'I know,' Harper agreed. 'I'm not expecting much. Particularly as Walker was banged up part of the year. This might help.' He picked up the folder on Frank Walker and slid across the desk. 'Yours,' he told Walsh. 'That eye of yours should scare people into answering, at any rate.'

Vivid, shining green and deep colours going from violet to near black. Enough to make people look twice. He gave a silent nod. His skin was still pale and clammy and he looked to be in pain.

'Are you all right?'

'Yes, sir. I think I might have hurt myself in that fight with Stead yesterday. Either that or I ate something that disagreed with me. It'll pass.'

'You didn't look well last evening, either. I want you to go to the doctor.'

'I'll be fine.' He gave a weak smile. 'Just some griping in my guts. I'll get over it. I'm fine to work.'

'The doctor,' Harper told him. 'This morning. That's an order. I need you fit for Mr Asquith.'

'Yes, sir.' Walsh gave a reluctant nod.

'Ash, you and Galt are going to ferret out the details of Mrs Woolcott's life. Down to the fine details, particularly anything involving the Cranbrooks or Walker.'

'Very good, sir.'

'Off you go, gentlemen.'

'What about me, sir?' Sissons asked when the others had gone.

Harper pulled out the plan for the prime minister's visit. Well over an inch thick now, and growing every day.

'You're good with all this stuff. Go over this once again. Find the flaws. There have to be some. Tell me if anything's missing, where there are weak points.'

'Very good, sir.' He sounded uncertain.

'Be honest and for God's sake, be critical.'

Sissons laughed. 'I'll be as thorough as I can.'

'Write down all your recommendations and give them to me before dinner.' He glanced out of the window. The fog was still thick enough to cut with a knife. 'Look on the bright side; at least you don't have to be out in this.'

Half past eleven, just as he was thinking about venturing out to eat, the telephone rang. Crossley's familiar voice at the other end of the line.

'I've had a word with my source close to the suffragettes, Tom. She didn't know of any plans in particular.'

She, Harper noticed. He had someone inside the group. That was going to be useful.

'That's good to know, sir.'

'Are you sure whoever gave you the information is sound?'

'Yes, sir, I am. Maybe I misunderstood.'

'Let's hope that's what it is.'

'Do we have anyone in with Alf Kitson's group?'

'We did for a little while.' The chief gave a sigh. 'He was rumbled and took a bit of a pasting. I haven't tried again.'

Wheels within wheels. He'd heard nothing about that.

He picked his way across the open market, hardly any traders out today, then along Boar Lane towards the railway station. Crossing the road meant taking your life in your hands; traffic appeared from nowhere out of the murk. He was grateful to duck through the door of the Griffin Hotel, feeling himself coddled in the warmth of a roaring fire and the fug of smoke from cigars and pipes and cigarettes.

Here they called it luncheon, not dinner. Much the same food he could have ordered in the market café, but brought by a waiter on a sparkling white plate and coffee to finish instead of tea.

A change of scene. A treat. An expensive one, he decided when the bill arrived. Not something he'd do often.

Back past the Corn Exchange and down Kirkgate. He knew the church was there, standing at the bottom of the street, but he couldn't even make out its shape, only a suggestion of something darker in the mist. He placed a hand on the wall of the graveyard. The stone was cold and damp under his touch.

It would be close to impossible to put the men through their paces in this weather. He'd go over in an hour and see what they'd been able to do.

As he marched back to Millgarth the sound of his heels on the flagstones faded as soon as it arrived. Only the occasional clang of a tram in the distance let him know there were vehicles on the street.

'Thank goodness you're here, sir,' Mason said as soon as Harper was through the door. 'We've been looking all over for you.'

'Why?' He could feel the urgency crackle in the air.

'It's Sergeant Walsh, sir. He's in hospital.'

'What?' He gripped the counter. The man had looked ill, but it must have been worse than he imagined. 'What's happened?'

'I don't really know, sir. All I can tell you is we had a telephone call about an hour ago saying he'd been found in the street, collapsed and unconscious. I've been trying to find out ever since.' He glanced at the clock. 'He ought to be at the infirmary by now.'

'I'll be over there. If you hear from Inspector Ash, tell him I need him as soon as possible.'

He moved quickly, dashing through the fog and careening into people, not caring who he pushed aside. His face was set, fists clenched tight in his pocket. He'd ordered the man to the doctor. It seemed he hadn't made it that far.

A nurse tried to stop him in the corridor; he showed her his identification.

'He's in the operating theatre,' she said. 'They brought him in with a burst appendix.'

Appendix, he thought. A familiar word, at least. Surely that wasn't too bad.

'How dangerous is it?'

She looked him in the eye before answering. 'Depending what happens, it can be fatal.'

He glanced desperately at the closed door ahead of him.

'Unless you're God, you're not going in there,' the nurse told him. 'There's a waiting room.'

'I need a telephone.'

A call to Millgarth. A car and driver to bring Walsh's wife to the infirmary.

'And send a message to Inspector Ash,' Harper said. 'Cancel the rest of today's exercise and tell him to report here.'

He picked up the receiver again and asked the operator for the Victoria, then explained to Annabelle.

'I'll be home when I'm home.'

'Yes,' she answered, 'of course. Do you . . .?'

'I don't think anyone knows at the moment.'

The waiting room was small, the chairs uncomfortable, but he dared not leave in case the doctor arrived with news. He felt cut off here, isolated from everything, simply willing the time to pass.

Finally the clump of boots in the corridor and Ash walked in, Sissons and Galt right behind him.

'Any word yet, sir?'

He shook his head.

'He didn't feel right after the fight arresting that man yesterday,' Galt said. 'But I never thought—'

'None of us did,' Harper cut him off. Who could have predicted something like this?

Another half-hour, and the door opened again. Harper and the others looked up, expectant and terrified. Walsh's wife, Sylvia. She looked lost, the tracks of her tears obvious through the powder on her cheeks.

They all rose.

'He's still in surgery,' Harper said. 'They'll let us know as soon as they're done.'

He was grateful to escape for a few minutes and find a cup of tea for her. Anything to be out of the room that stifled with silence. The corridors were empty, only the sound of coughing coming from the wards. Evening at the infirmary.

Ash accompanied him. He needed to talk, to think about something else for a few minutes.

'What happened this afternoon?'

'Waste of time, sir. The fog was too thick for them to see anything. They kept blundering into each other. If it's like that on the night, the best thing we can do is line up outside the Coliseum.'

'If it's clearer tomorrow, I want them out again.'

'Very good, sir.'

He was grateful for something solid to think about, anything that took his mind away from here. The emptiness, waiting, not knowing; it left him feeling hopeless.

'Walsh will be out of action for the prime minister's visit. Galt's going to have to run things inside the Coliseum.'

'He's only a detective constable,' Ash said. 'Some of the bobbies might resent having him in charge.'

'It doesn't matter. They'll have to lump it.'

By the time they returned, a surgeon with a bloody apron over his coat was talking to Mrs Walsh in the waiting room. Harper's chest grew tight, pressing so hard he felt he couldn't breathe.

'We've done everything we can.' The man sounded exhausted. 'I must be honest with you. The surgery went well, but the danger now is infection. That can happen when the appendix bursts the way his did. The next two days will be the test. If he survives those, he should be fine.'

She nodded her head, trying to blink back the tears.

Outside, Harper caught the surgeon as he walked away. 'Dominic Walsh, the man you operated on, is a police detective. How bad is it?' He dreaded the answer. But he had to ask.

The doctor stopped and looked him up and down. 'You're his senior officer?'

'I am.'

'Let me ask you: are you a praying man?'

The question shook him. 'No.'

'You might want to try it. Tell me: was he in a fight very recently?'

'Yesterday, when he was arresting someone. Why?'

'He must have taken one hell of a blow. That might be what started it.' The man shook his head. 'It's not the operation that's the problem, now, it's the infection that often follows. You heard me tell his wife. We've done everything we can. Now we have to wait . . .'

Harper forced himself to speak. 'What if there is an infection?'

'Then we'll do all we can to stop it.' He let out a long sigh. 'The truth is that too often we don't succeed.'

He turned away and vanished round a corner.

'I'll stay with Mrs Walsh, sir,' Sissons said. 'There's no sense in us all sitting here, and I know her and Dom best of any of us.'

'If—'

'If there's any news I'll telephone Millgarth straight away.'

NINETEEN

Harper stood on the steps outside the infirmary and pulled out his watch. Not even nine o'clock yet. He felt as if he'd been in there most of the night.

The air felt warmer; the fog had thinned to faint banners of mist.

'Bad business, sir,' Ash said as the men began to walk towards the Headrow.

'It is. And there's nothing we can do.' Pray, the surgeon had said. Right now, it didn't seem like such a bad idea.

'I'll take over from Sissons in the morning,' Galt offered.

Harper shook his head. 'I need all of you tomorrow. We still have work to do. And I have a new task for you, Mr Galt.'

'How is he?' Annabelle asked. She'd jumped up from the chair as he came in, searching his face for the truth.

'Not good.' He closed his eyes and ran a hand through his hair. He needed to sleep, to try and forget everything for a few dreamless hours. But he knew it wouldn't let him alone. 'It's the infection that might kill him.'

Too many had died lately. Billy first, then Taylor and the rest, tumbling like dominoes. He didn't know whether he could take one more. Especially not someone as young as Walsh, with two small children and a wife he loved deeply.

'Here.' She put a cup of tea in his hand. 'It's wet and warm.'

Harper drank, barely noticing the taste. It was something, a calming ritual.

'Is there anything I can do?' she asked. 'Sit with him? Look after their kiddies?'

'His wife's there.' He shook his head. 'I don't know. Maybe tomorrow.'

A long moment of silence before she said, 'I had another of those letters. The nasty ones.'

'The same person?'

'Yes.'

'Do you want me to look into it?'

'No.' Her voice was sharp. 'If this is what she needs to do, let her get it out of her system. Comes down to it, I'll take care of it myself.'

The anger was there, but it was buried far beneath the sorrow. He took her hand and pulled her close, wrapping her tight. Glad of the warmth, glad she was here.

The weather was mocking them. After two days of solid fog, the morning arrived clear, the promise of a pale lemon sun on the horizon. Men smiled on the early tram, staring out as if they were astonished to see everything in its usual place.

As he walked in to Millgarth, Sergeant Mason looked up from the other side of the front counter.

'Already rung the hospital, sir. No news. He's holding his own; that's all they'd tell me.'

That was something, Harper told himself. It was good. If Walsh could stay strong for a few more days, he'd be fine. Home free.

The men had already gathered in the detectives' room. Sissons was rumpled, bags under his eyes, yesterday's collar grimy and off-white. Galt looked rested, Ash as impassive as always.

'I'll go over to the infirmary later,' Harper began. 'I'm sure you already know there's nothing to report. But it looks as if the weather's smiling on us today. This afternoon we'll have the uniforms out and drilling properly. We've lost a day, so we don't have much time. Be hard on them. You all know what to do. This morning you're out hunting Taylor's killer again. Sissons, you pick up on what Walsh was doing.' He glanced up at the clock. 'Meet back here at noon. Ash, a quick word, please.'

'Yes, sir?'

'That man you took me to see. Heinrich. Why don't you ask him about Frank Walker and any connections to Taylor. He might know something.'

He'd considered it on the journey into town. Billy Larkin wouldn't have forsaken the White Stag just for a free drink and a couple of bob. He'd always given straight information in the past. It had to be worth digging a little deeper.

Ash smiled. 'Gladly, sir.'

'Ask if Cranbrook's connected to either of them, too. You never know.'

'I need a constable who's intelligent and can run,' he said to Mason. 'And big enough to hold his own.'

The sergeant thought for a few seconds, then smiled. 'I might have just the man, sir. He's on his beat at the moment. I'll send him to you when his shift is over.'

In the hospital room, Walsh lay under the covers. Small twitches in his arms and legs. Sweat on his face. Fever as he tried to fight the infection inside him.

His wife was asleep on the chair, the top half of her body sprawled across the bed. Then she stirred, raising her head and looking at him with bleary eyes before she quickly turned her head towards her husband.

'He'll be home and under your feet soon enough,' Harper told her. If he repeated it often enough, he might even begin to believe it.

'Maybe.' Her voice was dull, drained.

'You should go home yourself.'

'The children are with my ma. I need to be here. He might not . . .' She faltered on the words.

'He's strong,' Harper said gently. 'He'll come through it.'

She bristled. 'You don't know that. You can't. Even the doctors don't know.'

What could he say to her?

'I'm sorry. You're right. But we need to believe he'll come through it.'

'You believe what you like. I'll stay here with him.'

From one room to another. Mrs Woolcott moved her fingers a little as he talked. Flexed her wrist. Little by little, control of her body was returning to her. But still no speech. A soft moan, a quiet guttural cry.

He didn't know why he was here, why he kept coming back to see her. Until she could speak, she couldn't give him anything else. But he stood next to the bed, hardly even looking at her and letting his words wander. Walsh, Asquith's visit. Anything but Taylor's murder.

It was a kind of relief, simply getting it all off his chest. The worry, the fears. An audience that listened in silence, without judgement.

On his way out of the hospital, Harper spotted the doctor. 'Walsh,' he said.

'It's all going to depend on the next twenty-four hours. If he comes through that and he's no worse, he's turned the corner and there's a good chance he'll make it. But no guarantees,' he added.

Hopeful news. Another day and he might be out of the woods.

'What about Brenda Woolcott?'

The doctor gave a weary sigh. 'I'll tell you, Superintendent. Before I started this job, I didn't believe in God. But in the last five years I've seen my share of miracles. Recoveries that shouldn't have happened but did. I can't account for them. Mrs Woolcott has improved a little. My best assessment as a physician is that she'll probably never be back to normal. But miracles can happen. Does that satisfy you?'

'It's going to have to, isn't it?'

'Yes, and if you'll excuse me, I have twenty more patients waiting for me.'

Twelve o'clock on the dot and the men gathered in his office. Without Walsh here it felt as if there was too much space.

'Any news, sir?' Sissons asked.

'He's holding his own,' Harper answered, seeing the relief on their faces. 'Do you have anything for me?'

'I heard something interesting,' Galt said. 'Just a whisper . . .' He shrugged.

'Go on.'

'Cranbrook's business might be in trouble. Evidently he was relying on a contract to come through and it hasn't happened.'

'How reliable is that information?'

He shrugged. 'Like I said, sir. A whisper. I'm not sure how it affects our case, though.'

'Everything helps,' Harper said. 'Anyone else? No? Well, gentlemen, let's see what we can do with the uniforms. At least the weather's with us today.'

There was even a little warmth in the air as they strolled up the Headrow. Sissons and Galt moved ahead, deep in conversation. Ash and Harper stayed ten yards behind them.

'What did Heinrich have to say?'

'Off the top of his head, he didn't know about any link,' Ash replied.

'What do you think? Is that good or bad?'

'He's going to look into it. Sorry, sir, that's all I can tell you.'

'What about Cranbrook?'

'The same, sir. What do you make of Galt's little piece of news?'

'I'm not sure. Bad for him, if it's more than a rumour. But it might make it easier for us to prise the truth out of him.'

'I thought I'd go and see his wife tomorrow. I haven't had the chance today, what with everything else.'

'I might come with you. We can see what she has to say about her past. That could help.'

'You never know, sir. You never know.'

The constables were waiting outside the Coliseum, rank upon rank of them, lined up by their sergeants, standing at attention. God, Harper thought, most of them looked so young. Still uncomfortable in their helmets and heavy, scratchy uniforms.

He stood in front of them, scanning all the faces before he spoke.

'At least we can see each other today. Mind you, I'm not sure if that's a good thing or not.' That made them smile, set them at ease a little. 'You know why you're here. This afternoon you're going to become familiar with this area and the men who'll be in it when the prime minister is here.' He gestured at Galt, Sissons, and Ash. 'Obey them. They know what they're doing. I know it's just a few days away, but we'll have more training before the tenth. I want this visit to go off flawlessly. There's going to be trouble, I'll tell you that now. But you will deal with it calmly, quickly, and efficiently. You understand?' Nods of agreement, determined faces. 'Gentlemen, remember that you're Leeds City Police, and I know you'll do the city proud.'

A few people had gathered to watch. Near the top of Cookridge Street he spotted three women standing and staring intently. Mrs Baines with two others. Observing their enemy, he thought wryly.

A word with the sergeants who'd brought their men down. One bunch was made up of recruits, still in training.

'They're eager, sir, but still very raw, if you know what I mean.' He sounded embarrassed at the admission.

'I think we can all remember what that's like,' Harper told him with a grin. 'Still, they'll have a good chance to learn on the job.'

He'd station those men inside the hall. It should be the quietest place. With a little luck, they'd have nothing more to do than stand around and be bored by political speeches. If the demonstrators fought their way beyond the Coliseum doors, the night was already lost.

For an hour he watched, listened, moved between the groups. No drills yet, just making sure they were all familiar with what they needed to do. It was going to be a big operation, with none of the goodwill people had shown the king when he was here. A few grizzled faces had experience; they knew to expect the worst. The rest had no grasp of how rough things might be.

Finally, a little before five o'clock, Harper dismissed them, watching as the sergeants lined their men up and marched them off in smart formation. He glanced up the hill. Jennie Baines and her women were still there. Spying on them and making their plans.

Soon enough, the area seemed empty. Another few minutes and the streets would be teeming with people on their way home from work. He lifted his face to the sky. The day's pale sun had almost vanished, the first sense of night on the air, a chill that made him thrust his hands into his overcoat pockets.

'Well,' he asked his own men, 'what did you think?'

'We made a start, sir,' Ash replied. 'A little shaky, but we'll hammer them into shape.'

'Make sure you do. I don't want us to look like a bunch of fools when the whole country's watching.' Enough of that. 'Anyone care to join me at the infirmary?'

They stood, hushed. Walsh looked the way he had that morning, the sweat standing out on his face. He drew in a sharp breath and his arm moved.

Fighting for his life, Harper thought, and he didn't even know it. No sign of his wife, only the faintest hint of her perfume lingering.

Suddenly Walsh's eyes opened. Just for a fraction of a second, then they closed again. Enough to make them gasp.

It was painful to watch, knowing there was nothing Harper could do to help. Instead, he left, finding a nurse busy sorting bed linens down the corridor.

'Sergeant Walsh . . .' he began.

'Is still with us,' she said with a smile. 'He's no worse, and that's a very good sign. I made his wife go home so she could sleep for a few hours.'

'What are his chances?'

'That's for the doctor to say.' She pursed her lips and glanced around, making sure no one was close, then lowered her voice. 'If you were to ask me whether you should put money on his recovery, I'd say it's a good bet now.' She straightened again. 'But I never told you that.'

The nurse bustled away and he returned to the room.

'Time to leave.'

They were all quiet, chastened, each lost in his own thoughts. Dusk now, with night beginning to swallow the city.

'Go home,' he ordered. 'We've plenty of long days ahead of us.'

'I'd like to stay, sir,' Galt said. How could he refuse?

'Only until Mrs Walsh returns. I need you all sharp in the morning. We still have a murder to solve.'

But no home for him. Back to Millgarth to pore over more paperwork. Twenty minutes of it and he heard the tap on the door. Harper pulled off his spectacles and said, 'Come in.'

A young constable with a nervous expression, standing to rigid attention, exactly the way he'd been taught.

'Emerson, sir. PC 837. Sergeant Mason told me to come and see you.'

Ah, yes. The bobby he'd requested. Bright, able to run fast. He hoped the lad was up to it.

'I have a job for you. You're going to be working with me.' He explained the task, seeing the young man's eyes widen in astonishment. 'Two things. Get rid of the uniform for a few days. You'll be far less obvious in plain clothes.'

'Yes, sir.'

'And I want you to make yourself familiar with every street and ginnel between the railway station and the demonstrations.'

The young man bit his lip, then said: 'Begging your pardon, sir, but I already am. I was born in one of those courts by the old Cloth Hall. Know it all like the back of my hand.'

'Go over it all again,' Harper told him. 'I thought I knew the Leylands inside and out because I grew up there. Once I started going after criminals there, I realized I barely knew it at all. That's your job tomorrow. Walk every inch of that, again and again, until you can do it blindfolded.'

'Very good, sir.' The man beamed as if Christmas had arrived early. 'Thank you.'

'One last thing. Can you run?'

'I'm on the Leeds Police cross-country team, sir. Set a new record last year,' he added with pride.

'Then I'm sure you'll be fine.' That's me put in my place, Harper thought. He didn't even know the force had a cross-country team.

He turned the crank handle of the car and felt the engine come to life.

'I don't know what time I'll be back,' Annabelle told him. 'The meeting's out in Horsforth.'

Another burgess event, the third in a fortnight, educating women about democracy, making them hungry for the vote, but learning how to make their voices heard in a peaceful way. She'd been involved in more of them lately.

'Things are changing,' she'd told him as she slipped on a dark blue gown and waited for him to hook up the back. 'The Pankhursts and the suffragettes seem to think violence is the only way we'll get our voting rights. I don't believe that, Tom. You head down that road and people will end up hurt and killed. I won't be a party to it. I'll do it this way, stick with Miss Ford and Mrs Fawcett and the suffragists and do my bit.'

'What about Mary?' Harper asked.

She stared in the mirror as she pinned up her hair. Swift, practised movements; she hardly needed to look. But she was gazing into her own eyes as she spoke.

'She's old enough to work out what's right for her. We've taught her. God knows, with a copper for her da, she's heard what violence can do.'

'But she's not going to the demonstration,' he said with a smile.

'No,' Annabelle said. 'Not on your life.'

The fire burned bright and warm. Mary was on the settee, reading her book. *A Room With A View*. Precious few of those round Sheepscar, he thought. He settled in the chair and opened the *Evening Post*.

'I heard you and my mam talking, you know.'

He folded the newspaper and stared at her. 'Did we make any sense?'

But she wasn't going to be so easily distracted.

'I want to be serious for a minute.' Her voice was serious,

prickling with passion. 'Be honest. Do you think women are any closer to the vote than when Mam started campaigning?'

Fifteen years. He pressed his lips together and tried to find an answer that could do justice to all that time, to all the work he'd seen Annabelle perform.

'Yes,' he answered finally. 'It's slow, but I do believe it's coming.'

'We're still getting the brush-off from politicians. Mr Asquith wouldn't even include women's suffrage in his bill earlier this year.' Her voice rose. The kind of conviction that only came with youth or someone utterly certain they were right. Not wavering, not giving an inch. 'He refused to meet Mrs Pankhurst.'

'I remember,' Harper said. 'And after that, two suffragettes took a taxi to Downing Street and smashed his windows.'

'Can you blame them, Da? All the men do is break promises or ignore us altogether.'

That was what it was like to be young, to feel everything so deeply.

'They ended up with two months in prison.'

'They thought it was worth it. They stood up for what they believed.'

'Do you really think there's any sense in damaging property?' Harper asked.

'It was on the front page of every newspaper. It made people pay attention.'

'Do you think the demonstration here will make a difference?'

'It might,' she said. 'Everything helps.'

'No,' he told her. 'Not everything. If this is a roundabout way to ask if you can go, the answer's still no.'

'I know that,' Mary said. Her mouth turned down. 'You've said. Both of you.'

She managed to build a shell of resentment around the words. But he wasn't going to argue the toss. Instead, he looked at her and gently said, 'Yes, we have.'

Half an hour later and her chilliness had thawed.

'Do you want a cuppa, Da?'

'That'd be lovely.'

'Biscuits?'

'You read my mind.'

TWENTY

October the seventh. He saw the date on the newspaper. Three more days, then the prime minister would be here. Train pulling in at half past four. The entire schedule was imprinted on his mind. Harper folded his copy of the *Mercury* and stuck it in his pocket as he boarded the tram.

Three days to make certain everything was right. And knowing it couldn't be, that they had to be ready for the worst.

Through the door at Millgarth to see Mason smiling.

'Good news?'

'I've just been on the phone to the infirmary, sir. Sergeant Walsh has come around.'

Relief surged through him. Thank God for that.

'He's going to be all right?'

'Touch wood. The doctor was cautious, you know how they are, but he said it was a very good sign, sir. He's talking, not rambling.'

Harper chuckled. 'He must have woken up better than before, then. Thank you. That's the right way to start a day.'

It was plain on their faces; it gave them all heart. A sense of hope. Grins and chatter until he held up his hand.

'I'll go and see him later and pass on your wishes. For now, we have work, and the clock is ticking until the prime minister arrives. Don't forget that.'

'I don't think we could if we tried, sir,' Sissons told him.

'Then make sure you don't try,' Harper warned, but the mood had caught him, too. A sense of joy, that maybe everything would be well. 'What do we have on Cranbrook and Taylor and Walker?'

'Nothing to connect Taylor with either of them,' Ash said. 'That's according to what I've been told.' Heinrich, he thought. 'But it appears that back in 1893, Cranbrook and Walker were on a committee together.'

'Walker on a committee?' Harper asked in disbelief. 'You have to be kidding. What was it?'

'Helping the poor, sir.' He raised an eyebrow. 'Evidently Frank went through a period of wanting to appear a model citizen.' The smallest pause. 'It didn't last.'

'Hardly surprising. But that's the same year Andrew Sharp was taken . . . the timing's interesting.'

'I'm going to see Mrs Cranbrook today, if you remember, sir.'

'I do. We'll do that together. Galt, any more word on Mr Cranbrook's business troubles?'

'Nothing else so far, sir.'

'Then I'll let you get on. Ash, give me an hour and we'll be on our way.'

Walsh lay in the bed, eyes open and alert. His skin was pale, drawn tight over his bones, but he wasn't sweating. Harper opened the door and watched as the man turned his head, lips curling into a faint smile.

'Decided to join the land of the living again?'

'I thought it was time to wake up, sir. They say I've had a good sleep.'

His voice was shaky and weak. But he was here, he was alive.

'You certainly picked an interesting way to have some time off work.'

'You're always after us to be creative, sir.'

'I was talking about catching crooks when I said that.' He sat in the chair, placing his hat in his lap. 'Where's your wife?'

'I told her to go to the canteen and eat. She's been sitting here all night.'

'You have a good woman there.'

'I know, sir. Her mother keeps telling me the same thing.'

'We'll have you out of here in no time now. Back at work in a few weeks.'

'I'll be sorry to miss the prime minister's visit, sir.'

Harper stared at him. 'Don't ever turn to crime, Sergeant. You're the world's worst liar. Get your strength back. We need you. Everyone sends their best.'

Lucky, he thought as he closed the door. Barring something awful, Walsh would recover, he'd be perfectly fine. But it could so easily have gone the other way. If he hadn't been found for another hour, so many other things. It was enough to sober a man.

Two minutes with Mrs Woolcott, quiet, inconsequential words

as she listened without speaking, hardly moving, then he returned to Millgarth.

The motor car turned into the driveway of the Cranbrooks' house.

'You question her,' Harper said.

'Very good, sir.'

She swept into the room, dressed to the nines in a silk dress that fitted her perfectly, annoyance crimping her face.

'I have ten minutes before I need to leave. I hope this is important.'

'It is, Mrs Cranbrook,' Ash told her. 'Thank you for seeing us.'

'What do you want? My husband isn't here and we answered all your questions last time.'

'I wondered if you had the birth documents for Andrew and Marie. We know there are no birth certificates at Somerset House.'

A hesitation that lasted a heartbeat too long.

'They were both born abroad. At a clinic in France where there's very good care.'

'Then there will be documents,' Ash said. 'Might it be possible to see them?'

'Are you doubting me?' Her mouth hardened.

'Not at all, madam.' He smiled. 'It would just clear things up. I'm sure you understand.'

'No, Inspector, I'm not sure I do. What are you trying to say? You keep coming here, suggesting things . . .'

'If you could produce the documents, that would be an end to it all.'

'I don't know where they are. I'd have to look for them.'

'I can come back tomorrow, Mrs Cranbrook.'

'I might not have had a chance by then. We lead busy lives, Inspector.'

'It's important, madam.'

'Then I'll make sure we find them soon.' She glared at him. 'Is there anything else?'

'I believe you've had brushes with the law before.'

Her body stiffened. She drew in her breath. 'I was very young and stupid then,' she answered. Barely keeping a lid on her temper, Harper thought. 'Or do you intend to use that to damn me?' she finished.

'You might have known a few criminals.'

'I might,' she agreed. He could hear the control she forced into the words, trying to sound as if it was all folly. 'I suppose I did. But I'd already left all that behind when I met Robert. Since you've obviously looked into my record, you ought to know that.'

'Your husband knew a man named Frank Walker.'

'Who?' Her confusion was genuine. It meant nothing.

'He's a criminal,' Harper said.

She turned to face him. 'My husband knows many men, Superintendent. Business is like that. It doesn't mean he likes them. And it certainly doesn't mean he's done anything wrong.' Sarah Cranbrook straightened her shoulders and drew herself up. 'Now I need to go. I thought you had questions, not accusations. The maid will show you out.'

'We'll never get anything from her now,' Ash said on the drive back to Millgarth. 'I'm sorry, sir, maybe I took the wrong tack.'

'No, you did exactly the right thing. You rattled her. She doesn't have any documents. They never existed.'

They stayed silent until Woodhouse Moor lay behind them and they were into the haze and soot of Leeds.

'I want *all* the uniforms out drilling tomorrow and Friday. Push them. Make sure they know exactly what to do.'

'Very good, sir. I hear you've taken on Emerson.'

Did anything happen on the force without Ash knowing about it? 'All the gossip flows to you.'

A smile spread under the heavy moustache. 'He's my cousin's lad. Smart and eager.'

'A cross-country runner. That's what he told me.'

'He's won medals for it.'

'How long have the police had a team?'

'Donkey's years, sir. I was on it myself.' He patted his belly. 'When I was a young man, of course.'

Live and learn, Harper thought. Live and learn.

'Let's go and visit Mr Cranbrook,' Harper said suddenly. 'If that rumour about his business is right, he might be more willing to get the truth off his chest. Meanwood Road,' he told the driver.

The area stank. From the burning fumes of chemical works, the raw stench of the tanneries, and the leather of the boot factories. It caught in his throat as they stood at the entrance to Cranbrook's factory. How could anyone stand this day after day? But he knew the answer: they had no choice.

Ash's nose twitched. 'Let's hope his office smells better than the yard, sir.'

They had to wait, sitting side by side in a room while a secretary sat and typed. The only sounds were the clatter of her machine and the ticking of a clock. Finally, on the stroke of half past ten, a door opened, and Cranbrook appeared.

A few days appeared to have aged him by ten years. All the sleekness and shininess had gone, the confidence vanished. Worry hovered all around him. He seemed to move in jerks as he ushered them through to an office with warm wood panelling and a fire burning in the hearth. Not coal, Harper noticed. Apple wood to keep the air sweet for him.

'What do you want?' he asked. 'I'm very busy. My wife telephoned. She said you'd been out to the house. Practically accused her of being a criminal.'

'As we said to Mrs Cranbrook, we still need answers to a few questions, sir,' Harper told him. 'After all, we're talking about murder. It's important.'

It stopped the man for a second. His face twitched.

'What makes you think I'd know the first thing about murder? Or are you accusing my family of that, too? I make boots. Take a look around. It should be bloody obvious to a blind man.'

'We know what you do, sir,' Ash said. 'Very successful, too. And a self-made man.'

'That's right. When I started out in Kirkstall I didn't have two farthings to rub together. Learned my trade and took my chances.' He recited his history, but there was little pride in his voice, as if it was a lesson he'd learned somewhere and was repeating by rote. Then he seemed to gather himself a little. 'And I didn't do it so a pair of coppers with nothing better to fill their time could come in here and accuse my wife and me of whatever they like.'

'We haven't accused you of anything, sir,' Harper told him. 'Or Mrs Cranbrook. We're simply following up on things.'

'Your wife said the children were born abroad,' Ash said.

'If she told you, then you already know that. Why are you asking me?'

'As we said to her, we'd like proof of their birth, sir,' Harper said. 'Just to make sure everything is clear and legal. She said she'd look for it.'

'Then she will. Things have been hectic here. You'll receive your evidence in due course.'

It was time to come down on the Cranbrooks, to force their hands. And right now the husband appeared to be the weaker of the pair.

'Sir,' Harper said, 'I have to insist that you produce the papers by tomorrow. Do that, and we can resolve everything immediately.'

Cranbrook pulled himself up to his full height. 'And if I don't?'

'Then we'll be forced to take other measures. I trust you'll choose the easy course, sir.'

'I suggest you leave, Superintendent. The pair of you.'

Harper stood. 'If that's what you want. By the way, I believe you know a man called Frank Walker.'

'Walker?' He frowned, searching his memory. 'The only Walker I can recall is a businessman in Armley. We were on some committee years ago. Why?'

'No matter, sir. I hope we'll hear from you by tomorrow.'

Outside, they breathed through their mouths as they walked back to the motor car.

'What other measures can we take, sir?'

'None. But I'm hoping he won't know that.'

'Ten to one he's telephoning his lawyer right now. I have to say, he looks like a man whose world is falling apart.'

'He does, doesn't he?' Harper said. 'As long as he gives us our answers. There's nothing we can do about the rest of it.'

'A message from the chief constable, sir,' Mason said as he walked into Millgarth. 'Could you telephone him.'

'It's good news about Walsh,' Crossley said when he answered the 'phone. 'I went over to see him this morning.'

'Yes, sir. It really is.'

'I gather he's going to be off for a while. How's that going to affect your preparations for the prime minister's visit?'

'I'm moving my detective constable into Walsh's place inside the Coliseum. Should be quite placid in there.'

'Let's hope so. All hell's going to break loose if it's not. I wanted to tell you, Tom. I've been doing some thinking over the last few weeks.'

'Sir?'

'I've decided to retire at the end of this year. I've had a good run as chief constable, and with visits from the king and the prime minister, I'll be going out on a high note.'

He could scarcely believe it. Crossley seemed so comfortable in his position. Well-liked, in easy control of the force. He'd seemed wedded to the job.

'That's a pity, sir. We'll all be very sorry to see you go, believe me.'

He meant it. Crossley had always defended his men, a strong barrier between them and the world. He'd be hard to replace.

'I've sent in my letter, but I haven't told anyone else on the force.'

'I'll keep it quiet until you're ready, sir.'

'The reason I've mentioned it is that I think you should apply for the job.'

He was silent. Stunned. Absolutely no idea how to respond. The idea was preposterous. It was absurd. He was a lad from the Leylands. Common as they came. He'd never quite believed that he'd managed to rise all the way to superintendent. Chief constable? That was impossible. The Watch Committee would never accept it. Just a few years before, he'd put one of them in prison for corruption.

'I . . .' he began.

Crossley chuckled. 'I'm putting the idea in your head. Planting a seed. Please don't dismiss it out of hand, Tom. You have more friends on the council that you imagine. Talk it over with your wife. After this damned Coliseum event is out of the way, we'll discuss it again.'

'Yes, sir.'

He put the receiver back on the cradle. Chief Constable Tom Harper.

No. It couldn't happen. He'd dreamed it.

TWENTY-ONE

'He really said that? He's leaving?'

Annabelle stood in the kitchen, hands on her hips.

'Yes.'

'And he wants you to apply for the job?'

He smiled. 'Daft, isn't it?'

For a moment she looked as shocked as he'd felt when Crossley told him. Then her expression cleared and her eyes were shining. 'No, it's not. I think it's wonderful.'

But Harper shook his head. He'd had the chance to think on the way home. On foot, then the tram; hardly the way a chief constable travelled.

'What's wrong with it?' she asked. 'You'd be perfect for the job.'

'Me?' He laughed in disbelief. 'Come on, you know what I'm like. I already hate all the paperwork I have to do. It takes up most of my time. If I end up in a big office at the town hall, I'll be drowning in the stuff. If it's not that, I'll be going to meetings. That's not what I wanted when I decided to be a copper. Anyway, there's something else.'

'What?'

'You know who'll be on at me all the time. The politicians. Councillor this, Councillor that. The Home Office. Always on my best behaviour.' He raised his eyebrows. 'Honestly, can you see me lasting long with people like them and not speaking my mind? I can't play that game.'

She grinned. 'Not when you put it like that, I suppose.'

'All those formal occasions in full fig? A uniform with braid?'

'You'd look a right bobby dazzler. But no, I can't see you doing that,' she agreed with a laugh. 'I practically have to march you to the tailor to splurge on a new suit.'

'I'm flattered that Crossley thinks I could do the job, but it's not for me.'

'So what now?'

'Nothing,' he told her. 'I carry on, same as always, and hope the new chief is as good as the old one.' Enough. He'd said his piece, he'd told her. Time to change the subject. 'No more letters?'

'No.' She seemed to close up as she answered the question. 'Nothing. Just a note from Tetley's saying they can give me until the end of the month for an answer.'

'Made up your mind yet?'

She shook her head. 'I'm up and down so often I feel like I'm on a see-saw.'

'You'll know,' he told her. 'And you still have three weeks to decide.'

'Yes,' she agreed quietly. 'I suppose I do.'

'Da,' Mary called as he passed her door. She was sitting on the bed, a book on her lap.

He came in and settled on the stool in front on the dresser.

'I heard what you and my mam were saying. Do you really think she'll sell the pub?'

He could see the worry creasing her young face and understood what she meant. This wasn't just fretting about Annabelle's decision. This was about her own world, too. The Victoria was the only home she'd ever known. Sixteen years old, all her memories were held in these four walls and the streets that surrounded them. Leaving this would splinter her entire life.

'I don't know,' he told her honestly. 'It's her decision, and she's finding it difficult enough.'

'Yes, but . . .' She faltered.

'I like it round here, too. But we both need to accept that it's up to your mother. This is her pub. Do you know what she needs?'

'What?'

'To know that we'll be happy for her whatever she chooses.'

'Where would we go if she decides to sell?'

Harper shrugged. 'I haven't a clue. Nowhere too far, though, you can be certain of that.'

'It wouldn't be the same, would it?'

'No, of course not.' He smiled at her. 'There are worse things than new beginnings, you know. We all make them. I have, your mother has. You will in time.'

She sat, saying nothing. Sometimes it was hard to understand that the young woman who could argue so passionately for the vote was also still a girl. He patted her knee and stood.

'One thing about your mother,' he said. 'Whatever she decides, it won't just be the best thing for her. She'll make sure it's right for all of us.'

Early morning, grey, dampness in the air and enough of a chill to penetrate his bones and leave him stiff. Growing older, Harper thought.

In his office, he sorted through papers, seeing the light grow, hearing the change of shift, heavy boots tramping on the floor, then silence in the building again, just the constant sounds of the city as background.

He'd been at work for an hour before the men arrived, Galt still yawning, Sissons as eager as he'd been on the first day he arrived in plain clothes. And Ash, saying little but constantly amused at the world.

He looked at the inspector and realized that he'd worked with him longer than he ever had with Billy Reed. Seventeen years now. He trusted him, relied on him. He was comfortable with the man. Yet he didn't really know him, he never had. Harper and Billy had been friends, close friends for a few years, the kind that came along all too rarely. With Ash it was strictly work, always keeping a sober distance, respecting the difference in rank. But Billy was dead, and there would never be another.

He smiled at the squad gathered in his office. 'Ready for the day?'

They'd hardly begun when the telephone rang. Harper reached for the receiver, pressing it tight against his good ear.

'I'm glad I caught you, Tom.' Crossley's voice. 'This case with the Cranbrooks, is it very far along?'

'We've talked to him and his wife, sir. We're pressing them for proof that the children are theirs.' He felt the first prickle of something bad. The chief wasn't calling at this hour to catch up on events.

'I've just had the coroner on the line. Robert Cranbrook killed himself during the night.'

He wanted to say something, to reply, but the words wouldn't come. Only yesterday he'd been in the man's office, seen how lost he looked and the flare of his temper. And now that life had gone.

'He hung himself in the garage at his home. The chauffeur discovered the body when he went to fetch the car this morning. Left a note for his wife. The way I understand it, the business was crashing about his ears. He'd put in everything he had to try and save it.'

Harper thought of the woman in her parlour, of the girl climbing the stairs, never turning her head. Of the boy he hadn't seen.

'I'm sorry for them. That's awful news.'

'It is,' Crossley agreed with a sigh. 'When a man believes that's the only way out . . . Keep what you know under your hat.'

'I will, sir.'

'And that line of investigation is closed for the foreseeable future, Tom. I'm sure you understand.'

'Yes, sir. Of course.'

The line went dead. The men were all staring at him.

'Things have just changed,' Harper said.

It didn't stop them investigating Taylor's murder and the attack on Brenda Woolcott. The same person had to be behind both of them. Yet they were still nowhere. He kept trying to slide Frank Walker into the frame somewhere, but however much he hoped, the man didn't seem to fit. Billy Larkin must have had things wrong for once. That happened, even with the best informants.

'Go back over old ground,' he said. 'See if we missed something.'

They must have. The answer was there. Somewhere.

Once they'd gone, he pulled on his overcoat and emerged into the detectives' room. Emerson sat behind a desk, standing to attention as soon as he saw the superintendent. He wore a suit of thick, itchy wool. He'd almost grown out of it, an inch too short in the sleeves and the trouser legs.

'Where do you want me today, sir?'

'Are you familiar with every inch of ground between the town hall and the Coliseum?'

Emerson grinned. 'Yes, sir. Must have walked miles over it yesterday. Anyone watching would have wondered what I was up to.'

'We'll start drilling the constables at three o'clock. We'll be carrying on into the evening.' The young man's head bobbed. 'Until then I want you back in the area. Go over it again. Report to me outside the Coliseum at three.'

'Yes, sir.'

A row of three horse chestnut trees stood near the infirmary, full-grown, branches spreading high over the road. Dead leaves were scattered across the pavement, green and gold, and a lone conker in its spiny shell. He picked it up and broke it open against a wall, rubbing his fingers over the shiny brown nut.

When he was growing up in the Leylands, the nearest trees were in the tiny pocket park on the other side of North Street. Every autumn all the boys would go hunting for conkers, keeping the biggest and best, boring holes and threading string through them to play against each other. One year he'd had a champion, a twelver that had smashed open every opponent. Thirteen had proved unlucky. In less than two minutes, there was nothing left of his triumph. From victory to defeat in a moment. But wasn't that the way of the world?

For a moment he thought about Cranbrook, what he was thinking when he tied the noose and placed it around his neck. How deep was his despair? How black had the night looked? Worse than it had for Lawrence Armstrong?

He didn't understand, and hoped he never would.

'I asked the prime minister to delay his visit until you were well,' he said to Walsh. 'He sends his apologies but says it's impossible.'

'It does seem a pity that the rest of you will have all the fun, sir.'

'Never mind, we'll drum up some other excitement once you're back on duty.'

Walsh was propped against the pillows. He looked weathered, more lines on his face, far older than when he'd come into hospital just a few days before. The first traces of grey showed in his hair, and pain lingered in his eyes, a reminder that he'd been close enough to touch death.

But the doctor was jubilant. 'I don't know what you do with your men, Superintendent, but he's resilient. If he carries on at this rate, we'll be able to discharge him next week. *If*,' he repeated, with a physician's note of caution. 'There's still a great deal that could go wrong. Another infection, a relapse.' He shrugged. 'All we can do is wait and hope.'

Heartening news, though, and Walsh seemed brighter. Harper took the newspaper from his pocket.

'Something for you to read,' he said, and brought the sergeant up to speed on events.

'You're giving up on Frank Walker, sir?'

'Yes. I'd love him to be a part of it, but I don't see how he ties into it all. Cranbrook was on a committee with him around the time Andrew Sharp was taken. But what was he likely to say? "I've heard about you, Mr Walker, is there any way you can arrange to sell me a child?" I don't buy that for a second. We'll take Frank out of the picture and keep our eyes on the others. If anything comes up to hint at it, we can always go back to him.'

Walsh nodded. 'And Mrs Cranbrook is safe enough now. With what her husband's done, we can't go after her.'

'Safe from us, maybe,' Harper told him. 'But if the chief's right, there's no money left. The family's going to be poor.'

At the door he felt in his pocket, took out the conker and tossed it on the bed.

'A present for you.'

Walsh raised an eyebrow. 'Thank you, sir. I appreciate it. But I'd prefer a bar of chocolate next time, if you don't mind me saying.'

The file was thick, pages ready to spill out across the desk. He turned over the sheets, picking up the letter that had begun it all, seeing Charlotte Reynolds's writing.

> I am dieing now. Before I meet my maker I need to get something off my chest. Fourteen years ago a man was paid to steal a child. His name was Andrew . . .

Such a small start.

Charlotte Reynolds. When he'd spoken to her, she'd insisted that she'd put all she knew in the note. Back then he'd sensed something more, but he hadn't pressed her. Now, though, with her son-in-law dead because of it all, she might be willing to say something.

She was a woman who was fading out of life. Her cheeks were hollow, her eyes shone with pain, the skin under them deep and dark. Even less of her than the last time he'd been here, and that had been little enough. Her movements were stiff and measured.

'You might as well come in,' she said. 'No sense in all the heat going out the front door.'

The blaze was roaring, coal piled high in the grate. She settled into a chair, huddled in on herself, staring down at the floor. At her side, a small table held a tooth glass and tiny glass bottles, blue and green and brown. All the medicines to ease her.

'Is your daughter still staying with you?'

'Where else would she go?' Her voice was dull. 'Back to an empty house? She's sleeping. I had a turn in the night and she was up looking after me.'

'When I talked to you before . . .'

Her voice was sharp. 'What about it? I told you, if I'd known what would happen, I'd never have written that letter.'

'But you did,' he said gently, squatting by the chair so she had to look at him. 'There was more, wasn't there? Things you didn't put on the page.'

'No,' she replied. 'Why would I, after I said all that?'

'I don't know,' he admitted. 'But I'm certain you didn't tell me everything.'

'Nothing more to say. That's all I ever knew.'

It was a lie. If he hadn't been quite positive when he arrived, he was now. It was there in the shape of her mouth, the way she held her head. All he had to do was persuade her to give him the rest. The truth.

'Mrs Reynolds, two men have died. One of them was your own daughter's husband. There's a woman lying in the infirmary who will probably never talk or move properly again. I want whoever did that.'

'I said it before. I don't know.'

'Do you know someone called Frank Walker?' One final roll of the dice before he removed him from the game.

Harper held his breath, searching her face as he waited for her answer.

'No,' she said. 'I've never heard of him. Who is he?'

He believed her. There was no guile in her words. Nothing more than confusion in her eyes.

'I thought you might know the name.'

Charlotte Reynolds shook her head. He reached out and put a hand over hers. Even in the hot room she was as cold as a corpse, a ghost sitting upright.

'Please,' he asked.

The silence held for a long time. The fire crackled and slumped with a soft whoosh.

'Not yet.' She turned her head to watch him. 'Not yet. Before I go I'll tell you.'

'Why not now?' She didn't look as if she'd be alive much longer, but too much could happen. He might never hear her say the rest.

For the first time, she gave a smile. So faint that it barely existed.

'That's how it has to be if you want to know. There's a name, you're right on that. I'll put it in a note and tell my daughter to give it to you when I'm dead.'

She held all the cards. He stood, brushing off the knees of his trousers.

'Is there anything I can get you?'

'Some peace,' she told him. 'But I've never seen a bobby who could manage that.'

'We try.'

Mrs Reynolds raised a hand. It fell back to her lap. 'I'll send for you when it's time, and I'll say the name if I still can. Either way, it'll be there for you. Don't worry, you won't have to wait long. A few days, that's what the doctor said. A week if I'm lucky.'

'I'm sorry.'

She snorted, and it turned into a coughing fit. 'I'm not. It'll be a blessing to go.'

'Does your daughter know that?'

'I haven't said owt to her. But it's obvious, isn't it? Can't you smell the death in here? I can. I've been putting some of my medicine aside to make sure I go out easily. I don't think God will mind that, do you?'

'No,' Harper said. 'I don't imagine He will.'

Walking back to Millgarth, he wondered at the woman. The things she'd tell a stranger but not her own family. And the things she'd hold back, that she'd never have said if he hadn't found her and pressed her. He couldn't understand, couldn't see a grain of sense behind it.

But it was her choice, and all he could do now was wait for the name.

'Sounds like she has us over a barrel,' Ash said as they strolled down the Headrow and turned on to Cookridge Street, all the grand buildings ahead of them. The art gallery, the library, Board of Education offices. Tallest of all the town hall, the clock showing five minutes to three.

'She does. We can't exactly force her, can we?' Harper said.

'Wouldn't look good, sir.'

'I'd still like us to find him on our own. This way . . .' It felt like defeat, to depend on someone else.

'Happen we will, sir. There's still time. We're all working on it.'

'Let's hope we can.' He looked up and saw the ranks of dark

blue uniforms. 'For the moment, let's make sure this lot are ready for Saturday night. If we mess that up, we might all be back on the beat come Sunday.'

TWENTY-TWO

Harper watched them work, giving suggestions and orders. He marched one group down to the railway station, spreading them along the platform and outside the entrance. It was enough to make travellers stop and stare among the smoke and the train whistles, wondering what was happening.

For once, he was grateful for City Square and its statue of the Black Prince. He'd never cared for the way it broke up the flow of the roads, but now it made for a natural barrier. Harder for any mob to try and storm the prime minister's car.

Again and again they moved, until he was satisfied that it was drilled into their heads. After that he sent them back to the Coliseum and moved on to Quebec Street and the Liberal Club.

He was standing, inspecting the entrance, when Emerson came dashing along the street.

'Is there a problem?'

'No, sir.' The lad was barely out of breath, a grin as broad as the River Aire plastered on his face. 'I'm just practising finding you.'

'You've managed that. How are things up the hill?'

'Seem to be going smoothly, sir.'

'Right, I'll go back there, then on to take a look at the reserves.'

'Very good, sir.' The constable slipped away through the crowd on the street and round the corner.

There was something hypnotic about watching lines of men move. Sissons was drilling them on Victoria Square, giving his orders with blasts on the police whistle. Clever, Harper thought. With all the unemployed men around, shouting would never work, but that noise would pierce anything. Did he have enough constables there, though? Could they contain the demonstrators? And what happened if they couldn't?

There was a hush inside the Coliseum. Galt had the easy job:

men to guard the doors, others to stand around and keep watch during the speeches. Now they looked on as workers set up the scenery and props for tonight's variety show.

Harper stood in the dress circle, gazing down on it all, the gilt and red velvet, the heavy curtains that swished back and forth. Every seat would be filled on Saturday night, all of them eager to hear Asquith speak.

This would be the simple part. Outside was where there'd be trouble.

Ash seemed to have his bobbies in order, ready to contain Mrs Baines and the suffragettes. He'd been specific in his orders: no violence against the women. Reporters from every newspaper in the country would be there, and he'd be damned if Leeds was going to end up with a bad reputation.

Finally, he crossed Woodhouse Lane, over to Carlton Barracks. The sergeants were busy, supervising wave after wave of truncheon charges. But if the reserves were needed, that was how they'd come, ready to crack a few heads. With luck, they'd be kicking their heels over here for the whole evening. But he wasn't about to take any chances.

Last of all, the police horses. They moved with sweet precision, the riders guiding them with a twitch on the reins or a small movement of the legs. He'd seen them in action often enough, always astonished by their size and the way they worked.

'We'll be ready for you, sir.' The sergeant leaned down from his saddle, patting the neck of his animal. 'If this lot can control the football crowd outside Elland Road, we can keep a few men pressed back.'

'Don't take offence, but I hope I won't need you.'

The man laughed. 'My lads would be glad of an easy time. Sit around drinking tea and smoking. The army has a good set-up here. Almost as good as being at home. We'll be ready if you call, though. Down there in two shakes of a lamb's tail and we'll put the fear of God into them.'

It wasn't the fear of God he needed, Harper thought as he strolled back, but the rule of law. Maybe it would end up being the same thing. He hoped not.

They carried on past dusk and into the darkness. Over and over, until it was ingrained in their minds, moving without having to think.

Finally, as the town hall clock struck eight, he sent them all home. Late, well past the end of their shifts. Even with his bad hearing he could make out the mutterings of discontent.

'What do you think?' Harper asked his men as they walked back to Millgarth. 'Are they in good shape?'

'Coming along, sir,' Ash replied. 'If we have them out again tomorrow, they'll be ready.'

'Sissons, are you happy that your men can control the unemployed?'

'I believe so, sir.' But he heard the touch of doubt in his voice. 'They'll do their best.'

'I need some certainty.'

'I can't guarantee it, sir.'

'If things look as if they might tip the wrong way, send Emerson for the reinforcements. We're not going to let this get out of hand. Ash, are you sure you can contain the suffragettes?'

'Positive, sir. They can shout all they like, but they won't have a chance to get near the Coliseum.'

'Tomorrow I want the men ready at five o'clock. We'll keep it to three hours. Saturday afternoon, full inspection of everyone at two. Make sure they know to have those buttons shining and their boots polished. If the country's looking at us, we'll make sure we give a smart account of ourselves.'

'Any messages for me?' Harper asked the night sergeant.

'Not since I've been on, sir.'

Nothing waiting on his desk. All afternoon a feeling had gnawed at his stomach. Charlotte Reynolds on her deathbed, sending word to him, and he wasn't there to receive it. But she must have lasted through the day.

He glanced through everything else, none of it important enough to need attention tonight.

'If anyone wants me, telephone me at home. It'll be important.'

'I'll do that sir.'

He walked along Regent Street, skirting the bottom end of the Leylands, where he'd grown up; mostly filled with Jewish immigrants these days. Thursday evening and the streets were still alive with people, darting to and from the shops, standing and chatting. They had their lives, their joys, their fears. He knew half of them probably worked fourteen hours a day tailoring suits in the sweatshops, and lived crammed into tiny houses. A very few, the ones who'd earned some money, were already moving farther out, up Chapeltown Road. But most were stuck here.

Off in the distance a man began to sing in a high, beautiful voice that rang over the neighbourhood and made people stare. Yiddish words filled with sorrow and longing. He'd heard tales from those who'd come from Russia, Lithuania and elsewhere. Stories of why they'd needed to leave and the journeys they'd had to make. Things beyond his experience, outside his comprehension. Anyone who was willing to undergo what they had deserved a future in this country.

Not all of them were good, of course; he'd nicked several and sent them to prison. But most kept their heads down and tried to get by, exactly the same as everyone else.

Letting his mind wander was welcome relief. Yet as he came to Sheepscar and the junction with Roundhay Road, the floodgates opened again and it all rushed back. Had he forgotten anything? Would the men be fully prepared? Was he underestimating Mrs Baines? Would the lines hold?

And underneath all that, always the thought of trying to find Taylor's killer.

At the entrance to the Victoria, he stopped for a moment and exhaled. Get a grip, he thought. This was his job and he did it well; Crossley would never have suggested he apply to be chief if he didn't. It would all pass. Asquith's visit would go smoothly. He'd find his murderer.

Right now, though, he needed sleep.

Friday morning. No fog, but grey, a faint mist hanging in the air. The type of day when the dampness clung to everything – branches, railings, pavements. And no word from Charlotte Reynolds. The only thing waiting was a note from the chief constable.

'Mr Cranbrook will be buried this morning.' Harper sat in his office and passed Crossley's message on to his men. 'Food for thought. I'll go and keep my eyes open for anyone who might be of interest to us.'

'Do you really think they'd be stupid enough to attend the funeral, sir?' Galt asked.

'Yes,' Harper told him. 'I do. One thing about people, they never cease to surprise me.'

'The super is right,' Ash agreed. 'You get some strange people turning up for funerals. We've broken a couple of cases that way. Thank God most criminals aren't that bright.'

Sissons opened his mouth and closed it again. Time to take them off that subject before they started reminiscing.

'Now,' Harper said with a smile, 'anyone had any more thoughts about anything else we need to do when the prime minister visits tomorrow?'

The interment was set for eleven at St George's Field. Plenty of time to do some work and stop by the infirmary.

A little before ten he stood in Brenda Woolcott's room. A little more movement in her limbs, the doctor had told him. Piece by fragile piece, her body was coming back together. But no one could say how long it would take or how far it would go.

'Medically, there's very little more we can do,' he explained. 'Just wait. She needs care. She can't look after herself, and there's no family. It seems she has no money.'

'Isn't there somewhere she can go? There must be others like her.'

'A ward at the workhouse,' the doctor said. 'That's where she'll end up if there's no improvement in the next few days.'

'And there won't be, will there?'

'No,' the man agreed. 'Barring a miracle.'

He spent ten minutes with her. Idle chatter: the weather, the prime minister's visit, anything but the case. This might be the last time he'd see her; at least he could let her remember a friendly face.

Finally he said goodbye and walked to the other end of the building. Walsh had been moved to a ward. He looked cheerful. Almost back to his old self until he tried to shift in the bed. Then he winced and pain showed on his face.

'Sure you don't fancy joining us tomorrow? You can direct things in your nightshirt.'

'Very generous, sir. But doctor's orders: I have to avoid demonstrations and public gatherings for the moment.'

'Any more word on when you'll go home?'

'Tuesday, they say, all being well.'

'Have they told you how long before you'll be back on duty?'

'Two or three weeks. But nothing strenuous at first. Light duties.'

'Don't rush things,' Harper ordered. 'Crime will still be waiting when you return.'

Walsh grinned. 'No doubt about that, sir. Is everyone ready for tomorrow?'

'We will be. We'd better be.'

A few more minutes and he stood, bringing something from his pocket and laying it on the blanket. A bar of Fry's Chocolate Cream.

'Never let it be said I don't look after my men.'

'Very kind of you, sir.'

'Just look after yourself. It's not the same without you around.'

Another grin. 'As long as you mean that in a good way, sir.'

A walk up to the cemetery, past the new university, almost to Woodhouse Moor. Bleak and grey. Plenty had come to see Cranbrook laid to rest. Councillors, business owners, bankers, all gathered to mourn. One or two he knew; most of the faces meant nothing.

But no one to spark his curiosity.

Instead, he watched the Cranbrook children. Almost adults now. It was his first opportunity to see them properly. Marie was shorter than Mrs Cranbrook. She looked lost in her heavy black coat, leather gloves on hands that clutched tight at a small reticule. A wide black hat, shoulders slumped in grief. As she lifted the dark veil to dab away the tears, he caught a glimpse of her face. Nothing like the pair who brought her up, but the exact image of Mrs Davis. If he'd ever harboured the slightest doubt, that swept it away.

Andrew stood tall, back straight, elegant in his suit, the overcoat unbuttoned. A slim young man. But it was his expression that caught Harper's eye. The mix of fierce determination, trying to hold everything inside, and paralysing fear, as if he'd just realized he was the man of the family now, responsible for something that was falling apart around him.

There would be money tucked away, Harper was certain. Not a fortune, but they'd never starve. Mrs Cranbrook would fade into a quietly genteel life. The children . . . a mix of contacts and sympathy would see them buoyed through life.

As the vicar asked Sarah Cranbrook to sprinkle earth into the grave, he turned away. No clues here and he had too much to do.

Still no word from Mrs Reynolds. She was managing to cling to life. For a moment he considered another visit, a chance to persuade her to give him the name. No. It was too ghoulish, hovering like a carrion crow waiting for death. Let her have a little peace, if that's what it was.

And maybe his men would turn up something.

But their faces held no joy as they came into the office a little after three. Galt first, shaking his head. Sissons looking dejected. Finally Ash, thoughtful and silent.

'Whoever he is, he's getting away with it,' Harper said.

'He *thinks* he is, sir,' Ash corrected him.

'No, for the moment he *is*. He murdered Taylor, he might as well have killed Brenda Woolcott. He severed the links. He must believe he's free and clear.'

'And we're left waiting for a woman to pass us his name before she dies.'

He could hear the frustration coiled in the inspector's voice. Exactly the same as the rest of them. But they'd exhausted everything else. 'We don't have much choice at this stage.'

'Surely it's not *how* we find out that matters, sir,' Sissons said. 'What's important is that we end up with the name and make the arrest. The information is still coming to us.'

'I don't like it,' Harper told him. 'Even when we arrest the man, we've failed.' He sighed. 'Still, there's nothing more to be done about it until Sunday. We're going to be a damned sight too busy.' He glanced at the clock. 'Time to go and put the men through their paces once again.'

TWENTY-THREE

By eight o'clock, the men were moving exactly the way Harper wanted. He'd worked them hard, hurrying between the Coliseum and Victoria Square to supervise. As they drilled, council carts arrived with the barricades and began unloading them along the pavement.

Emerson earned his pay, constantly darting between locations, sprinting off with messages and suggestions and dashing back with questions.

All this made the king's visit back in the summer seem

straightforward. The only thing to do then was guard the route and watch out for drunks. He'd had so many coppers for the occasion that the trick was to stop them falling over each other's feet. It had all gone off smoothly. Too smoothly, he thought now as he watched the constables preparing for pitched battles.

Little pools of light from the streetlamps cast shadows over their faces. But he needed them capable of working together in the darkness. That and discipline would give the police the advantage tomorrow night, and he'd need all of it.

He sent Emerson back down the hill with a final message, waiting until even he could hear the boots marching up Cookridge Street before bringing everyone to attention.

'You've done a good job.' His voice rang into the night and he spotted a few smiles. 'We're going to be ready. But' – he allowed the pause to hang in the air – 'remember it's the prime minister visiting Leeds tomorrow. The home secretary will be with him, and he's the man in charge of the police for the whole country. He's going to be looking at us all. Even me.' Harper grinned. 'That means spit and shine for everyone. Buttons, badges, numbers, I want them all gleaming. I know your boots are going to end up dirty, but they'll start the day polished so bright they glow. It's going to be out with the dubbin and the rags. Do you understand?'

A few groaned, some looked glum at yet more work. Most stared, blank. Probably the best he could hope for; these men had put in a fourteen-hour day so far, and tomorrow would be longer.

'I'll be inspecting you in the afternoon. Maybe you don't care either way about Mr Asquith or Mr Gladstone. But you do care about Leeds City Police. That's why you joined the force. It's why I'm here. So we're all going to look good and put on our best faces. Go home and enjoy the good night's sleep you've earned. Dismiss.'

He watched them disperse. Two minutes and the street was empty, only Harper and his squad remaining. It would be different tomorrow night. They'd be going at it hammer and tongs.

'Stirring speech, sir,' Ash said.

'As long as they look presentable and do their best.'

'They will, sir,' Sissons told him. 'And they're ready to knock some heads together if it's needed.'

'It'll be needed,' Harper said. 'I can feel it in my water.'

That had been Billy's phrase. It made him smile.

'We thought we'd pop in on Walsh for five minutes, sir,' Ash said. 'If you'd care to join us . . .'

He shook his head. 'I was there this morning. And I still have a few things to do at Millgarth.'

He relished walking alone. But Leeds wasn't quiet. It was Friday night, just another half-day of work ahead for most people. The pubs were packed, the gin palaces throwing light on to the street. Busy at the music halls, people already queueing for the second house.

No one noticed him as he strolled along the Headrow. Trams passed, bells clanging, empty eyes staring from the windows.

At Millgarth the constables were dragging in the first of the drunks. Harper pulled out his pocket watch. Twenty past eight. About right. They'd have their chance to sleep it off before going in front of the magistrate tomorrow morning. A few shillings' fine and bound over to keep the peace. The alcohol tax was what some of them called it.

In his office he glanced through the notes and reports waiting for his attention. No word from Charlotte Reynolds, and he began to wonder. What if there was nothing to tell after all? That he was waiting for a name he'd never hear. She could already be dead, laid out at home.

No. He had to believe. If he didn't, he had nothing at all, no chance of discovering who killed Adam Taylor and left Brenda Woolcott trapped inside her helpless body.

The Victoria was full. He had to squeeze between men who breathed beer fumes on him. Behind the bar, Dan and another barman he'd never seen before were run ragged by customers lined up four and five deep for service. Off in the corner, someone thumped out a tune on the old piano and voices picked up the chorus of *Poor John*.

By the time he pushed through the doors and climbed the stairs, Harper felt as if he'd survived a rugby scrum.

'You'll be making money tonight,' he told Annabelle. 'I can't remember the last time I saw it so busy.'

'A couple of retirement parties,' she explained. 'I popped my head round the door earlier.'

'Who's the new man with Dan?'

'He's just in for tonight. Lives on Henbury Street, lost his job last week. His mam asked if I knew of anything.' She pulled his plate from the oven, still warm. 'Ready for tomorrow, do you think?'

'I hope so. Is Mary out again tonight?'

'At the Palace with her friends. We should go sometime; it's been an age since I had a good sing-song at the music hall.'

'Once all this is over and I can breathe again,' he promised. 'Has she said anything more about the demonstration?'

'Not a dickie bird.' She raised her eyebrows. 'You know how she is, talks your ear off about some things, dead silence on others.'

'As long as she keeps her promise not to go.' He finished the last bite of sausage and mash, reached across and poured himself a cup of tea. 'It's going to be a battle royal.'

'What about the suffragettes? Do you think they'll cause much trouble?'

'I honestly don't know.' A moment's silence. 'Anyway, I've had enough of that for one day. Have you had any more thoughts about selling the pub?'

Annabelle gave a wan smile and played with a loose strand of hair before pushing it back behind her ear.

'Right now I'm inclined to sell. Look at me, Tom, I feel as if I haven't really known what to do with myself since I stepped down from the Guardians.'

'You still speak for Miss Ford and the suffragists.'

She nodded. 'I know, but it's hardly full-time, is it? One night a week, sometimes two. I'm too comfortable here, that's the problem. I need something to give me a good kick.'

'And you think selling the pub will do that?'

'I hope so. What do you reckon?'

He squeezed her hand. 'I think that whatever you decide to do will be fine. We'll be happy wherever we live. It'll be a big wrench for Mary, though.'

'She'll adjust. A few more years and she'll be getting married and off somewhere new, anyway.'

'I suppose you're right.'

'I'm always right, Tom Harper.' She tried to sound firm and cheerful. The act didn't quite work this time; indecision burrowed under her words. 'In the end, anyway.' She cocked her head. 'We have the place to ourselves. Maybe we deserve an early night for once.'

'You read my mind.'

He wanted to sleep. Annabelle had dropped off. He heard Mary come home, the soft click of the latch, the familiar sounds as she prepared for bed. The pub emptied, conversations slowly fading as men walked to their homes. And then the greater quiet of night. Not silence, he knew that, even if his hearing couldn't catch the noises that were always there.

Everything was spinning in his mind. Tomorrow's visit, finding Taylor's killer. It all clutched at him, not willing to let him go and rest. Maybe he dozed here and there, but by four he knew there'd be nothing more.

Harper dressed, standing in the kitchen and polishing his boots as the kettle came to a boil. A cup of tea, a hunk of bread and butter, shave in cold water and he was out of the door and into the morning.

It looked like any other autumn day. Grey, dull, a hint of moisture in the air. But he knew it was different. The tension was rooted deep in his body and it wouldn't leave until tonight, when everything was done. For good or ill.

So early, the streets were quiet, not even time for the morning shift yet. But still the haze hung over the city, the taste of soot he'd known every single day of his life. Something for the prime minister to relish when he stepped off the train. Welcome to Leeds.

Time to distract himself with all the paperwork he'd ignored for two days. At least he couldn't see the creeping hands of the clock with his head bent over the pages. He read, signed his name and moved them from one pile to another.

At seven, the telephone rang.

'I thought I'd find you in,' Crossley said. 'Did you have trouble sleeping, too?'

'Barely a wink, sir.'

'I know how you feel. Is everything ready? Is there anything else you need?'

'I think we'll be fine, sir,' he said with more confidence than he felt. But he had the reinforcements in reserve; it would only take two minutes for them to arrive. 'Thank you, though.'

'I'll leave it in your hands, then, Tom. If there's anything at all, telephone me.'

'I will, sir.'

'I'll see you at the railway station.' He chuckled. 'I'll be the one in the fancy uniform.'

No uniforms for his squad. They wore their working suits, clothes made to last. The only concession to the occasion was Ash in his best bowler hat. But they were the ones who'd be in the thick of things.

'We still have the morning,' he told them. 'Let's use it well and see if we can find the man who killed Taylor.'

'Is it official that we're doing nothing about the Cranbrooks, sir?' Galt asked.

'For now,' Harper said. 'If we discover something fresh . . .' He shrugged. 'If that happens, we'll see.' He glanced at the clock. 'Let's do what we can. Here at one. Make sure you all have a good dinner. There won't be a chance to eat this evening. It's going to be a long day.'

After they'd gone, he tried to return to the papers. But his mind was racing, thoughts flickering one after another. He laid down the pen, tucked his spectacles in his pocket and put on his coat.

The street was empty. Nobody lurking. His hand strayed to his pocket, feeling the reassurance of the cosh. Just in case. He stopped in front of a house and knocked on the door. But it wasn't Charlotte Reynolds who wrenched it open. Instead, it was Roberta Larner, the daughter, skin taut over the bones of her face. She looked washed out, empty.

'What do you want?' No colour or tone in her voice, all the emotion bleached away by exhaustion.

'Your mother . . .' Harper began.

'She's still in the land of the living. Just.'

He could feel her contempt, but he still had to ask. 'Can I see her?'

'Won't do no good.' She narrowed her eyes. 'I know why you're here. She told me she promised you something. Wouldn't say what.'

'That's right.'

'It's there on the mantelpiece, in an envelope. Made me swear I wouldn't look.' She stared at him. 'I keep my word.'

'I understand.'

'So come back when she's dead. I'll make sure you know, just like she asked. Nowt here for you before then. And nothing for me after. Not with my husband gone, then her.'

Only an empty world ahead of her.

A nod, a tip of his hat, and Harper turned on his heel. At least they'd caught the man who'd killed John Larner. That didn't help when her husband was in his grave. The law was one thing. But justice? Sometimes he wondered if it truly existed.

Beef stew, piping hot, with slices of bread to sop up the juices. From the café he looked down at the market, bustling with shoppers on a Saturday. The well-heeled and the poor, side by side, buying their potatoes and carrots, children captivated by toys on display at one of the stalls. A rising welter of noise.

The waitress took his plate and he ordered suet pudding and custard for afters. That should keep him going. A final sip of tea, then he paid the bill and strolled down George Street to Millgarth.

He could feel the worry rising through his body and tried to push it down. Plenty of time for that later. The men were waiting, fidgeting and restless.

'Any luck this morning?' Harper asked. Nothing more than the three of them shaking their heads. 'Why don't we go over to the Coliseum? It'll be better than sitting here twiddling our thumbs.'

They were ready. Wary as they walked, as if something might happen. Not for a few hours yet, he told himself.

Rows of barriers stood, ready to close the Headrow at half past four and give the prime minister's party an unimpeded journey to the theatre. Workmen stood around in their heavy jackets, with nothing to do but smoke and talk. Victoria Square was blocked off, waiting for the unemployed to arrive and begin.

Farther up the hill, barricades cut off Vernon Street. Would they stop the suffragettes, Harper wondered, or would they try to flood over them? More barriers were ready at the top of Cookridge Street. A few more hours and no one would be entering from Woodhouse Lane.

So far, so good. The street sweepers had been out, removing all the rubbish and sweeping up the dirt. There'd be plenty more soon enough, and who knew what they'd be cleaning up in the morning?

The police were waiting at Carlton Barracks, spread out across the parade ground. Harper talked to the sergeants and waited as they shouted their orders, watching as the men dashed into their ranks and stood to attention. Thank God all those years were far behind him. All the pointless ceremony.

He walked along the rows, a smile and a word for those he recognized, picking out the obvious failings – dull buttons and unshined boots. Who really cared about the rest? They were here to do a job.

Finally, he stood in front of them.

'You heard me talk yesterday. There's no need to repeat myself. It's a big day for us, and it'll probably be a difficult one. Just do your jobs and make Leeds proud. I know you will.'

Another half-hour and they began to march, the kind of spectacle to stop traffic and make people stare. There was no doubt: they looked bloody good, and he was proud to be one of them.

By two o'clock they were at their posts. Nothing left to do but wait.

'Where do you want me, sir?' Emerson seemed to appear from nowhere.

'You might as well stay close to me for now. Not much to do at the moment.' A quick smile. 'Never mind, you'll be busy enough later.'

'That suits me, sir. I've never been one for doing nothing.'

Harper moved from one area to another, making the final checks. His mouth felt dry, his nerves crackling. The town hall clock seemed to move too slowly. And then, as if time had speeded up, suddenly it was five minutes past four.

'The railway station,' he told Emerson. 'Better make yourself smart. We're going to meet the prime minister.'

Mrs Baines had gathered a group of women on City Square. Only fifteen of them. If this was the best she could scrape together, he wouldn't need to worry too much.

Harper raised his hat as she approached. In return, Jennie Baines stared daggers at him.

'At least the weather's on your side,' he said. 'Dry.'

'Wouldn't matter if it was raining cats and dogs,' she told him. 'We'd still be out here. What do you think, women aren't built for the wet?'

'I'm just making polite conversation.'

'You might as well save your breath. We're here, and we'll be at the Coliseum later.'

'That's your right. As long as everyone's peaceful.'

'I remember what you said.'

'And will it be?'

She stared at him and smiled. A few of the women murmured. He looked at their faces. Young, old, rich, poor. But all of them determined, ready for anything.

'I don't want trouble,' he continued. 'I've told you that before. My men are under orders to treat you politely and with dignity.'

'I'm pleased to hear it, Superintendent.' Her voice dripped sarcasm. 'I'll believe it when I see it.'

'All I ask in return is the same.'

'Then perhaps you should tell Asquith to treat us that way when you see him.'

The murmuring grew louder. Nothing he said would alter the way they behaved later. Harper tipped his hat again and walked on.

'She scares me,' Emerson said as they crossed the road.

'That's what she wants. Worry the men and inspire the women. Let's see how she does outside the Coliseum.'

Two large black motor cars were parked, drivers in place, engines running. Ready in case the train arrived early. A group of constables stood at the station entrance, surrounded by the noise and people trying to move around them.

No more than a few more yards and he was in among the dirt and the smoke. Thick hisses of steam. A sharp whistle, then the sense of harnessed power as a train started to pull away, the sound hitting a crescendo before softening as the locomotive gathered momentum. Everything was movement.

Harper looked around. It all seemed ordinary. No sign of anyone lurking. Just the everyday travellers and people waiting for arrivals. He let out a breath, then he was aware of someone running.

A constable in uniform, his face red as he gasped for breath, boots skidding over the tiles. A hasty salute.

'I was looking for you up by the Coliseum, sir. Message for you from Millgarth. Sergeant Mason says to tell you it's important.'

'What does he want?' He felt fear creeping up from his belly.

'Don't know, sir. He just told me to give you this and get back sharpish.' He thrust a piece of paper in Harper's hand and ran off.

Your wife telephoned. Vital you ring her as soon as possible.

He opened his watch. Twenty past four. God Almighty. Asquith was due in ten minutes.

'You keep watch,' he told Emerson. 'If anything happens, come and get me immediately.'

In the station master's office, he lifted the receiver, waiting impatiently for the connection.

'What is it?' he asked as soon as Annabelle was on the line. 'The prime minister's arriving any minute.'

'It's Mary,' she said, and he stopped, unable to say a word. 'She told me she was going to do some shopping after work this afternoon.' Annabelle caught her breath. 'She telephoned half an hour ago. She's going to the demonstration, Tom. I'll swing for the little madam, behaving like this.'

Christ, he thought. Bloody girl.

'I can't do anything now. Nothing.' He tried to think. 'I'll tell Ash.'

'I'm coming down there.'

'Don't—' he began, but she'd already gone.

Damn the girl. They'd *told* her, but she had to go and bloody defy them. Now she was going to be trapped in the middle of a war and there was nothing he could do to help her. If she was hurt, injured . . . not just her. Annabelle, too.

He dared not let himself think about it. Not now. Not—

'Sir,' Emerson said, 'the chief constable is looking for you.'

TWENTY-FOUR

'Are you all right, Tom?' Crossley asked. 'You look like you've just had a shock.'

He tried to gather himself. A deep breath and a smile that felt utterly false.

'Some news, sir. I'm fine.'

'Anything I need to know?'

'No, sir.' God forbid.

'Good,' the chief said with a doubtful look. He looked uncomfortable in his dress uniform with the glittering gold braid on the cap. 'The train's two minutes away. Make sure your men are ready.'

'Very good, sir.'

'The mayor and the councillors are on the platform. As soon as you're set, present yourself there.'

'Sir?' He didn't understand.

'I want you with me.'

'Me?'

'Of course.' Crossley smiled. 'You didn't think you were going to get off that lightly, did you?'

'But . . .' He looked down at his suit. A good one, but not his best, not when it was likely to end up filthy or torn. 'I don't even know how to address him.'

'Mr Prime Minister is the proper way,' Crossley said. 'Don't worry, it'll only be a quick handshake then you can nip off. Get your men in place and come along.'

He couldn't think; his thoughts were flying all over the place. Still, he managed to give out his orders to the men. He needed to let Ash know, so he could keep an eye out for Mary and Annabelle, but he couldn't send Emerson with a message yet; he needed the lad here in case of trouble. And as few people as possible had to know about her. Very slowly, he exhaled, silently cursing the girl.

All the great and the good of Leeds were assembled, standing in line as if they were on a school outing. The Lord Mayor wore his chain and robes. About the only thing missing was the ceremonial mace. Councillors in frock coats and high wing collars, clutching top hats in their hands. He joined the end of the line.

Crossley leaned towards him. 'Is it going to go off smoothly, Tom?'

'I hope so, sir. I really hope so.'

But the gnawing in the pit of his stomach told him how bad it was going to be.

Exactly on time, the train arrived with a wild screech of brakes and plumes of smoke. Without thinking, Harper came to attention.

Three large men in suits and mackintoshes climbed down to the platform, spreading out and looking around with practised eyes. Special Branch; they had to be. After them, Mr Gladstone, the home secretary, mouth hidden under a heavy moustache. And finally the prime minister, his white hair cut short and severe, and a plain, vigorous face.

He looked so ordinary; that was the real surprise. He might have been any successful businessman walking across Park Square in his overcoat and hat. But then the politician shone through, as if someone had thrown a switch. He began to smile and glad-hand all the waiting men. A word or two, a grin here or there. A professional at work.

Finally he was close. Crossley introduced himself, then said, 'This is Superintendent Harper. He's in charge of the policemen looking after your visit.'

Mr Asquith extended a hand. A firm enough handshake, but the skin of his hand was completely smooth and soft. A man who'd never done a day's manual labour in his life. But why would he expect anything different?

'Then I trust you'll all be good at your job, Superintendent.' He smiled again, showing clean, white teeth. His breath smelled like wine.

Harper fumbled for a reply. 'The best we can, Prime Minister.'

'Good, good.'

And he was gone, the men from Special Branch hovering close as he began to move through the station.

'You'd better get busy, Tom,' Crossley said. 'And let's all pray it stays quiet.'

He hurried out. Constables were lined up. Crowds had gathered, hundreds of them who'd appeared in the last few minutes. The group of women around Mrs Baines had grown too, almost thirty of them now.

But a line of coppers faced them. Harper stood and watched as the politicians emerged. As soon as they saw Asquith, the suffragettes began to shout, ragged chanting like a chorus at the football ground.

Harper turned to Emerson. 'Get yourself to the Liberal Club. Warn them he's on his way. Then take a look at the other places.'

He saw the prime minister glance up at all the noise, mutter something to the man at his side, and duck into the first motor car. As soon as the door closed, the driver moved away, the other setting off behind it.

Immediately, people started to disperse. This moment had passed smoothly. But there were plenty of others ahead.

He gave a quick word of praise to the sergeant and men and sent them off to guard the route along Park Row.

Quebec Street was quiet. Only the motor cars idling by the kerb hinted at anything out of the ordinary.

A word with the two constables outside the Liberal Club, then he was crossing the road, watching, ready, trying to push Mary from his mind for now. Further ahead a figure was running, dodging between people on the pavement as it approached. Emerson.

'Has something happened?'

'No, sir.' He caught his breath. 'Mr Sissons said to tell you the unemployed men are assembling on Victoria Square. About four hundred so far and growing all the time. Alf Kitson's up on a stepladder, addressing them.'

'Is everything still calm?'

'For now, sir.'

He had a little time. But he needed to start making decisions. A few hundred angry men made for a volatile crowd. If the mood turned, they could become a mob in seconds.

'Go back up there,' Harper said. 'Stay close to Sissons. If he asks for reinforcements, you come and see me.'

It was October, the late afternoon turning chilly, but he was sweating, armpits clammy, shirt sticking to his back. And things had barely begun.

He needed to be by Vernon Street, to pull his daughter from the crowd of women and keep his wife safe. But he had his duty, and that had to come first. For now he *had* to stay here, to keep an eye on everything.

Waiting. The copper's bane. All it did was give him more time to think and worry. What was going on up there? Scenes played out in his head. Mary injured. Arrested. He shifted from foot to foot, anxious to be on the move as the minutes passed.

He stirred as the doors to the building opened. The people passing barely glanced up as a stream of men emerged and entered the cars.

Harper ran, cutting through the back streets to the Headrow. Barricades in place, traffic stopped for the prime minister. Carters and drivers sat, smoking and swearing.

He paused for a moment, staring at the growing numbers on Victoria Square. There had to be close to five hundred now. Kitson was still shouting through a megaphone, whipping them up. Harper tried to sense the mood. Dark, growing stormier by the second, but still contained. For how long, though? He saw plenty of angry faces and raised fists. What did they have to lose? They had no jobs, no money. Just bitterness and poverty.

He looked for Sissons but couldn't spot him. Still, the coppers seemed to be moving with purpose, forming their lines to hold the crowd in place. They were in control. For now, at least.

Police numbers were heavier along Cookridge Street. The crowds on the pavement stood five and six deep. A few children had been pushed to the front to wave their Union Jack flags. People were smiling, as if they were at a party, ignoring the angry, yelling men just a few yards away. Two worlds, right next to each other, as different as they could be.

He hurried up the hill, crossing Great George Street, passing the Mechanics' Institute. Ash stood in the middle of the road, tall, bulky in his overcoat and new bowler hat.

He nodded towards the Coliseum. 'Almost full in there, sir. They're just waiting for the guests of honour. Everything in order?'

'No.' He pointed at the suffragettes, close to a hundred of them now, penned in on Vernon Street. 'My daughter's in with them and Mrs Harper is on her way down here.' He could hear how frantic he sounded. It didn't matter. He didn't care.

There was too much to juggle. The prime minister would arrive at any moment. The last of the audience was filing into the hall. Businessmen in expensive suits, tickets checked at the door before they could gain entry.

Mrs Baines was addressing the women, her voice loud and strident. And somewhere among them . . .

'It's probably just a matter of time before the unemployed break out,' Harper said.

'We have the reinforcements, sir.'

He shook his head. 'I'm holding them back for when we really need them. We'd just better be prepared for the worst. It's not far away.'

'We'll manage, sir. You leave things up here with me. I'll have that lass of yours out of there.' He marched away, shoulders back, shouting orders at the constables.

Harper stood. For a moment he felt utterly lost, out of his depth. Too much was happening, his head was on fire. This was like trying to keep a dozen balls in the air, knowing that if one fell, chaos would follow.

Suddenly, off in the distance, he made out a faint swell of cheering. He cocked his head, leaning his good ear towards the sound. It was definitely there. Asquith's procession was drawing closer, all those people by the side of the road happy to have a sight of their prime minister. A tiny glimmer of sanity among the madness.

He ran his palms down his cheeks.

Everyone was relying on him to make sure the politicians were safe. Let the demonstrators bray all they liked, that wasn't going to do any damage. Words might fill the air, but they couldn't wound. Nobody would die from them. But if it went beyond that – *when* it did – he'd stop them.

A final breath and he was ready.

The first of the motor cars came in sight. A chorus of boos, a clamour of shouting from the women. He searched their faces for Mary. Couldn't see her. A swift prayer to keep her safe. Her and Annabelle.

He put a hand in his pocket and felt the comforting shape of the cosh. Just in case.

The first vehicle pulled up by the doors of the theatre. The big men came out, staring around, eyes worried by everything they saw. The air crackled. The home secretary emerged, bundled through the doors and into the building. Then the prime minister, suddenly looking weary and old.

The booing reached a crescendo. The loud, hard voice of Jennie Baines carried over the noise.

'The unemployed question is more a woman's question than a man's. If a man brings home a small wage, enough for himself and his family, but not to save anything, it's the woman who suffers most. Especially when she has to face the landlord.'

Different words, but hardly a million miles from the speeches Annabelle had given when she was campaigning to be elected as Poor Law Guardian. She'd spoken them at meetings, though, in halls and at hustings; she hadn't been trying to whip up a mob. And down the hill Alf Kitson was doing exactly the same thing.

A few more minutes and it would come to a head. Soon. Very soon.

A line of coppers stood, nervous, not sure what to do as they faced down the women. Mrs Baines was still speaking, her voice ringing out.

But Asquith was inside the Coliseum, all the dignitaries behind him; and the motor cars had pulled away. There was just the street, the women, and Kitson's men down the road.

And only the police to stop them.

He saw Ash, taller and broader than most of those around him. He was pointing and giving orders.

'Any problems?'

'Not yet, sir. Just some pushing against the barriers. Soon enough, though.'

Then the question he dreaded asking. 'Mary?'

'Haven't seen her, sir. If she's in the middle of that lot, it might be a while before I can spot her. She's safe enough for now. No sign of Mrs Harper, either.'

One small blessing.

Then Emerson was standing by them. He was panting hard, his face red, eyes wild.

'Sergeant Sissons says that Kitson is finishing.' The words tumbled out in a rush. 'He's urging them to come up here.'

'Can Sissons hold them?' Harper asked.

Emerson shook his head. 'He doesn't think so, sir. There are over six hundred now and they're all keyed up. I heard—'

The superintendent glanced at Ash. The inspector's face showed nothing.

'Go back down there,' Harper said. 'Tell him to contain them as long as he can, then start falling back. But I want it to be *orderly*, you understand. Make sure he knows that. Orderly. It's vital. I'm relying on you to keep me informed.'

'Yes, sir.' He gave half a salute and sprinted back down the hill.

'I hope you have a plan, sir,' Ash said.

'So do I. And I hope it bloody well works.' For a second he wished he'd kept Emerson close. He needed a second messenger. Harper looked around and found a copper standing by himself. 'You. Do you remember where Carlton Barracks is?'

'Yes, sir,' he answered in surprise. 'Of course I do.'

'Go over there. My compliments to the sergeant and tell him we need the reinforcements to make their way over here. Horses at the front. Have you got that?'

'Sergeant, bring reinforcements, horses at the front.'

'Good. Now *run*.' He watched the man disappear, then looked up at the sky. Coming on towards dark, a little light remaining to the west. Time had slipped by without him even noticing. He took out his pocket watch and snapped open the cover. Half past seven. Inside the Coliseum, the speeches would have started. They'd go on for another hour, at least.

To his left, Mrs Baines was still yelling, her voice as strong as ever. The suffragettes were restive, straining against the barriers, but only a few of them looked threatening. He was satisfied that the police would keep them penned.

It was the men who scared him.

Emerson was returning, dashing up the hill. A few of the women called out to him. A pair blew him kisses and laughed.

'They're beginning to move, sir. Some of them are breaking up the barricades to use as weapons.'

'Is Sissons holding them?'

He shook his head. 'His men are starting to fall back, sir. They're using their truncheons.'

Like a war. He cursed himself. He hadn't expected the unemployed to arm themselves. Dammit, he should have anticipated that. Where were the bloody reserves? He glanced over his shoulder. No sign yet. It wasn't far to the barracks. They should already be here.

'Go back down there. Tell him to make sure they don't get around him.' If that happened, it was all over. They'd overpower the coppers and flood up the hill. He made a quick decision. 'Stay with Sissons. Be ready if he has any more messages.'

'Very good, sir.'

The air was heavy, humming with the promise of violence. He strode over to the row of uniforms guarding the doors of the Coliseum. Their faces were hard and drawn. Burly men, experienced, tough.

'Make sure no civilian gets past you. If any of ours are wounded, help them through.'

'Is it going to be that bad, sir?' one of the men asked.

He turned to face the copper who'd spoken. 'It is,' he said. 'Be prepared. Your job is to keep that mob out. Do whatever you need.'

Ash pulled at his sleeve. 'No sign of your daughter yet, sir. I've been looking. But I thought I caught a glimpse of Mrs Harper in with the women.'

Christ.

TWENTY-FIVE

Then, for a moment, there was utter silence. Harper stared around in confusion. Had his hearing failed completely? But Jennie Baines was simply gathering her breath. She began to speak again, building the pitch higher. And then . . .

He seemed to catch something that rose up the hill. A deep roar that sounded as if it might have come out of hell. He stood, transfixed. Two seconds, three, and he realized what it was. The unemployed had broken through. They were pushing up Cookridge Street, hundreds of them moving, shouting. Full of blood lust.

Mrs Baines was louder. The women were a force now, rocking the barricades, shifting them. But Ash's men were holding firm.

Where were the bloody reinforcements?

He could make out the men in the distance. Kitson was at their head, turning to urge them on. Those around him were carrying pieces of wood, lashing out at everything. At the coppers trying to force them back. At anything at all. They had fury in their eyes and hatred on their lips. They were taking their revenge against a world that had no use for them.

They were rolling like a tide. Sissons's men were fighting hard, but they were outnumbered. Not a snowball's chance in hell. They brought down their truncheons, but they were taking three blows for every one they gave.

Kitson whirled like a madman, swinging the top of a barrier like an axe, crashing down on a policeman's helmet and sending it spinning away. He kicked out and the copper fell, lost on the ground.

Without thinking, Tom Harper started to run towards him. He needed to drag that bobby out of there before he was trampled.

He tried to squirm through the mass of men. Blue uniforms and old jackets were tangled together. Everyone was shouting and screaming. Something hit him on the back and he staggered forward, pushing into someone else. Another blow, not as hard, and he turned, pulling the cosh out of his pocket.

The man had a brutal grin on his face. Hardly any teeth. He

pulled the stick back, ready for a third strike. Too slow. Harper's cosh caught him on the point of the elbow and he began to howl with pain. Another step, close enough to smell the old sweat and stale beer. Harper brought his forehead down on the man's face, feeling the nose break, then pushed him away.

He looked down, searching. Men were on the ground, curled up into balls, trying to make themselves small. Groaning, crawling. But he couldn't see a copper.

Harper fought his way back out, cracking the cosh down on wrists and shoulders. He found a little space and stopped, breathing hard. There was a cut on the back of his hand. He felt something trickle down his neck and touched it with his fingers. They came away bloody.

He needed to be out of here, back where he could see what was happening. Where were those damned reserves? His men were taking a battering. A lungful of air and he ploughed his way back through.

Finally he was free of the battle, able to think again, close to the entrance to the Coliseum. The constables were standing shoulder to shoulder, truncheons drawn and ready.

The suffragettes had toppled the barricades and were swarming through. He saw a copper grab Jennie Baines around the waist and start dragging her away. She struggled, but he didn't let go. Two women grabbed her wrists and a pair of his men took hold of them, too, lifting them off their feet as they kicked out helplessly. A copper tackled another one and pulled her from the crowd. It stopped them long enough for the rest of the policemen to surge into the gap and start pushing them back. Maybe that would be enough. He just hoped that Mary and Annabelle were away from there, because he couldn't do a thing for them now.

The unemployed men were still gaining ground. Kitson stayed at the front, swinging his weapon. Blood streamed from a wound on his head, but it didn't slow him. His eyes were filled with madness. No words from his mouth, just snarls that sounded more animal than human.

If the reinforcements didn't arrive in the next two minutes, the police were going to be forced back against the Coliseum.

All around, noise. Men, women. Yelling, screaming. The sounds blended, towering over the night.

He caught a movement from the corner of his eye and turned.

A man had broken from the crowd, running at him. A knife glittered in his right hand. His left arm hung useless. Lips pulled back in a snarl.

Harper waited until he was close and brought the cosh down hard on his wrist. The bones shattered and the blade tumbled to the ground. The man bent over and Harper kicked him between his legs, happy to see him crumple.

'Come on, lads. We're almost there.' Kitson, battling for every foot of ground. Still twenty-five yards from the theatre, trying to press his men forward.

Then it came. Sharp, like a hammer on stone. Harper looked over his shoulder and saw them. Finally. The line of police horses, six of them abreast, seemed to fill the road. The animals moved steadily, coming closer and closer. In the centre, the sergeant had a grin plastered across his face. He raised his arm, shouted something, and the riders flicked at the reins, quickening to a trot.

A few more seconds and they were pressing against the crowd. For a moment the mass of bodies held. Then they started to give. Inches at first. Then a foot, a yard.

Behind them, the reinforcements, truncheons held at port. Harper darted across to the sergeant.

'What took you so long?'

'Sorry, sir. The man you sent was attacked. We came as soon as he delivered his message.'

God Almighty. 'How is he?'

'Didn't look too good when I saw him.'

He pointed out Kitson. 'I want him arrested and all those right around him.'

The sergeant nodded. 'Right you are. Do you care if he ends up hurt, sir?'

'No,' Harper answered. 'I bloody well don't. No need to be kind to any of them.'

Two sharp blasts on the whistle and the horses moved aside, creating a gap. The reserves rushed in, fresh, full of fire.

Now the tide would turn. He leaned against the wall and watched. Bit by bit they started to push the demonstrators back down the hill. The horses penned them in, letting the police do their work. Now the noise all came from the coppers.

They'd won. It would still take time, but soon it would be all over. He turned his head and saw the suffragettes, safely back behind the barriers. Still shouting, but not as loud, not as angry without Mrs Baines there to lead them.

He needed to go down the hill, to make sure it all ended without a problem.

First, though, he found Ash. The man looked battered and bruised, his tie askew, the new bowler hat now as beaten and dusty as his old one.

'Quite a scrap, sir.'

Harper tilted his head towards the fight that was moving down the hill. 'Not done yet.'

'Your Mary's safe. I had a constable slip in and snatch her out. She wasn't happy, but she's over in the Art College. No harm done.'

He closed his eyes for a second and let himself breathe in the news. 'Thank you. What about Mrs Harper?'

'Neither hide nor hair, sir. At least she wasn't one of those arrested. We took Mrs Baines and three others.'

He stared at the ground around the suffragettes who remained. Three hats and a broken umbrella lay on the cobbles.

'Move them on,' he said. 'They must be nearly done talking inside by now.'

'Very good, sir. You look like you took a leathering yourself.'

'I probably did. I daresay I'll feel it in the morning. Good work. And thank you again for Mary.'

Down the hill they were still battling. But the police had the upper hand now, moving efficiently, steadily. Professionally. It was under control.

Harper slipped into the Coliseum. Everything was fine in here, as if nothing at all had happened outside. A quick peek into the auditorium. Asquith stood on the stage, voice droning.

In the manager's office he picked up the telephone. When the operator came on the line, he said: 'Victoria public house, Roundhay Road.'

The long wait, hearing the bell as it rang on the other end. Be there, he thought. Be there. Please.

'She's fine,' he said as soon as Annabelle answered.

'You're sure?'

'Ash said she was. He has one of his coppers looking after her.'

'I started to come down. The hackney got as far as Eastgate,' she told him, 'then I told him to turn around.'

'Just as well. It's been a mess and it's not quite over yet. I need to get back.'

'You're . . .?'

'Alive and kicking.'

'I'll see you when you come home. And that little miss is going to get a piece of my mind.'

The remnants of battle were scattered around on the cobbles. Dozens of caps. A shoe. Pieces of broken lumber. A man who lay on the ground, moaning. His friend knelt by him.

Harper passed them, moving steadfastly towards the noise. The men were back on Victoria Square now, what remained of them, at least. No more than sixty left, surrounded by coppers and horses.

All the fight had gone out of them. Even from a distance he could feel it. Whatever they'd wanted to achieve, it hadn't happened. But they'd come closer than they probably realized.

He pushed himself between the uniforms. A copper turned, truncheon raised, stopping in embarrassment when he saw the superintendent's face.

In the centre of the ring, men huddled together. Defeated, broken. A few wore sullen faces. Most were simply exhausted.

'Go home.' He shouted loudly enough to catch their attention, his voice rising over the noise. 'If you're carrying anything, drop it and leave. Do that and we won't arrest you. But anyone still here in two minutes will be going in the cells. That's not a threat, it's a promise, and you'd best believe I mean it.'

A few murmurs, but the offer was enough. It let them leave with some pride intact. He watched as they began to drift away. They were done.

Sissons's face was a mass of bruises. The lapel of his coat was torn, the knee of his trousers ripped. Emerson stood by his side, face still shining and elated from the fighting.

'I'm sorry, sir,' Sissons said. He looked distraught, almost in tears. 'We tried to contain them. Honestly, we did. There were just too many.'

He thought he'd failed. Harper smiled and clapped him on the shoulder.

'I don't think you ever had much chance. Six hundred determined men? You did well to keep them back as long as you did.

And you all fought well.' That perked him up a little. 'Many of ours injured? I saw one go down.'

'Scrapes and bruises for the most part, sir. One with a broken arm. I sent him to the infirmary to have it set. A few with cracked ribs.' A wan, stunned smile. 'Not too bad, all things considered.'

'Not at all.'

Given how brutal it had all been, they'd come off remarkably lightly. Better than many of the demonstrators. But he wasn't going to worry about their injuries; they'd brought it on themselves.

The horse sergeant rested in his saddle. Harper patted the animal's neck. 'You turned the tide.'

The man grinned. 'These beasts are good at that, once you've trained them right, sir. I'm sorry we didn't arrive sooner. That messenger.'

Yes. He needed to go up to the barracks and check on the constable.

The night seemed quiet, hushed. Hard to believe that only a few minutes had passed since it was filled with so much noise and pain.

'You might as well take your men home. There won't be any more problems tonight.'

'Thank you, sir.' He saluted. 'Glad we could help.'

A single word and the horse patrol wheeled away, lining up and moving off towards the Headrow.

The last of the stragglers were dispersing now. Quite a few limped heavily, leaning on their friends as they walked. It was done.

'Dismiss your men,' he told Sissons. 'Give them my thanks. Tell them they've done a job to make us all proud.'

'I will, sir. How was it up the hill?'

Harper thought for a second before he answered.

'If I never experience anything like that again, it'll be too soon. I'll see you in the morning.'

'Do you still need me, sir?' Emerson asked.

'No, you're done for the night. A sterling job, I'll make sure it goes on your record.'

The lad beamed.

He saw small, dark puddles of blood on the stones as he climbed back towards the Coliseum, remnants of the madness that had arrived and passed. The audience was filing out, eyes moving around warily, seeing all the debris with a mix of distaste and relief.

The two big black motor cars drew up outside the entrance, the sound of their engines filling the street. All the suffragettes had gone. Only the barriers and the litter showed where they'd once been.

Suddenly there was movement. The Special Branch coppers spilled out into the night, alert and ready. There was nothing for them to do but stand. All the danger had passed. A brief glimpse of the prime minister as he ducked into the vehicle, then he was gone.

Crossley stood, turning his cap in his hands as he surveyed the scene.

'How bad was it, Tom? We could hear quite a bit, even in there.'

'Bad, sir,' he replied. 'It was a proper riot. They came close.'

The chief narrowed his eyes. 'How close?'

He paused before replying. No point in lying about it. The truth would come out in the next day or two, anyway.

'Much closer than I'd have liked. The constable I sent for reinforcements was attacked, so they were late arriving. Once they showed up, we started to push them all back.'

'How are our men?'

'I haven't had a chance to check everywhere yet, sir. But I haven't heard of anyone too bad. The worst seems to be a broken arm.'

The chief raised his eyebrows. 'That's all? You were lucky. You look like you were in the wars yourself.'

Harper shrugged. He'd forgotten about the wounds; they were minor. 'All done and dusted now.'

'Many arrests?'

'Mrs Baines and three other women. I haven't checked about the men. Kitson's in custody, though.'

'It'll hardly be the first time for him. He'll probably apologize, pay the fine and agree to be bound over to keep the peace.'

'He deserves six months at least.'

'I wish it worked that way.' Crossley smiled. A car horn sounded. 'Send your men home with my gratitude. I still have to go to a blasted dinner at Gledhow Hall.' He began to turn away, then stopped. 'Tom, good work tonight. All of you. I'm sure the prime minister will be pleased when I tell him.'

'Thank you, sir.'

But he didn't care what Asquith thought. He ached to go over to the Art College and find Mary. She was going to have to wait a little longer, though; there were things that needed his attention first. His duty. At Carlton Barracks a colonel received him in his office.

'Your man didn't look at all good when he arrived. Taken a beating, by the look of it.' He spoke in a languid drawl, as if nothing in the world was of any consequence.

'How bad was he? Is he still here?'

'Turned out to be walking wounded. I had the medical officer patch him up and send him on his way. Your people will owe the army for the hackney.'

'Send us the bill,' Harper replied coldly. Let them wrangle over that for a few years. He realized that he didn't even know the constable's name.

Ash and Galt were still outside the Coliseum. In the morning the council would have their crews out. By dinnertime there would be hardly any trace left of the destruction. All the debris would have vanished. As if nothing had ever happened.

'Surveying the field of battle?'

The inspector's moustache twitched. 'Looks so peaceful now, doesn't it, sir?'

'I'd rather see it like this than the way it was. You missed all the fun, Mr Galt.'

'Sorry, sir, I was otherwise engaged. I think I'd have preferred being out here. Might have been more interesting.'

'It was certainly that.' He turned to Ash. 'Any more word on injuries?'

'There'll be some who don't report for work tomorrow, sir. But it seems better than I expected. I thought we'd have a few cracked skulls.'

'Thank God there weren't. I saw at least one of ours go down.'

'He must have managed to crawl out. In the end the men were more trouble than the suffragettes.'

No surprise at all. Exactly as he'd predicted. 'How many of them in custody?'

'Twenty-two in all, sir. Alf Kitson took quite a hammering from our boys once they had him. He's going to look a mess in court.'

'He had it coming.' He sighed. 'We were very lucky tonight.

It was touch and go for a few minutes. But don't you dare ever repeat that to anyone. Go home. We'll talk about it all in the morning.'

He had to pound hard on the door of the Art College before the caretaker arrived to open up, grumbling and muttering under his breath.

Mary sat at a table, across from a very young, red-headed constable, the pair of them chattering away, oblivious to the world. Harper stood for a moment, watching them. They looked so innocent, so removed from everything that had happened outside. His daughter laughed, a happy, carefree sound that seemed to fill the room.

That was what it was like to be young, he thought, to be able to put everything behind you so easily.

He let his heels ring down on the floor. The bobby hurried to his feet, hands scrambling for his helmet.

'PC Miller, sir.' He came to attention, hands pointing down the sides of his trouser legs, face reddening.

'At ease, Constable. I'm grateful to you for looking after my daughter. I understand you're the one who brought her out of the crowd.'

'Yes, sir. The inspector's orders.'

'Thank you.'

'It was my pleasure, sir.' His face turned almost beetroot red. 'I hope . . .'

'It finished well,' Harper told him. No need for details. He'd hear them from his friends. As for Harper himself, he'd have to go over it time and time again. 'The men have all gone home. Your duty's done for the evening.'

'Goodnight, George,' Mary called as the bobby left. 'Thank you.'

He heard the door close and stared at her. Happy she was safe, that nothing had happened. And furious that any of this was necessary. She'd given her word and then broken it.

'Time we were on our way.'

'Yes, Da.' Meek and mild as she gathered her reticule and pinned her hat in place.

TWENTY-SIX

He didn't say a word as they walked. The fire of the night was still roaring through his blood. Better to stay quiet than snap her head off. There'd be enough of that once they were home. Annabelle would lift the roof off the Victoria.

Images from the evening replayed in his head like a moving picture, juddering, shaky, in and out of focus. The faces, the anger. The raw, bitter violence.

He'd intended to walk all the way, to let the journey drain everything from his system. But by the time they reached Briggate he was beginning to feel all the aches and pains. At the hackney stand he opened the door of a cab.

'In you go.'

Mary obeyed, quick, silent, pushing herself away into the corner as if she wanted to be invisible. He gave the driver the address.

The familiar clop of hooves, the squeak and jouncing of ancient springs as they moved along the road. More soothing than any motor car. They'd reached North Street before he finally trusted himself to speak.

'You gave us a promise.'

'I know, Da. But . . .' He didn't need to hear the words to know what was coming. For too many years he'd listened as people spoke like this. In the interview rooms, at pub tables, shadowed in dark ginnels. First the admission of guilt, then the list of excuses. 'I had to do it. Mr Asquith lied to us. You've read what he said. I've heard you and my mam talking about it. He told us he'd support votes for women, but when he stood up in Parliament, he didn't do it. This is my future, Da. I didn't have any choice. I had to protest.'

'No,' he told her. He kept his voice level, hoping to sound calm and sensible. 'Just because his promise isn't worth the breath he uses, that doesn't mean yours has to be the same. Do you know your mother was on her way down?'

'What?' Her eyes widened in alarm. 'I—'

'She got halfway and turned around. She was terrified for you. So was I.'

'I didn't want you to worry—'

He rode over her words, trying hard to keep his anger below the surface. 'For God's sake, what did you think we'd do? You want us to treat you like an adult, then you go and do something like this. You were there tonight, you saw what happened. My men were beaten. We came this close to a full-blown riot. You promised me you wouldn't be there. You told your mother the same thing. We believed you.'

She didn't reply until the hackney reached Sheepscar. 'I'm sorry, Da.'

Too late for that, he thought. Much too late.

The pub was busy, all the windows bright. He pushed through the crowd with Mary in front of him. Up the stairs, towards the light shining under the door. Annabelle sat at the table, a book open in front of her. But she didn't look as if she'd read a word all night.

She stood, waiting until Mary had taken off her coat and hat, then took her daughter by the shoulders, staring into her face. A bleak, unknowing look. The two women gazed at each other for a moment.

'Go to bed. We'll talk about this in the morning.' Her voice could have frozen boiling water.

The bedroom door closed and she turned to him. 'Are you hurt?'

'It's nothing.'

She stroked the cut on his hand and the bruises starting to form on his cheeks. 'Doesn't look that way to me.'

'I'll be fine.' He could feel himself starting to deflate, all the energy vanishing.

'How is she?' Annabelle asked.

'No damage done. I think she was pulled out before things turned bad.'

'Any of the women arrested?'

'Four.'

'And the men?'

'That was rough.' He didn't want to talk about it any more tonight. Just some rest, a chance to forget for a few hours.

'What are we going to do about her?'

Harper sighed. 'I don't know. I wish I did. I don't know if we can trust her again.'

She nodded sadly. Everything broken, and who knew how to mend it?

As he stripped his clothes off he saw all the marks across his body. He couldn't even remember most of the blows, but he'd feel them tomorrow. Ten minutes past eleven. He had no idea where the evening had gone. Everything had passed in a blur. Lying in bed he could feel his muscles begin to tighten. Breathe slowly, gently, he told himself. Let it all go until the morning.

Annabelle was already up and moving around as he eased his way out of bed and dressed. His skin was a mass of greens and blues and purples. Every muscle complained. Harper lowered himself gingerly on to the chair. Porridge and tea. Exactly what he needed.

'How do you feel?' she asked.

'Stiff. Painful,' he told her with a rueful smile. 'Old.'

'You were dead to the world.'

He'd needed that, to let it all seep away. Sleep was wonderful medicine.

'You might want to see this,' Annabelle said, pushing the *Leeds Mercury* across the table.

WILD STREET SCENES IN LEEDS. Big, bold type. He read the story, trying to square it with his memory. God knew where the reporter had been; he hadn't spotted any. Some of it was accurate, but it tried to heighten the role of the suffragettes.

'It wasn't quite like that. The women weren't the real problem.' His eyes moved to the closed door of Mary's room. 'Have you talked to her?'

'She hasn't poked her nose out yet. I'm not going to shout, though; I've decided that. But there's one thing: apart from work, she's not going anywhere for a month.'

He nodded his agreement. Probably a light punishment compared to those who'd been arrested.

Movement helped. By the time he'd walked to Millgarth he felt easier, the worst of the kinks and aches worked out of his body. For a moment he thought about Billy and how he'd laugh. He'd have been in the thick of things, battling hard alongside the coppers and enjoying every second. No, he corrected himself. That was what the young Billy would have done. The older one was more reserved and thoughtful. But he'd never come to know him too well.

'How many reported sick today?' he asked Sergeant Mason.

'Four in this division, sir. I don't know about any of the others.'

It could have been much worse. After yesterday they all deserved the day off, but fat chance of that.

'There was a constable beaten on his way to Carlton Barracks yesterday. Can you find out who it was?'

'I'm sure I can, sir. How about a cuppa in the meantime?'

Harper grinned. 'You read my mind.'

The men were waiting, Ash and Sissons looking as battered as he felt. Only Galt seemed fresh, but he'd been tucked away inside the Coliseum, safe from it all.

'Well,' Harper said, 'we survived.'

They grinned and started to laugh. A survivor's reaction, he thought. They'd made their way through the madness.

'What now, sir?' Ash asked.

'I need a report from each of you to pass to the chief. And the big question – could we have stopped it going as far as it did?'

'We could have stopped them at the bottom of the hill if the reserves had arrived earlier,' Sissons said.

'They would have, if the messenger hadn't been attacked on his way.' His voice was sober. 'I'm just glad they came when they did. At least the newspapers didn't complain about us.'

Ash's moustache twitched as he grinned. 'First time for everything, sir.'

'I'm proud of you all,' Harper told them. 'You did everything you could, you fought hard.'

'That was the men, sir,' Sissons said. 'They deserve the credit.'

'They do,' he agreed. 'I'm sure the chief will send out a letter to read at roll call. But don't sell yourselves short. You were in command, you kept order. And,' he added, 'we won. Write it all up for me, then we can do some real police work. I want the person who killed Adam Taylor. He's the one responsible for snatching Andrew Sharp and Marie Davis. Don't forget, that's where it all begins.'

'Won't that mean involving the Cranbrooks, sir?' Sissons asked. 'I thought the chief wanted us to steer clear after the suicide.'

'We will,' Harper said. 'Until we have evidence. After that . . . I think those children deserve to learn the truth. Then they can make up their own minds what they do about it.'

He'd made the decision on the way into work. He'd finish this case properly and ensure that the children saw some measure of justice.

No message from Charlotte Reynolds; it was the first thing he'd looked for among the papers waiting on his desk. She must be tougher than she looked; either that or reluctant to drink that last draught she was saving. Clutching on to life. Even when you were in pain and dying it could be hard to let go.

He couldn't return to her house.

He needed to write his own report, to try and make sense of all that had happened the night before. Put some order into the jumble of thoughts. He was halfway through when Mason placed another paper on his desk.

'The tally from last night, sir. All the divisions. Twenty-three off injured, most expected back in the morning.'

'Thank you.' Just as well today was Sunday; everywhere would be short-handed.

'The constable you asked about is PC Dixon, sir. C division.'

'Any word?'

'He's one of those on the list. He'll probably be gone two or three days.'

'I see.'

As he finished writing, Harper added a note suggesting that Dixon be given a commendation.

He stood and stretched, staring out of the window at a grey day. Every part of his body was tender.

'Penny for them?'

He turned to see Crossley in the doorway.

'You'd probably end up with change, sir.'

The chief smiled. 'How are your men?'

'They've all looked better, but they're here.'

'I've been doing the rounds of the stations. We took a hammering, Tom, no doubt about that. Still, we came out on top and the newspapers praised us. I'll call that a victory of sorts.'

'Our reports are on my desk for you, sir.'

'I'll take them with me. But tell your men I appreciate what they did.'

'I will, sir, thank you. How was the dinner?'

Crossley grimaced. 'Disagreed with me, I was up half the night. Pheasant, God only knows how long it had been hanging. It smelled off. And the pâté wasn't much better.'

Rich food like that. Another reason not to apply for the chief constable's post. He wouldn't even know which knife and fork to use.

'I hope it passes soon.'

'That makes two of us. Still, at least the first act of this drama is done.'

'Sir?' He didn't understand.

'There's still court tomorrow. That's what Mrs Baines always wanted. Her day in the dock. A pulpit.'

'It should be over in a few minutes, sir.'

'Let's hope you're right. I need you there to give evidence. Make it clear to the magistrate just how serious this was, so he can hit them with heavy fines. Maybe prison.'

'Yes, sir.'

One more damned thing to do. He'd given evidence often enough in his life and always hated it. Oily lawyers ready to pounce on every sentence and twist it.

'After what happened, we need to make examples out of her and Kitson,' the chief said.

He didn't reply. What could he say? Every wound and bruise agreed. But he wasn't going to stand up and lie. He'd tell the truth and nothing but the truth.

Harper handed Crossley the reports.

'Make sure you pass on my praise to your men, Tom.'

'Don't worry, sir. I will.'

'And you worked wonders last night. The prime minister and the home secretary send their gratitude.'

'Thank you, sir.'

He should have been swelling with pride. Instead, he felt empty, simply glad that it was all over. At least no one had mentioned the fact that his daughter had been at the demonstration. Small mercies.

By the time the men straggled back, he'd made his way through all the papers needing his attention.

At dinnertime he'd walked over to the infirmary. Five minutes with Brenda Woolcott. She'd regained a little more movement in her arms and legs, but speech still defeated her. She wanted to talk, he could see it in her eyes, hear it in the noises she made, but desire wasn't enough; that part of her brain refused to respond and no doctor knew how to start it up again.

Five minutes, telling her what had happened a quarter of a mile from where she lay, and he gave her a faded smile.

'I'll see you again soon. Maybe you'll feel better by then.'

He felt bleak as he left. But Walsh greeted him with a grin.

'You look like you enjoyed yourself, sir. Very colourful.'

'I won't say it was fun. You look in better shape than me and you're in a hospital bed.'

'Not for much longer, sir. There's no sign of sepsis, so they're packing me off home on Tuesday. With luck, I'll be back on duty by November.'

By then the Sharp case would probably be over. One way or another.

It seemed like a day when the city was catching its breath, recovering from everything that had happened the night before. He walked by the Coliseum, stood and looked at the building, trying to remember all he'd seen. The overwhelming noise. None of it remained now. The streets were clean, the blood washed away, the barriers removed. A broken window – the only one smashed during the evening – still needed repair. To look at the scene, nothing had ever happened in this place.

Life marched on. Another day, another month, another year.

'All people want to talk about is the riot,' Galt complained. 'I've not had a straight answer from anyone all day.'

The others nodded; exactly the same. So many people weren't quite ready to let it go yet. He could see the frustration on their faces. A whisper, a name, that was all they needed. And they couldn't scrape it up anywhere.

'Never mind, maybe you'll have more luck tomorrow. I stopped in to see Walsh; he's being discharged in two days.'

That cheered them. A good way to end.

'What did you do?' he asked as he stood in the kitchen.

'I read her the Riot Act,' Annabelle said. 'Quietly and calmly. Laid it all out. She apologized.'

'She did that last night.'

'Mary said sorry to you,' she corrected him. 'This was for me. I told her that until the end of November she was going to come straight home after work and not set foot outside the door in the evening or on weekends.'

A month and a half. That should be long enough to impress their feelings on the girl.

'I told her something else as well. About trust. I pointed out that I'm not daft enough to go into business with someone I can't trust. If she wants me to lend her the money to start this secretarial agency of hers, she's going to have to convince me she's worth the risk. That means no trouble from now until she's eighteen. Not a foot wrong. What do you reckon?'

He smiled. 'Very effective. It'll make her think about what she really wants.'

'Oh, I know what she wants, Tom. So does she. I'm not trying to stop her being a member of the WSPU. She can believe whatever she chooses. That's fine. Even go on marches if she likes, as long as we give her the nod. But I'm not having a repeat of last night. I was tearing myself apart here until you rang.'

'It's all done now.'

'No.' She tried to smile, but her mouth barely moved. 'It's not. *This* might be over. But the suffragettes are going to get worse. I can see it. If there's one thing come out of last night, it's that I know what I have to do now. Work with Miss Ford and her group. Educate women. Help them. None of this violence.'

'You already do that,' Harper said.

Annabelle shook her head. 'I've been playing at it since I left the Guardians. High time I dived back in properly.'

'It's been worthwhile, then. After a fashion.'

'I suppose it has.' This time the smile was real.

'What about the pub? Made any decision on that yet?'

'One thing at a time, don't you think?'

TWENTY-SEVEN

Monday morning and his best suit for court. Sitting on a bench in the corridor, kicking his heels until he was called to give evidence. The same old swearing-in, the same tattered Bible they'd always used. He stood in the witness box, staring at the defendants. Mrs Baines and three other women at the front. Crammed behind them, the men. Kitson stood with his face misshapen, the cuts still livid on the skin.

Harper hid nothing as he told the story. No lies, no exaggerations. What happened was quite enough.

'Would you say Mrs Baines was inciting the women?'

'Yes, I would. She was whipping them up. I did hear her shout "Break down the barricades."'

'I see. And would you say she and Mr Kitson were acting in unison?'

He waited, knowing every eye was on him. Were they?

'No,' Harper answered finally. 'I have no reason to believe that was the case.'

When he'd finished, the room was silent for a few seconds.

'Questions?' the magistrate asked. When none came, he said, 'You may step down.'

A few other witnesses. Then the magistrates conferred quietly and called over the clerk. More soft words, too quiet for his hearing. And then: 'This is a very grievous matter of public disorder. You attempted to disrupt a visit by the honourable gentleman who holds the highest elected office in the land, and you did it with extreme violence, as the superintendent explained. I shall come to Mrs Baines and Mr Kitson in a moment. Before that, all the others are fined one pound and bound over to keep the peace for a year. Do you agree to that?'

The men nodded, relieved to be let off so lightly. But the three women next to Jennie Baines refused.

'In that case, I have no alternative but to sentence you to five days in prison, to be served at Armley Gaol. Take them away.'

That left just two in the dock. Harper sat upright, alert, wondering what the magistrate was planning.

'Without any doubt, the pair of you were the instigators and ringleaders of this. You incited those who followed you. That puts you in a different position entirely. Given everything that happened, we feel we have no choice but to commit your cases to be heard in the Crown Court next month.'

A gasp of disbelief. It didn't make sense. Everything could have been dealt with here, done and out of the news in a day or two. Now it was going to blow up into something much bigger. Every newspaper in the country would cover it. Leeds would stay on the front pages for weeks.

Harper marched over to the chief constable's office.

'They did what?' Crossley asked in astonishment. 'For God's sake, what were they thinking? There's absolutely no good reason behind it. I don't imagine you've heard what happened in London yesterday. Mrs Pankhurst stood in Trafalgar Square and urged everyone to gather in front of Parliament when the Commons opens its session today. A summons went out this morning for her arrest. "Inciting the public to do a wrongful and illegal act." Between that and Baines going on trial, the suffragettes just found a huge wave of publicity. They'll be over the moon.'

'Probably exactly what they wanted.'

'I've no doubt about it.' The chief tossed down his fountain pen in disgust. 'This is going to roll on for the rest of the bloody year.'

'I just wanted to let you know.'

'I wish I could say I was grateful, Tom. It isn't exactly how I wanted to end my career.'

The news had already reached Millgarth; he saw it in Mason's astonished look. But he didn't want to stop and discuss it. The chief was right; this would stay in the newspapers for weeks. Mrs Baines had achieved a distinction; she'd become the first suffragette to be committed to trial by jury.

In his office he searched through the messages. Nothing from Charlotte Reynolds. He didn't want her to die, but he ached for this case to be over. And she was the one holding the answer to it all.

The first reporter arrived at noon, Russell, the red-headed Liverpudlian from the *Mercury*.

'What do you think of the magistrate's decision, Superintendent?' he asked with a broad grin.

'It's not my place to comment on it, Mr Russell. You should know that. If you have any questions, you should talk to Chief Constable Crossley.'

'His office says he's not available. And you were in charge on Saturday night, weren't you?'

'You already know I was.'

'Then you must have some feelings on the matter.'

'If I do, they're my own feelings and I'll keep them that way.'

'Not going to give me a thing, even if it's not for publication?'

Harper smiled. 'Not a word. You've had a wasted trip.'

The man shrugged. 'Ah well. If you don't try, you'll never know. That's what my mammy used to say.'

The same response to reporters from the *Post* and the *Evening Post*. The chief had done the sensible thing by ducking out of the way.

'If any more reporters show up, I'm out,' he told Mason.

'Very good, sir. And while you're not here, would you be ready for a cup of tea?'

'And a biscuit?' he asked hopefully.

'I'll see if we can stretch to that, sir.'

'I might have something, sir,' Galt said. 'A fellow I know claims he remembers something from long ago.'

'Go on.' The men had gathered in his office, looking bone-weary and defeated. Only Galt had that glimmer of hope on his face.

'It's not directly related to child-snatching. But he claims that Brenda Woolcott's husband knew Harry Matthews. He thinks they grew up together or something.'

Harry Matthews. The bookie who'd employed Taylor after Harper had kicked him off the force.

'That's very good.' He glanced at the faces. 'I tell you what. Sissons, why don't you see how far Matthews and Taylor go back.'

'I don't see Harry as a killer, sir,' Ash said.

'Nor do I,' Harper agreed. 'But let's take a look, anyway. I want every connection to Matthews explored. We've got nothing else.'

It was something fresh, another line to pursue. It would probably peter out to nothing, but at least it gave them fresh purpose. Was that the name waiting for him in the envelope at Mrs Reynolds's house?

He'd intended to go straight home. But his feet took him in the other direction, up the Headrow, past the town hall and on to the infirmary.

He stood at the entrance to the ward. Brenda Woolcott's bed was empty. Harper looked at the nurse on duty.

'Have you moved her?'

She stood and came towards him. The sympathy in her eyes told him all he needed to know.

'Mrs Woolcott started thrashing around this morning. We tried to calm her and called the doctor. She had a stroke. It was too much for her. I'm sorry.'

He nodded. All because of the attack. Another murder to lay at someone's door.

'Were you a relative?' the nurse asked.

'No,' he answered. 'Not family. Not even a friend, I suppose. Just a copper.'

He moved on, a lone figure among the crowds on Great George Street. Lost in his thoughts. He'd felt an odd kinship for the woman trapped inside her own body. Maybe the end was a blessing; he could never really know. But it was a little more emptiness in his life, one more missing person.

She couldn't have given him much information, nothing beyond yes and no. But maybe enough to know if they were going in the right direction. Now even that was over. No relatives he knew about, and she didn't have any money. Her body would end up in an unmarked grave at St George's Field. Another forgotten life.

By the time he reached Sheepscar he could feel every single ache in his body and he was weary. The Victoria was almost empty, just a few regular customers tucked in their usual places. Behind the bar, Dan was reading the evening paper.

'They're going to trial, are they?'

'More money for the lawyers,' Harper said. 'At least they'll have a fat Christmas.'

Mary sat at the table, reading and wearing a sullen expression. Annabelle bustled through from the kitchen, plates in hand.

'I thought we'd wait for you. All eat together.'

Meat pie, the gravy thick and rich. But all he could do was pick at it.

'Something wrong?'

'No,' he told them. Then, 'Yes. Someone died. A victim, a witness. The thing is, it might have been the best thing for her.'

'That's out of your hands, Tom,' Annabelle said.

'I know. It still doesn't make it any easier. It just seems there's been too much death lately. Ever since Billy.'

'You should ask Mrs Reed to stay,' Mary said.

Long ago, when Mary was young, Elizabeth Reed had been Aunt Elizabeth, an honorary family member. Now everything was more formal.

'That's not a bad idea,' Annabelle agreed with a nod. 'A change of scene for a few days might do her good. I'll write to her in the morning, see if she fancies it.'

As soon as they'd finished eating, she was bustling around.

'I invited myself to a burgess meeting tonight. There's another on Wednesday, too. Tom, could you be a love and turn the crank on the car for me?'

Five more minutes and she was gone, the sound of the engine slowly vanishing into the distance. Upstairs, Mary was washing the pots.

'Doing penance?'

'Helping.' She stared down, scrubbing hard to clean the metal of a pan. 'I really am sorry, Da.'

'How did you feel when you were in the middle of it?' Harper asked.

'I was scared,' she said after a moment. 'All those people, and the men were so angry. I saw about Mrs Baines in the newspaper. What do you think will happen?'

'I don't know,' he told her. 'It'll be interesting to see. It's not my business any more. My part ended on Saturday night. It's up to the courts now.' He patted her shoulder and left her to work.

'What have you found on Matthews?'

'A few bits and pieces, sir,' Ash said. 'Take a guess who liked a flutter on the horses while he was on the force and placed his bets through Harry.'

'Adam Taylor,' Harper replied.

'Bang on the money.'

Him and half the force, most likely. All it meant was they knew each other back then. It proved nothing at all.

'Do we have any connection between Cranbrook and Matthews?'

'Not *Mr* Cranbrook, sir.' Sissons looked up. 'But Mrs Cranbrook knew him before they were married. She must have – they grew up on the same street. He's a few years older than her.'

'Well, well, well.' Now things were far more interesting. He remembered what Ash had said: *you go round and round in circles, then something will pop*. 'You won't have heard, but Mrs Woolcott died yesterday. She had a stroke. We have her husband knowing Harry, Taylor knowing Harry, Mrs Cranbrook knowing Harry. Seems like he's been at the centre of the web without us even realizing it. No wonder he sent Taylor away when he learned a letter had been sent to us.' He stood. 'Mild, meek Harry. I think it's high time to pay a visit, gentlemen.'

* * *

Sissons and Galt waited in the ginnel in case Harry tried to escape through the back door. The street was empty, the sky overcast, the hint of a chill in the breeze that whipped through the neighbourhood. Not enough to cleanse the air in Hunslet, though. It still stank of oil and hot steel, probably would until Doomsday. A chimney belched smoke, and fine particles of soot gathered on their coats.

Harper knocked on the front door, Ash standing by his side. He could feel the anticipation rising. A young man opened the door, a flash little fellow in his cheap suit, pomaded hair and pencil moustache.

'We're looking for Mr Matthews.'

'He just popped down to the shops.'

'Then we'll wait inside.' Harper brought out his identification. 'It's getting parky out there.'

He pushed his way past and through to the scullery. No sign of Matthews.

'Has he been gone long?' Ash asked.

'Ten minutes. But—'

'Harry's always pleased to see us,' Harper told him. He examined the betting slips on the table. No one would end up rich from wagers like these. But a bookie could make a comfortable living. 'Are you his new assistant?'

'I am,' the young man replied.

'And what's your name?' Ash stood close to the lad, towering over him with a smile.

'Ralph. Ralph Enderby.'

'A word to the wise, Ralph. You might want to look for other employment. This job might not last much longer. Still, as you're here, you can make yourself useful and put the kettle on.'

Ten minutes became a quarter of an hour, then twenty minutes. Harper glanced at Ash. The inspector shook his head.

'How far away is this shop? The other side of Leeds?'

'Five minutes,' Enderby replied.

'Harry must know we're here,' Harper said. 'He's skipped.'

'Maybe he saw us on our way over, sir, or someone tipped him the wink.'

Yes. Matthews wasn't coming back here.

Outside, he looked up and down the road. Not a soul to be seen.

'You might as well fetch the others.'

'He could try to sneak back if he learns we've gone,' Ash said.

'Leave Galt to keep watch.'

As they walked back to Millgarth he tried to think. Where could Harry be? He was desperate, on the run for his life. Where would he go? Who was still alive and knew enough to convict him?

Two women. Charlotte Reynolds and Sarah Cranbrook.

Time to make his own bet and hope it was the right choice.

TWENTY-EIGHT

Charlotte Reynolds. It had to be. Had to be. Too many people out at the Cranbrooks. He'd take the easy target first. The closest one.

Harper's mouth was dry as he ran, feeling his bruises with every step, the others keeping pace right behind him. Matthews had a head start. He could already have killed and vanished.

At the corner of the street, he stopped and gathered the men around.

'We'll knock. If there's no answer, kick in the door.'

'I hope you're right about this, sir,' Ash said.

'So am I.' He grimaced. 'So am I.'

A final breath and he brought his fist down hard on the wood. One-two-three. He held his breath. No sound inside. No feet moving across the floor. And then a muffled shout from upstairs.

'Now.'

Ash rammed his shoulder against the door. Nothing at first. The second time it gave a little, straining against the lock. A third and it flew open.

'Ash, with me. Sissons, search down here.'

Harper led the way up the stairs. Charlotte Reynolds lay in the bed, eyes closed. She was bleeding from a cut on her chest. He placed his fingers against her neck. No pulse.

The other woman was on the floor, legs tight against her body, curled up into a ball.

'She's still alive,' Ash said.

'Sissons,' he shouted, 'get out there and blow your whistle. I want an ambulance here as soon as possible.'

Pain creased Roberta Larner's face. She'd bitten down on her lip, hard enough to make it bleed.

'How bad?' Harper asked.

'Can't tell, sir.'

A knitting needle was clutched in her fist. Gently, he pried her fingers open, took it and looked at the tip. Blood. It looked as if she'd wounded Harry Matthews.

'What about the other one, sir?'

'Dead.' Matthews had killed again. Only one place he could go from here. 'You stay. Make sure she gets to hospital. I'm going to the Cranbrooks. He's on his way there.'

In the living room, a thick envelope with his name in pencil stood on the mantel. He pushed it into his pocket. Time to read it later.

Harper ran, pounding and weaving along the streets. His body screamed, every bruise, every wound. But he dared not slow down. He swerved between carts and buses, dodged in and out of people. Stumbled on the cobbles and kept going.

One hundred yards from Millgarth and his lungs were bursting. In his mind he saw Charlotte Reynolds, Brenda Woolcott, Adam Taylor. So close to the end of it now.

No more dead. No more. There had already been too many.

'Send for a car,' he ordered Mason and leaned against the counter, drawing in lungfuls of air. His pulse was pounding in his ear.

Two minutes and he was in the back of the vehicle as it headed up Eastgate.

'Quick as you can,' he said, then slit open the envelope with his thumbnail.

Harper jumped down as the motor car slowed to a stop.

'Come with me,' he called over his shoulder to the constable who'd driven him, and sprinted for the front door. The cosh was still in his coat and he drew it out. Ready.

Not locked. Not even closed. He entered cautiously, trying to be silent, straining his bad ears for any sound at all. Behind him, a footstep as the constable followed him. Harper held up his hand.

Then he caught it. A soft murmur. Sounds from the end of the hall. Quietly, he moved along, hardly daring to breathe. He stopped, trying to pick out voices. A woman. The deeper tones of a man.

His fingertips touched the handle and started to press down. Just for a moment, time stood still.

Very quietly, he entered the room. Sarah Cranbrook was on her feet, pale, shaking. Andrew had his arms around his sister. And Harry Matthews turned.

His right hand gripped a knife, the blade dulled with blood. His eyes were wild, caught in some idea he might murder his way out of this after all. Blood stained the thigh of his trousers.

Harper didn't wait. Couldn't give him the time. He launched himself at Matthews, sending him crashing down on the floor. Matthews snarled. He tried to raise his arm, to bring his weapon down.

Harper swept across with the cosh and caught nothing but air. Matthews was rolling, trying to pin him down. This time the cosh caught his chest, but there was no power behind it. Harry had the strength of madness in him.

He couldn't let Matthews get on top of him.

He fought, squirming. Trying for any hold. Any advantage. But inch by inch, the man was gaining.

The knife was so large, so deadly in Harry's hand. Harper had his fist clamped around the man's wrist, pressing, keeping it away. But it was still coming down.

One last chance.

He pushed, heaving the man away. For a few seconds he believed he could do it. Then the pressure grew again. Harry shifted, forcing his way over his body. The blade started to move closer and closer to his face.

And then.

In an instant, the pressure vanished. Matthews slumped on top of him. The blade clattered to the floor. Harper squirmed free. He tried to stand, legs so weak he had to hold on to a table to keep himself upright.

With his truncheon in his hand, the constable looked apologetic. 'I'm sorry, sir. I had to wait until I could take a clear swipe at him. I couldn't risk hitting you.'

Harper nodded, staring down at the ground. He was shaking, not ready to speak just yet. Matthews was unconscious. He kicked the knife out of reach.

Mrs Cranbrook sat perfectly still. The children still hugged each other, unmoving. Just like a tableau, he thought, like figures made from wax. Unreal.

It was a minute before he could trust his voice. But once he started to speak, it grew easier. 'Put the cuffs on him. Telephone for a wagon.' He pointed at the knife. 'Take that with you, too.'

'Yes, sir.'

'And thank you.' He tried to smile. 'I'm glad you didn't wait any longer.'

The copper scooped up the blade, snapped the handcuffs over Matthews's wrists, then grabbed him by the collar and dragged him out across the polished boards. He was still alive, at least for a while. Long enough to end his days on the gallows. As the door closed, Mrs Cranbrook said, 'That was very brave, Superintendent.'

He stared at her, closed his eyes for a moment, then opened them again.

Broken. That's what they were. He looked around the room. For the first time he noticed the boxes along the walls, filled with books, paintings in gilt frames, the glass dome of a clock.

'No servants?' he asked.

'I had to let them go,' she replied. 'We'll be leaving here by the end of the month. My husband had mortgaged it all.' A wan smile. 'And lost it.'

This was the time, he thought. The perfect moment to press her for the truth. When she was weak and the walls had crumbled. Here, now, where the children would hear it.

'You've known Harry for a long time, haven't you?'

'I knew him,' she replied quietly. 'Years ago.'

'How much did you pay him for the children?'

'I—' She turned her head to look at them. 'He's lying. You're mine. Both of you.'

Harper took out the letter and unfolded it. He'd read it in the car. He offered it to Andrew, to Marie.

'It's in here. Some of it, at least.'

Andrew wouldn't move. He stared at his mother, his expression unreadable. But Marie extended her hand and took the papers.

'Don't believe a word of it,' Mrs Cranbrook told her. 'I gave birth to you.' Her voice was brittle, on the verge of falling apart. Her eyes were frantic.

'Adam Taylor,' he began. 'Brenda Woolcott. Charlotte Reynolds. Harry killed them all to keep it quiet.'

'I don't know any of them.'

'Maybe you did, maybe you didn't,' Harper said. 'But they're the ones who made it all happen. Andrew Sharp, snatched from Harmony Court in 1893.' The boy stiffened. The superintendent could see the confusion in his eyes. 'Your mother was so distraught that she died two months later. To the day. Marie Davis, taken from Armley in July 1895.' The girl looked up from the letter to stare at him. 'Your father has never stopped believing you're alive. After three years your mother had to tell herself you were dead. That was the only way she could keep going.' Best not to finish that story, to tell her that John Davis was now in prison for murder. It would wait. Maybe forever. That would be up to her.

He cleared his throat. 'Why?' he asked. 'If you couldn't have children of your own, you could have adopted from the workhouse. Babies, if you wanted them.'

She kept her head high. 'I told you, Superintendent. These are my children.'

'You raised them, Mrs Cranbrook, but you never gave birth to them.'

'They were born abroad. I told you that before.'

'And you said you'd produce the documents to prove it,' he told her. 'You haven't. They don't exist.'

'They do. I was going to find them, then my husband . . .'

He turned to Andrew and Marie. 'You were born in Leeds. Both of you.'

The girl had finished reading. She tried to pass the letter to her brother, but he pushed her hands away.

'I . . .' Marie began. But she didn't know what to say. Who would? The world was already falling apart in front of her. He'd just smashed the last pieces of it. The real wonder was that she was still standing. She was stronger than she appeared.

'I'm sorry. But it's true. All of it.'

'It's not,' Sarah Cranbrook said. But her voice was weak. Andrew placed a hand on his mother's shoulder. At first she flinched, as if she wasn't sure why it was there. Then she covered it with her palm, looked up at him and gave a grateful smile.

'You have two brothers and two sisters,' he told Andrew.

He shook his head. 'I have a mother. She's here. I think you should go now. Thank you for what you did with that man. But you've arrested him. It's over.'

The man of the house, ready to make the decisions, to step into his father's shoes.

'Over?' Harper stared at the boy in disbelief. 'Three people have been murdered to keep this quiet. Another is badly hurt. That's not over.'

'And what about me, Superintendent?' Mrs Cranbrook asked. 'What are you going to do about me?'

'Nothing,' he replied. He gazed around the room. Soon it would be empty, she'd be gone to some small, anonymous life. 'I've said what I needed to. You started all this. You'll carry the guilt.'

He was in the hall, almost at the front door, when he heard footsteps behind him. Marie, still holding the letter.

'You forgot this.'

'Thank you.' He refolded it, put it back in his pocket. From here it was her choice. He'd told them, that was all he could do.

'You said my parents are still alive.'

'That's right.'

'I'd like to see them.'

'Whenever you want. Just contact me at Millgarth Police Station and I'll take you.'

She looked up at him, so earnest, so young. So lost.

'I never quite felt as if I belonged here,' she said. 'Now I suppose I know why.'

'Maybe that's it, Miss Cranbrook. Your brother seems to see it differently.'

'Andrew's always been certain of his place in the world. Mama made sure of that.'

'But not you?'

'I'm a girl, Superintendent. We're made for other things. That's what I've always been taught.'

He thought of Annabelle. Of Mary, just a year older than the young woman in front of him. They knew the world wasn't like that.

'Come and see me when you're ready, Miss . . . Davis. I'll arrange everything.'

Outside, the constable was waiting by the car. 'They came and hauled him off, sir. He started to come to as they put him in the van.' His expression softened. 'Are you all right, sir? That was a bit of a scrap. Short, but . . .'

'Fine.' It was already receding. He felt as if he'd lived a year since then. 'You did well. How long did it last, anyway?'

'No more than a few seconds, sir.'

Was that all? It had felt like five or ten minutes.

'Sure you're fine, sir? You look a bit peaky, that's all.'

'Yes.' He sighed. 'I just had to tie up a few ends in there, that's all. Let's go back to Millgarth.'

TWENTY-NINE

As he entered the detectives' room the men all rose and turned towards him. Harper perched on the edge of a desk.

'Harry Matthews was out at the Cranbrooks. He's been arrested.'

'Anyone else hurt, sir?'

He considered the question. 'Not by him, anyway. How's Mrs Larner?'

'Better than she looked, sir,' Ash replied. 'He managed to stab her twice, but she's not in danger.'

That was good news, at least.

'She'll be able to give evidence, then.' Harper took out the letter and placed it on the desk. 'That's what Charlotte Reynolds left for me. Much more in there than I'd expected.'

'Very detailed,' Ash agreed as he finished and passed it to Galt. Sissons read over his shoulder.

'Mrs Cranbrook arranged the first snatch with Matthews. He hired Mark Reynolds to find a suitable baby and take him.' Harper shook his head. 'A chain. And if it hadn't been for Charlotte Reynolds and her dying conscience we'd never have known about it.'

'That was Andrew, sir,' Galt said. 'What about Marie?'

He shrugged. 'Nothing in the letter; she didn't know about it. So, unless Harry tells us, I doubt we'll ever have the real answer. But I'd bet good money it involves Brenda Woolcott.'

'We don't have the evidence to charge Matthews for her or Taylor,' Ash said. 'No judge will accept that letter in court.'

Harper knew that well enough. For once, though, it didn't matter.

'We have him for Charlotte Reynolds,' he said. 'More than enough. We can hang him for that. Never mind the rest.'

'What about the Cranbrooks?'

'Harry wasn't the one who did the damage out there. I did. I had them read the letter.' He paused. 'Mrs Cranbrook is still denying it all. Either Andrew believes her, or he doesn't want to know.'

'What about the girl?' Galt asked.

'I seemed to strike a chord there.' He shrugged. 'But we'll see.'

Harper glanced at the clock. 'Let's call it a day and hope tomorrow's quiet. We could do with it.'

He sat in his office, trying to find some sense, some hope in it all. The names of the dead flowed back through the years, starting with Alexandra Sharp and stretching all the way to Charlotte Reynolds. And all because Sarah Cranbrook couldn't have children. But her husband had money so she got what she craved, never mind the cost to anyone else.

And even now she was denying it all. No truth, no redemption. But he'd never apologize for telling those children who they really were. They deserved to know, to understand how they'd ended up in that world.

He was about to leave when the telephone bell began to ring.

'November the nineteenth,' Crossley said.

'Sir?' What was the man talking about?

'That's the trial date for Jennie Baines and Alf Kitson. Make sure you're available.'

'I will, sir.' Maybe that would bring down the curtain on 1908.

'Big scenes in London today, Tom. Thousands of unemployed in Parliament Square at the moment. More arriving all the time. The place is packed with coppers trying to keep it all safe.'

'I hope they have better luck than we did.'

'Just be glad we're in Leeds, eh?'

'Always, sir. Always.'

The parlour above the Victoria was warm. A fire burned in the grate, the curtains were drawn against the night. Only eight o'clock but he was already trying to stifle his yawns.

'Mrs Baines will be in court next month,' he told Mary.

She looked up from the book she was reading. 'What do you think will happen, Da?'

'That depends on what she wants. The judge, too, how severe he's feeling. And who defends her,' he added.

'She'll want to be a martyr,' Annabelle said.

'Mam.'

'She will. You mark my words on that. Causes need martyrs. It's how they attract people. Maybe that's why the suffragists don't make the headlines.'

Mary glared at her and stormed off into her room.

'You shouldn't,' Harper said.

'Why not? It's the truth. I don't mind if she supports them, but she needs to hear it. Anyway, don't you think I'm right?'

He considered the idea. 'Probably,' he replied. 'Mrs Baines has already made her contribution. The first suffragette to be tried in Crown Court.'

'She won't be the last. Not by any means. Tell me, Tom, do you really think Saturday is as extreme as it'll get?'

'No.' He wanted to relax, to let everything go away, Instead, he was in the middle of a political discussion. All from one piece of information. He should have kept his mouth shut. 'I don't imagine so.'

'Nor do I. I don't know, maybe that *is* what we need if we're going to end up with the vote. They're right in that all we've achieved so far are broken promises. And women like Mrs Baines and the Pankhursts are going to become heroines to plenty of girls.'

'Like Mary.'

'Yes.' She leaned a head on his shoulder. 'I don't know the answers, Tom. I used to think I knew the questions, but I'm not even sure of that any more.'

'The world's changing.'

'We're growing older,' Annabelle said. 'I've made up my mind about one thing, though. I'm not going to sell the pub.'

He felt his heart lift. He'd follow wherever she went and never question her decision. But this place was home. He was comfortable here. Happier than he'd been anywhere. Sheepscar wasn't rich, not even close. That didn't matter. He saw enough of the wealthy areas to know he'd never fit in there. None of them would.

'I'm glad,' he told her. 'What made up your mind?'

'I finally realized we belong here. Daft to think anything else, really. Anyway, it'll make whoever wrote those letters look like a fool, won't it? Put her nose out of joint.'

'Did you ever find out who sent them?'

She shook her head and her hair tickled his face. 'Never tried. Doesn't matter, anyway.'

'No,' he agreed, 'it doesn't.'

November 19, 1908

They came out of court to the November mist. Soot and dirt hung in the air, and people coughed as they passed. Every autumn it was the same, bronchitis that settled on the lungs until spring came around again.

Crossley paused and lit a cigar. 'Mrs Baines gave a good defence,' he said. 'But she damned herself when she said the court wasn't legitimate.'

'Six weeks in Armley,' Harper said. 'That'll give her plenty of time to think.'

'She'll be out before Christmas. The Home Office won't dare keep her in. Too much bad publicity.' He smiled. 'At least the woman has the courage of her convictions. I had to laugh when Kitson agreed to be bound over instead of going to prison. Not exactly full of bravery, was he?'

'No one's going to be following his lead again.'

'It's the women we'll need to watch out for in future.' He stared at the traffic flowing past. 'Your sergeant is back on the job, isn't he?'

'Walsh? Yes sir. Light duties for now. He could easily have died from that ruptured appendix.'

Crossley sighed. 'A very fragile thing, life. That's why I decided to retire. Enjoy it while I can.'

'A few more weeks and you'll be free.'

'Yes,' he agreed. But he sounded more wistful than joyous. 'Sure you won't apply for the post, Tom? It might suit you. Especially after a good result on that murder.'

Harry Matthews would hang in the new year. He'd given a full account when they interviewed him, even answered the question that had vexed Harper. Why warn Brenda Woolcott only to attack her later? It was simple. He wasn't the one who'd done it. He had no idea who'd tipped her the wink; it could even have been about something else. He'd searched for her, but he'd never found her or hurt her. Someone else had done that. An unknown man. Was it true? Maybe, and if so there was another mystery they'd never solve.

Harper smiled at the chief. 'I'm positive, sir. The job's not for me. But thank you, anyway.'

'You're taking a few days' leave, aren't you?'

'Going to the coast, sir.'

The chief looked up at the sky. 'Not exactly the best time of year for the seaside. But you've earned it.'

Elizabeth had sidestepped the invitation to visit Leeds. Instead, she'd suggested the Harpers come to Whitby.

'It'll have to be after the trial,' he'd said when Annabelle told him. 'I can't go until that's off my plate. What about Mary, though?'

'She'll be working.'

'You know what I mean. After what happened.'

'Her punishment will be over by then,' Annabelle said. 'This will be a good way to show we trust her. And a good sea breeze will blow out the cobwebs for you and me. I think we both need it, don't you?'

The air was sharp, the smell of salt clear and clean in his nostrils. The waves rose and curled and foamed as they crashed against the shore. Harper turned the stem of the rose in his hand as he stood by the grave. Still a mound of dirt, dark and damp.

No headstone yet. Next year, after the earth had settled over the coffin. Elizabeth had shown them the design. Simple, just the name, year of birth and death, and *Rest in Peace*. Why would anyone need more than that? he thought. The only way people lived on was in the memory of the ones they left behind.

Marie Cranbrook had come to see him, long after he'd given up on her. He'd already been to see Andrew's sister, exactly as he'd promised. Told her he was still alive, but that he intended to keep to the only life he'd known. He'd watched her face fall. But he was a copper, not a priest. All he could do was tell her.

'You said you could take me to see my parents,' Marie said. 'My real parents.'

It was there on her face, the way she'd needed time to build up her courage. She was anxious, scared. Utterly terrified, but doing it anyway.

'I can.' At least he could take her to her mother. She'd need to be the one to explain why Marie couldn't see her father, what he'd done for the love of his daughter. 'I'll have them bring the car round and we'll go now.'

Before her nerve failed.

Beginnings, endings. And in between, life was so fragile.

He bent over, laid the rose on the earth and walked away.

AFTERWORD

Prime Minister Asquith and Home Secretary Gladstone did visit Leeds on Saturday October 10, 1908, to address a crowd at the Coliseum (the building that is now the O2). It was the second big occasion for the city after Edward VII had come earlier in the year.

Suffragettes – members and supporters of the WSPU – under the direction of newly appointed regional administrator Jennie Baines, did demonstrate. She and three other women were arrested, and the evening became known as the Suffragette Riot. However, just down the hill, six hundred unemployed men really did hold their own demonstration. I've fictionalized things, but Alf Kitson, noted as an anarchist, was their leader, and he was arrested. Remarkably, the only property damage really was a single broken window.

Mrs Baines became the first suffragette to be tried by a jury and received a six-week sentence after refusing to accept the legitimacy of the court. However, she was released before Christmas. Called 'our brave soldier on outpost duty' (a condescending way to look at Leeds) by Emmeline Pankhurst, as she emerged from Armley Gaol she was met by a crowd and a band, placed in a carriage drawn by 'women attired in the clogs and shawls of the Yorkshire millhand' – no one knows why – and taken to breakfast at the Queen's Hotel. The next day she received similar treatment in London.

I'm grateful, once again, to Vine Pemberton Joss for her detailed information on the events of October 10 and their aftermath. Any error or deviation from fact is strictly mine.

My thanks, too, to everyone at Severn House; everyone does such a great job for their writers. It's hard to single anyone out, but I'm hugely indebted to Kate Lyall Grant and my wonderful editor, Sara Porter. My agent, Tina Betts, is a treasure. And I've worked with Lynne Patrick, who has the thankless task of going through these books and finding my errors and typos, for a full decade now. I value all she does more than she'll ever know.

To all the book bloggers and reviewers – we all thank you for everything you do. Libraries, you're so vital. And readers, however you come to the book – thank you.

Last, but far from least, my love to my partner Penny, always supportive of what I do, as well as being my best critic.